The Loom of Ms. Jenny

Johan Sparr

Copyright

Also by Johan Sparr

The StainedSteam Saga
Phantom of StainedSteam
The Near Voice of Empathy
The Loom of Ms. Jenny

Watch for more at www.johansparrbooks.com.

Prologue: The Cosmic Weaver's Loom

L ord Everett Wentworth's boots whispered against the cobblestones as he slipped through the shadowy alleyways of London. The night air nipped at his face, carrying the scent of coal smoke and damp stone. His cloak fluttered, revealing a flash of his finely tailored waistcoat beneath.

"Blast this infernal wind," he muttered, tugging the fabric closer. His steel-grey eyes darted from shadow to shadow, every sense on high alert. Centuries of survival had honed his instincts to a razor's edge.

The vampire aristocrat's steps slowed as he approached a nondescript brick wall. He ran a gloved hand over the rough surface, feeling for the hidden mechanism. With a soft click, a section of the wall swung inward.

Wentworth paused, nostrils flaring as he scented the air beyond. "Well, old boy," he whispered to himself, "once more into the breach."

He stepped through, the door sealing silently behind him. The musty air of the hidden passage embraced him like an old friend, a stark contrast to the wind outside. His breath formed delicate, shimmering clouds in the darkness.

As Wentworth descended the narrow stone staircase, the sounds of the city above faded away. The clip of his heels against the steps echoed in the eerie quiet. Here, in this secret realm, he moved with fluid grace, as if the very shadows empowered him.

His pale fingers trailed along the rough wall, tracing ancient symbols carved into the stone. Runes and sigils flickered to life at his touch, pulsing with otherworldly energy.

"Awaken, old friends," Wentworth murmured in a long-dead tongue. The air crackled around him, responding to the magic that flowed through his veins.

The passage seemed to come alive, stones humming with recognition. Wentworth felt a surge of pride. Here, hidden beneath the bustling streets of London, he was truly in his element – a creature of shadow and mystery, as timeless as the very earth itself.

"Now," he said, a wry smile playing on his lips, "let's see what other secrets you've been keeping, shall we?"

LORD EVERETT WENTWORTH'S footsteps echoed softly against the ancient stone walls of the labyrinth. The air hung heavy with the weight of centuries, thick with dust and forgotten secrets. His pale fingers traced the glowing lines of the map he held, its ethereal light casting eerie shadows across his angular features.

"Well, well," he murmured, a hint of amusement in his voice. "What secrets do you hold, I wonder?"

The map pulsed in response, as if alive. Wentworth's dark eyes narrowed, focusing on a particularly intricate pattern.

"Ah, there you are," he whispered, his lips curling into a satisfied smile.

With a graceful motion, he turned down a corridor that seemed to materialize out of nowhere. The labyrinth shifted around him, walls melting away and reforming at his command.

"It's been far too long since I've had a proper challenge," Wentworth said to himself, his voice carrying a hint of excitement. "These modern nights can be so dreadfully dull."

He paused at a junction, his keen senses alert for any sign of danger. The air shimmered with an otherworldly energy that made his skin tingle.

"Now, now," he chided gently, addressing the labyrinth itself. "There's no need for hostility. We're old friends, you and I."

Wentworth reached into a pocket of his finely tailored coat, withdrawing a small pouch. With practiced ease, he sprinkled a fine powder into the air. It glittered as it fell, forming intricate patterns that pulsed with a soft, soothing light.

The labyrinth seemed to relax, its defenses lowering ever so slightly.

"That's better," Wentworth nodded approvingly. "You remember the old ways, don't you? As do I."

He continued his journey, each step purposeful and measured. The map in his hand glowed brighter as he drew closer to his goal, whatever that might be.

"I do hope this isn't all for naught," he mused aloud, a hint of impatience creeping into his voice. "I've grown rather fond of this coat, and I'd hate to see it ruined by some ancient booby trap."

As if in response, the ground beneath his feet trembled slightly. Wentworth chuckled, unfazed by the subtle threat.

"Oh, come now," he said, his tone light but with an undercurrent of steel. "We both know you're not going to harm me. I'm far too interesting for that."

The trembling subsided, replaced by a feeling of grudging acceptance. Wentworth nodded, satisfied, and pressed on.

With each step, the air grew thicker with magic, crackling with potential. Wentworth's eyes gleamed with anticipation, a predatory smile playing across his lips.

"Whatever lies at the heart of this maze," he whispered, his voice filled with determination, "I will uncover it. After all, that's what I do best."

LORD WENTWORTH'S BOOTS struck the ancient stone, each step echoing through the vast circular chamber. Dust swirled in the stale air, clinging to his skin like a second layer. He blinked, more out of habit than necessity. His vampiric eyes pierced the gloom effortlessly.

"By the gods," he whispered, his voice barely a breath.

The chamber stretched before him, a masterpiece of impossible architecture. Pillars soared upward, their tops lost in shadow. Intricate carvings writhed across their surfaces, alive with movement in the dim light. Wentworth's steel-gray eyes widened as he traced the forms, recognition dawning.

"These aren't mere decorations," he mused, running a hand through his salt-and-pepper hair. "It's a language... a history older than time itself."

His gaze dropped, and he froze. A mosaic sprawled across the floor, its complexity staggering. Celestial bodies danced in patterns that defied logic, yet pulsed with undeniable truth.

"All my years," Wentworth muttered, his brow furrowing, "and I'm but a child before this wisdom."

At the chamber's heart stood a raised dais, smooth and unmarked. Wentworth approached with measured steps, each footfall deliberate. His weathered features reflected a mix of reverence and barely contained hunger.

The air thickened as he neared the platform. Static electricity made the fine hairs on his neck stand on end. His heart, usually steady through centuries of adventure, quickened its pace.

"After all this time," Wentworth breathed, a smile tugging at his lips, "I stand on the precipice of true power." He paused, chuckling softly. "And yet, I can't shake the feeling I'm in over my head."

He placed a hand on the dais, feeling ancient energies thrumming beneath his palm. "Well, old boy," he said to himself, "nothing ventured, nothing gained. Let's see what secrets you're willing to share."

Wentworth closed his eyes, focusing on the energy pulsing through the stone. "Come on, you ancient mystery," he coaxed, "show me what you've got."

Suddenly, the air crackled with intensity. Wentworth's steel-gray eyes snapped open, widening as glyphs began to glow on the dais surface.

"Well, I'll be damned," he whispered, a mix of excitement and trepidation coloring his voice. "Looks like you were just waiting for the right touch."

As the chamber came alive around him, Wentworth couldn't help but grin. "Into the unknown we go," he muttered, bracing himself for whatever came next. "Let's hope my centuries of experience count for something here."

HIS FINGERS TREMBLED as he reached into his cloak, his steel-gray eyes gleaming with anticipation. He pulled out a set of braziers, their cold metal etched with symbols that seemed to writhe under his gaze.

"Steady now," he murmured to himself, his voice barely a whisper in the cavernous chamber. "We've come too far to falter."

With practiced precision, he placed each brazier around the dais. The metal clinked softly against the stone floor, echoing in the silence. Wentworth paused, his raven hair with silver temples catching the dim light as he tilted his head, listening for any disturbance.

Satisfied, he produced a matchbox from his pocket. The strike of the match sounded like a thunderclap in the quiet room. As he touched the flame to each brazier, colors erupted - deep purples, vibrant teals, and shimmering golds that defied nature itself.

Wentworth stepped back, admiring his handiwork. "Beautiful," he breathed, a rare smile tugging at his lips.

Next, he pulled out a piece of chalk, its surface glittering with crushed gemstones. Kneeling on the cold floor, he began to draw. His hand moved swiftly, tracing arcane symbols that pulsed with power.

"Blast," he muttered as his hand slipped, marring a delicate curve. "Focus, old man. You're not some green acolyte."

He corrected the mistake and continued, sweat beading on his brow as he worked. The completed pattern seemed to shift and dance in the otherworldly light of the braziers.

With a grunt, Wentworth stood, brushing dust from his knees. He reached into his coat, feeling for a hidden compartment. His fingers closed around cool metal and smooth stone.

One by one, he placed the artifacts within the circle. A crystal skull that hummed with psychic energy. An obsidian dagger, its edge gleaming wickedly. A small hourglass filled with glowing sand.

As each item found its place, the air grew thick with magic. Wentworth's skin tingled, and he shivered despite the warmth.

"Almost there," he whispered, his voice tight with anticipation.

Finally, he produced an ancient tome. Its cover seemed to drink in the light, and strange symbols crawled across its surface. Wentworth opened it carefully, his eyes scanning pages filled with forbidden knowledge.

He began to chant, words in long-dead languages spilling from his lips. The chamber responded, walls pulsing with an inner light. The mosaic floor beneath his feet began to glow, as if awakening from a long slumber.

Wentworth's voice grew stronger, more confident. The ritual was working. Soon, very soon, all his centuries of waiting would pay off.

As the final word left his lips, he allowed himself a moment of triumph. "And now," he said to the empty room, his eyes gleaming with fierce joy, "we wait."

EVERETT POSITIONED himself at the dais's edge, his bearing majestic and authoritative. He inhaled deeply, bracing himself for the impending events. The burden of generations weighed on him, yet he cast it aside. This was his time.

"It begins," he murmured, to himself.

As he opened his mouth, the words that flowed forth were unlike any human tongue. They resonated with a primal power, each syllable seeming to pluck at the very strings of reality. Wentworth's voice, usually smooth as silk, now carried an otherworldly timbre that filled every corner of the chamber.

The air around him began to shimmer, like heat rising from sun-baked cobblestones. As his chant continued, something extraordinary happened. Ancient voices, ethereal and haunting, joined his incantation. They whispered and sang, their tones blending with his own in a chorus that spanned ages.

"Can you hear them?" Wentworth thought, a thrill running through him. "The voices of those long past, awakening to my call."

The mystical glyphs carved into the ground throbbed with an unearthly radiance. Every stroke and arc flashed in precise synchronization with Wentworth's utterances, producing a mesmerizing ballet of brilliance. The relics positioned deliberately around the ring started to vibrate, their forces coalescing into a harmony of unbridled, primal energy.

Wentworth felt the chamber respond to his presence. The very stones beneath his feet thrummed with awakened magic, vibrating in tune with his chant. The walls seemed to breathe, expanding and contracting in slow, measured beats.

His eyes, normally a deep steel-gray, now glowed with an inner fire. They reflected the arcane energies swirling around him, twin pools of barely contained power. His pale skin took on an unearthly sheen, as if lit from within by the same force that now permeated the chamber.

As the ritual reached its crescendo, Wentworth's voice rose to a fever pitch. The echoing voices grew louder, creating a chorus that seemed to stretch across time and space. The air crackled with tension, magical energy building to a breaking point.

"Almost there," Wentworth thought, gritting his teeth against the strain. "Just a little more..."

The power surged through him, threatening to overwhelm his senses. But Lord Wentworth stood firm, a pillar of focus amidst the swirling chaos of magic. He was the conductor of this otherworldly orchestra, and he would see it through to its thunderous finale.

WENTWORTH'S VOICE ROSE to a fevered pitch, the ancient words tumbling from his lips with practiced precision. As the final syllable echoed through the chamber, reality itself seemed to shudder.

"By the dark powers, it's working," he breathed, his steel-gray eyes widening in anticipation.

The air at the chamber's center began to ripple and twist, like heat rising from sun-baked cobblestones. Wentworth's gaze locked onto the spectacle, his centuries-old heart quickening in his chest.

"Come forth," he whispered, willing the artifact into existence.

Slowly, achingly, a massive form materialized on the central dais. At first, it was nothing more than a hazy outline, a ghost of potential. But with each passing moment, it gained substance, edges sharpening, colors bleeding into view.

Wentworth's breath caught in his throat. "The Cosmic Loom," he murmured, awe coloring his usually composed voice. "After all this time..."

The loom that stood before him was a masterpiece of celestial craftsmanship. Its frame shimmered with the light of distant stars, constellations trapped in an endless dance of shadow and radiance.

Wentworth's keen gaze traced the intricate designs etched into its surface—stories older than time itself, their origins lost to the ages.

He leaned in, nostrils flaring as if he could scent the power emanating from the artifact. The threads running through the loom's mechanism pulsed with an otherworldly glow, each filament a universe unto itself. Realms upon realms unfurled within those gossamer strands, a tapestry of infinite possibilities.

"Fascinating," Wentworth breathed, his usual predatory stillness giving way to barely contained excitement. "Each thread... a lifetime. A world. An entire history."

As he studied the cosmic weaver, understanding dawned in his steel-gray eyes. His spine straightened, resolve settling into the very marrow of his bones. This was no mere magical trinket—this was the key to reshaping reality itself.

A slow smile spread across Wentworth's face, revealing the tips of his fangs. "Every dark deed, every sacrifice," he mused aloud, "all of it... worth it. For this."

He circled the loom, drinking in every detail. Centuries of plotting had led to this moment, and the reality before him surpassed even his wildest imaginings.

"With this," Wentworth said, his voice barely above a whisper, "I could rewrite the very fabric of existence. Bend the cosmos to my will." He paused, a dark chuckle escaping his lips. "The world thought me monster enough before. Just wait until they see what I become with the power of creation at my fingertips."

The vampire lord stood transfixed, basking in the glow of infinite potential. The Cosmic Loom hummed with promise, threads of destiny waiting to be woven anew.

WENTWORTH'S EYES GLEAMED with a mixture of reverence and naked ambition as he gazed upon the artifact. The air around him crackled, heavy with potential and the weight of unwritten destinies.

He inhaled deeply, savoring the moment. "Centuries of plotting," he whispered to himself, "and countless sacrifices. All for this."

The loom beckoned, its threads shimmering with the brilliance of a thousand suns and the inky darkness between stars. Wentworth's footsteps echoed in the chamber as he approached the dais. Each step felt momentous, as if he traversed not mere feet but eons.

As he drew closer, the intricate patterns of the shimmering threads came into sharper focus. His hand, adorned with an ornate ring passed down through generations of his line, reached out towards the loom. The vampire lord's fingers trembled ever so slightly, betraying the magnitude of this moment.

"Steady now," he murmured, feeling the heat emanating from the threads. It was warm like fresh blood, yet cool as the void of space. A sense of fulfillment washed over him. "This is my birthright," Wentworth thought, "the culmination of a destiny set in motion long before my mortal birth."

He stood at the precipice of change, not just for himself but for all of existence. The weight of that responsibility should have been crushing, yet he felt only exhilaration.

"The power to reshape reality itself," Wentworth breathed, his body quivering with anticipation. "It's finally within my grasp."

He paused, a wry smile playing on his lips. "I wonder if the other lords could see me now. Would they still call me mad?" He chuckled softly, the sound echoing in the vast chamber. "Mad with power, perhaps. But mad nonetheless."

Wentworth's fingers hovered mere inches from the loom, the anticipation building to an almost unbearable crescendo. "Well," he said to the empty room, "here goes everything."

WENTWORTH'S FINGERS quivered, hovering mere millimeters from the shimmering threads of the cosmic loom. His heart pounded in his chest, a drumbeat of anticipation and trepidation. This was the moment he had been preparing for, the culmination of centuries of planning and sacrifice.

As his fingers brushed against the threads, a blinding flash erupted from the loom. Wentworth's eyes widened in shock as an invisible force slammed into him, sending his noble form hurtling backward. He crashed against the ancient stone wall with a sickening thud, crumpling to the floor in a heap.

The cosmic loom pulsed with energy beyond mortal comprehension, its threads whipping about in a frenzy as if possessed by a furious tempest. Wentworth struggled to his feet, his normally graceful movements now clumsy and disoriented. He stared at his hand in disbelief, wisps of acrid smoke rising from the enchanted glove. The fabric was charred and crumbling, the ring passed down through generations was now black and lifeless.

"Impossible," Wentworth whispered, his voice hoarse with disbelief. "How can this be?"

Centuries of planning, and countless sacrifices, all for naught. Despite his noble heritage, despite the power coursing through his immortal veins, despite meticulous preparation - he was not the chosen one. The loom had judged him and found him unworthy.

The realization hit him like a physical blow, and Wentworth stumbled, bracing himself against a nearby pillar. His mind reeled, unable to comprehend this turn of events. How could he, Lord Everett Wentworth, vampire aristocrat and master of the arcane, be denied?

The loom's energy continued to surge, bathing the chamber in an otherworldly glow. Wentworth felt small, insignificant in its presence.

For the first time in centuries, fear gripped his heart, cold and unyielding.

"Who then?" he demanded, his voice echoing through the chamber. "Who is the chosen one?"

But the loom remained silent, its secrets locked away in the depths of its shimmering threads. Wentworth stood there, his pride shattered, his dreams of power and dominion crumbling to dust around him.

THE COSMIC LOOM'S LOW hum filled the chamber, its eerie vibrations seeping into Wentworth's bones. He stood motionless, his pale fingers trembling at his sides. The weight of his failure pressed down on him, threatening to crush his centuries-old spirit.

Suddenly, a whisper slithered through the air, bypassing his ears and burrowing directly into his mind. Ancient, powerful, and utterly alien, it sent shivers down his spine.

"The loom awaits its true master," the voice intoned.

Wentworth staggered backward, his normally graceful movements clumsy and uncoordinated. His crimson eyes widened in disbelief, darting around the chamber as if searching for the source of the otherworldly voice.

"Impossible," he muttered, his voice barely a whisper. "I am the chosen one. I've prepared for centuries."

The voice continued, unperturbed by his protests. "Your efforts are impressive, Lord Wentworth, but ultimately futile."

Wentworth's shoulders sagged, his usually impeccable posture crumbling under the weight of his failure. He ran a hand through his raven-black hair, disheveling the carefully styled locks.

"If not me, then who?" he demanded, his voice rising in pitch. "Who could possibly be more worthy than a vampire lord with centuries of knowledge and power at his fingertips?"

The voice remained calm, its tone almost pitying. "The true wielder of the loom's power is yet to come."

Wentworth's fists clenched at his sides, his sharp nails digging into his palms. "This can't be happening," he muttered to himself. "I've sacrificed too much for this moment."

"These actions have merely set greater events in motion," the voice proclaimed, its final words sending a chill through Wentworth's undead heart.

He stood frozen, his mind reeling. The implications of those words washed over him like a tidal wave of dread. He'd believed himself to be the architect of destiny, but now he realized he was merely a pawn in a game far beyond his comprehension.

"A pawn?" Wentworth spat, his voice dripping with contempt. "I, Lord Everett Wentworth, reduced to a mere chess piece?"

But the voice had fallen silent, leaving him alone with the cosmic loom's incessant hum and the crushing weight of his shattered ambitions.

WENTWORTH'S USUALLY graceful movements abandoned him as he stumbled out of the chamber, his feet tangling in his haste. The loom's rejection reverberated through his mind, a cosmic warning that shattered centuries of carefully cultivated composure.

"No, no, no," he muttered, his voice trembling. "This can't be happening."

His feet carried him swiftly through the labyrinth, each step taking him further from the power he'd coveted for so long. The sound of his own ragged breathing echoed off the stone walls, a harsh reminder of his mortality in this moment of desperation.

Behind him, precious artifacts lay scattered and forgotten. He dared not look back, fearing what he might see if he did. The weight of his failure pressed down on him, crushing his spirit with each passing moment.

"Centuries of planning, wasted," he hissed through clenched teeth.

As he fled, the walls of the ancient maze seemed to close in around him. Shadows danced at the edge of his vision, taunting him with whispers of what might have been. The air grew thick and oppressive, adhering to his flesh like a moist burial cloth.

Wentworth's mind raced, unable to comprehend the magnitude of what had transpired. He, who had walked the earth for centuries, who had bent mortals and immortals alike to his will, now found himself running like a frightened child.

"Get a hold of yourself," he snarled, trying to regain some semblance of control. But the tremor in his voice betrayed his fear.

Back in the chamber, the cosmic loom remained on its dais, indifferent to the vampire lord's hasty retreat. The air thrummed with residual energy, a sense of expectancy hanging heavy in the stillness. It was as if the very fabric of reality held its breath, waiting for the next act in this cosmic drama to unfold.

As Wentworth's footsteps faded into the distance, the chamber seemed to pulse with an otherworldly light. The loom's threads shimmered and shifted, weaving patterns too complex for mortal minds to comprehend. It stood as a silent sentinel, keeper of secrets yet to be revealed.

A voice, neither male nor female, whispered from the loom, "The unworthy shall not command the threads of fate."

The words hung in the air, a final judgment on Wentworth's failed ambition.

Really Bad Day

The fog clung to William Blackwood's coat like a second skin as he navigated London's labyrinthine streets. His boots barely made a sound on the slick cobblestones, a testament to years of practice moving unseen through the city's underbelly. The night air assaulted his heightened senses with a cacophony of scents: acrid smoke, the metallic tang of fear, and something... else. Something that made the hairs on the back of his neck stand at attention.

William paused, tilting his head to one side. The usual nighttime symphony of drunken revelry and distant carriages faded into white noise as an unfamiliar sound pricked at his ears. A low growl rumbled in his chest, unbidden, reminding him of the beast that lurked just beneath his skin.

"Bloody hell," he muttered, flexing his fingers as phantom claws itched to burst forth. "Can't even have one quiet night, can I?"

He passed a row of dimly lit taverns, wrinkling his nose at the stench of cheap gin and unwashed bodies. Two gentlemen, more alcohol than blood in their veins by the smell of them, stumbled out of a nearby establishment.

"Evening, gents," William nodded, his piercing blue eyes already scanning past them, searching the shadows between buildings.

One of the drunks hiccupped, squinting at William. "Oi, mate! You look like you could use a drink!"

William's lips quirked into a half-smile. "Perhaps another time. I'm afraid I'm on the hunt tonight."

The other drunk guffawed. "On the hunt, he says! What're you huntin', fancy man? Rabbits?"

"Something like that," William murmured, his gaze fixed on a flicker of movement in a nearby alley.

As the drunks stumbled away, still chuckling, William's eyes narrowed, cutting through the gloom with preternatural clarity. A figure darted from one shadow to another, too quick for human eyes to track.

"Well, well," he whispered, his hand instinctively gripping the ornate hilt of his cane sword. "What have we here?"

His muscles coiled, ready for action. The thrill of the chase sang in his veins, a potent reminder of why he'd chosen this life as a supernatural PI. William's keen eyes darted around the dimly lit alley, every sense on high alert. A sudden rustling from a nearby stack of crates sent electricity coursing through his body, awakening the predator within.

"Come out, come out, wherever you are," William called softly, a wry smile playing on his lips. "Let's see what manner of beastie is causing trouble tonight."

He took a step forward, gravel crunching beneath his boots. The stench of rotting garbage and stale urine assaulted his nostrils, but beneath it all, he caught a whiff of something else – the unmistakable musk of a supernatural creature.

William's hand hovered over his cane sword, fingers itching to draw the blade. "I know you're there," he said, voice low and dangerous. "And I know you're not human. So why don't we skip the cat-and-mouse game and have a proper chat?"

A low, guttural growl emanated from behind a rusted dumpster. William's grip tightened on his weapon.

"Last chance, you mangy cur," he growled back, baring his teeth. "Show yourself, or I'll drag you out by your scrawny tail."

The crate shook violently, and a pair of glowing red eyes appeared in the darkness. William's heart raced with a mixture of fear and exhilaration. He'd faced his share of monsters and demons, but each encounter only fueled his desire to protect the innocent from the horrors that lurked in the night.

As the creature began to emerge, its form still shrouded in shadow, William's mind raced. Vampire? Rogue werewolf? Or something far more sinister? Whatever it was, he was determined to uncover the truth and keep London's unsuspecting citizens safe from the dangers that prowled their streets.

"Right then," William said, drawing his cane sword with a flourish. The silver blade gleamed in the dim light. "Let's dance, shall we?"

The creature lunged forward with a bone-chilling howl, and William met the creature with a skilled backhand cut. Another night, another monster – just another day in the life of London's only supernatural private investigator.

THE GAS LAMPS FLICKERED, casting long shadows as William's boots clicked against the cobblestones. London's fog clung to him like a damp shroud, carrying whispers of dread that seemed to seep into his very bones.

"Another night, another mystery," he muttered, his breath visible in the chill air.

William's mind wandered to Mrs. Abernathy, her weathered face streaked with tears as she clutched his sleeve. "Please, Mr. Blackwood," she'd sobbed. "My Tommy, he's vanished!"

The memory of the boy's room flashed before him - rumpled sheets, a half-eaten piece of toast, and that damned open window. It was like the lad had simply evaporated into thin air.

Then there was Mr. Finch. William could almost smell the banker's expensive cigar, abandoned on the front step where he'd last been seen.

"Bloody hell," William growled, kicking at a loose pebble. It skittered across the street, disappearing into the mist.

Inspector Holloway's gruff voice echoed in his head. "We're stumped, Blackwood. These cases... they don't make a lick of sense."

William snorted. "When do they ever, old friend?"

But it wasn't just the human world on edge. William had seen it in the shadows, in the wary glances of those who dwelled beyond the veil of normalcy. Vampires huddled in their havens, pale faces etched with worry. Rouge werewolves, usually solitary, now moved in packs, fur bristling at every sound. Even the Fae, those mischievous tricksters, seemed to have lost their spark.

"What are you all afraid of?" William whispered to the night.

He paused at a crossroads, closing his eyes and inhaling deeply. The scent of fear was there, acrid and sharp. But underneath... something else. Something old. Ancient. It prickled at the back of his neck, raising goosebumps along his arms.

William's eyes snapped open, scanning the empty streets. "Show yourself," he challenged the darkness.

Only silence answered.

With a sigh, he ran a hand through his hair, feeling the weight of expectation pressing down on him. The human world still eyed him with suspicion, while the supernatural community kept him at arm's length. This case could change all that.

"No pressure, eh?" William chuckled humorlessly.

He gripped his cane sword tighter, the silver handle cool against his palm. Lives hung in the balance, threads in a tapestry he couldn't yet see.

"Right then," William squared his shoulders, his voice low and determined. "Let's unravel this bloody mystery."

He strode along the fog-shrouded street, continuing his nightly patrol, ready to face whatever lurked in London's shadows.

WILLIAM'S NOSTRILS flared as an unfamiliar scent tickled his senses. His eyes, sharp as a hawk's, locked onto a cloaked figure darting through the shadows of a narrow alley. The stranger's furtive movements set his nerves on edge.

"Well, well," he muttered under his breath, "what have we here?"

Without a sound, William melted into the darkness. His footsteps, honed by years of practice, made no more noise than a cat's paw on velvet. He matched the stranger's pace, keeping a careful distance as they wound through London's maze-like underbelly.

The cloaked figure moved with purpose, occasionally throwing glances over their shoulder. William's heart pounded, a mix of excitement and apprehension coursing through his veins. This was no ordinary late-night wanderer.

"Steady on, old boy," he whispered to himself, pressing his back against the damp brick of a building as the figure paused. "Don't get ahead of yourself."

The dance continued through the city's darkest corners, a silent game of cat-and-mouse that seemed to stretch for an eternity. Finally, the cloaked stranger halted before a nondescript door wedged between two crumbling buildings.

William watched, barely daring to breathe, as the figure fumbled with a key. Their movements were hurried, almost frantic. As they struggled with the lock, their sleeve rode up, revealing a flash of embroidery.

William's eyes widened. The symbol on the cuff was like nothing he'd ever seen - an intricate weave of lines and curves that seemed to shift and dance in the dim light. He blinked, wondering if his eyes were playing tricks on him.

"Bloody hell," he breathed, "what in God's name is that?"

Before he could ponder further, the figure slipped inside, the door closing with a soft click. William stood alone in the alley, his mind racing with questions.

"My, what a predicament I've wandered into," he muttered, raking his fingers through his locks. "I reckon there's no choice but to forge ahead. As they say, inquisitiveness may have done in the feline, but its revival came through gratification."

With a sardonic grin, William faded into the darkness, prepared for whatever escapade awaited him.

WILLIAM'S KEEN EARS twitched at the sudden crescendo of voices and hurried footsteps echoing from around the corner. He tore his gaze away from the enigmatic door, his investigator's instincts kicking into overdrive. Curiosity burned in his chest as he followed the commotion, rounding the corner to find a street cordoned off by a sea of blue uniforms and yellow tape.

His hand instinctively reached for the worn leather wallet in his coat pocket. As he approached the nearest officer, a stocky man with a salt-and-pepper mustache, William flashed his credentials.

"William Blackwood, private investigator," he said, his voice steady and authoritative. "Mind if I take a look?"

The officer's eyes narrowed, skepticism etched across his weathered features. He scrutinized the identification, then gave a curt nod. "Alright, Mr. Blackwood. But don't touch anything."

As William ducked under the barrier, a familiar voice called out. "William? What are you doing here?"

He turned to see Jaxon, his friend and sometimes-rival, striding towards him. Jaxon's curly brown hair, thin beard, wire glasses, and hazel eyes were sharp, with glinting curiosity.

"Same as you, I'd wager," William replied with a wry smile. "Following the scent of trouble."

The moment they stepped inside the crime scene, the acrid stench of violence assaulted William's heightened senses. His nose wrinkled involuntarily. Overturned furniture littered the floor like fallen soldiers, and shattered glass crunched beneath their boots with each step.

But it was the walls that captured William's attention. Strange, arcane symbols covered every inch, pulsing with otherworldly energy that made the hair on the back of his neck stand on end.

"Good God," Jaxon whispered beside him. "What in blazes happened here?"

William didn't answer immediately. His nostrils flared as he caught a whiff of something hauntingly familiar. His blue eyes widened in recognition. It was faint but unmistakable - the same scent he'd picked up from the cloaked figure earlier.

"Jaxon," he said quietly, "take a look at these markings. Carefully."

They moved closer to examine the symbols, mindful not to disturb any evidence. William's keen eyes darted from one marking to the next, his mind racing.

"Some of these I recognize from my studies," he murmured, more to himself than to Jaxon. "Ancient runes, occult sigils. But others... I've never seen anything like them."

Jaxon nodded, his brow furrowed in concentration. "It's like a twisted alphabet soup of the arcane."

As William surveyed the room, pieces of the puzzle began to slot together in his mind. The disappearances, the cloaked figure, and now these arcane markings - they were all connected. A chill ran down his spine as the implications sank in.

"This isn't just another supernatural disturbance," he said, his voice low and tense. "Something far more sinister is at play here, Jaxon. This case... it's bigger than we imagined."

Jaxon's hazel eyes met William's blue ones, understanding, and determination reflected in both. "Looks like we're in for one hell of a ride, old friend."

William nodded grimly. "Indeed. And we'll need to tread carefully from here on out. The game is afoot again, my friend."

WILLIAM'S KNEES CREAKED as he crouched, his keen eyes tracing the intricate lines of a symbol etched into the floorboards. The air hung heavy with the musty scent of neglect and something... else. Something he couldn't quite place. His fingers hovered over the marking, not daring to touch.

Heavy footsteps echoed through the decrepit room, each thud as familiar to William as his own heartbeat. He straightened, his back protesting the sudden movement, and turned to face the doorway.

Inspector Graves filled the frame, his broad shoulders nearly scraping the sides. The weak sunlight filtering through grimy windows caught the silver in his hair, a stark contrast to his perpetually furrowed brow. His steel-gray eyes narrowed as they landed on William, a cocktail of resignation and suspicion swirling in their depths.

"Blackwood," Graves growled, his voice rough as sandpaper. "I should've known you'd turn up here like a bad penny."

William's lips quirked into a tight smile. "Inspector. Always a pleasure to grace your crime scenes."

Graves grunted, shouldering his way into the room. His gaze darted from the overturned furniture to the strange markings on the walls, his frown deepening with each passing second. "Well? What've you found that my men haven't? And spare me the flowery language, if you please."

William chose his words carefully, aware of the delicate dance they always performed. "The symbols are... unusual. It's not your typical act of vandalism or gang territory marking. And there's a scent-" He caught himself, noting the skeptical arch of Graves's eyebrow. "I mean, traces of an unfamiliar substance. It could be connected to the other recent disturbances we've been seeing."

Graves's brow furrowed so deeply William half-expected it to stay that way permanently. "You're not talking about those disappearances, are you? That's a separate investigation, Blackwood. Don't go connecting dots that aren't there."

"Perhaps," William said, his tone measured. "But I suspect there might be a connection we're overlooking."

The inspector's jaw clenched, the muscle twitching visibly. William could almost see the gears turning behind those steely eyes, trying to reconcile what he was seeing with his understanding of the world.

"Look, Blackwood," Graves said, his voice low and gravelly. "I appreciate your... unique perspective. God knows it's been useful before. But I can't have you running around, stirring up panic about some grand conspiracy. The papers would have a field day."

William held up his hands, placating. "I'm merely following the evidence, Inspector. Same as you. Though perhaps with a slightly different lens."

Graves sighed, the sound seeming to come from the very depths of his soul. He ran a calloused hand over his face, suddenly looking older, every one of his years. "Fine. What else can you tell me? In plain English, if you don't mind. None of that mystical mumbo-jumbo."

William shared his observations, carefully skirting around anything overtly supernatural. He could see Graves struggling with the information, his ingrained skepticism warring with the undeniable strangeness of the scene before them.

Finally, the inspector spoke, his words coming slowly as if dragged from him. "I don't like it, Blackwood. Any of it. But I can't deny something odd is going on." He paused, clearly wrestling with his next words. "I'll keep you informed of any developments. But you keep me in the loop too, understood? No running off on your own and getting yourself killed. I don't need that paperwork."

William nodded, a genuine smile tugging at his lips. He knew this reluctant agreement was the best he could hope for. "Of course, Inspector. You have my word. Though I must say, your concern for my well-being is touching."

Graves snorted, already turning to leave. "Don't flatter yourself, Blackwood. I just don't want to explain to the Chief why our resident oddity ended up face-down in the Thames."

As the inspector's heavy footsteps faded, William turned back to the room giving Jaxon a wink, his mind already racing with possibilities. The game, as they said, was afoot.

WILLIAM'S PIERCING blue eyes darted across the room, his gaze sharp and focused. The sound of Inspector Graves' heavy footsteps echoed from the adjacent chambers, a constant reminder of the ticking clock. He locked eyes with Jaxon, both of them silently acknowledging the urgency of their search.

"Anything?" Jaxon whispered, his voice barely audible.

William shook his head, frustration etching lines on his forehead. "Not yet, but there's got to be something we're missing."

As he moved past a fallen curtain, a metallic glint caught his eye. William's heart quickened. He crouched down, his fingers brushing against the heavy fabric as he pulled it aside.

"Jaxon," he hissed, "come look at this."

Nestled beneath the curtain was a small, ornate box. It was no larger than William's palm, its surface adorned with intricate patterns that seemed to dance in the dim light. William reached out, his fingers hovering just above the object.

A faint thrumming of energy pulsed against his skin, barely perceptible but unmistakably magical. William's breath caught in his throat.

"Do you feel that?" he asked Jaxon, his voice low and urgent.

Jaxon nodded, his eyes wide. "What is it?"

William glanced over his shoulder. The human officers were still occupied, their voices a low murmur as they cataloged evidence. Inspector Graves stood in the doorway, deep in conversation with a junior constable.

"We can't let them find this," William muttered, his decision made in an instant.

His hand closed around the box. It was cool to the touch, heavier than its size suggested. He tried to open it, but the lid remained stubbornly shut.

"Locked," he said, frowning. "But how?"

"We'll figure it out later," Jaxon urged. "Just take it."

William slipped the box into his coat pocket, the weight of it pressing against his side like a secret burden. He straightened up, schooling his features into a mask of neutrality as he rejoined the bustling activity of the crime scene.

"Find anything interesting, gentlemen?" Inspector Graves called out, his bushy eyebrows raised in question.

William forced a casual shrug. "Nothing out of the ordinary, I'm afraid. Just more questions than answers."

As he moved about the room, offering observations and theories to the human investigators, William's mind raced. What connection did this box have to the disappearances? What secrets did it hold? The magical aura it emitted was unlike anything he'd encountered before - subtle, yet undeniably powerful.

He caught Jaxon's eye across the room, a silent understanding passing between them. They had taken a risk by removing evidence from the scene, but some instinct told William this was too important to leave in the hands of those who couldn't understand its true nature.

The responsibility settled on him like a physical weight, matching the heft of the box in his pocket. Whatever this object was, William knew it was now up to them to uncover its secrets - and face whatever consequences might follow.

WILLIAM'S BOOTS CLICKED softly against the cobblestones as he slipped away from the crime scene. The mysterious box in his pocket seemed to grow heavier with each step, its weight a constant reminder of the night's events. He ducked into a narrow alley, seeking refuge from prying eyes.

Leaning against the cold brick wall, William met Jaxon's gaze. A slight frown creased his brow as he considered their predicament.

"Well, that was a close call," Jaxon whispered, his voice barely audible above the distant city noise.

William nodded, his senses on high alert. "Too close. We need to figure out what's in this box before anyone else does."

The night air swirled around them, carrying a mix of scents. Smoke from distant chimneys mingled with the lingering aroma of street vendors' wares. Underneath it all, William detected a faint trace of something otherworldly. He closed his eyes and inhaled deeply, his heightened senses picking up nuances no human could detect.

"You smell that?" William asked, opening his eyes to look at Jaxon.

Jaxon shook his head. "Nothing out of the ordinary. What is it?"

"Something... not of this world," William replied, his voice low and tense.

He ran a hand through his dark hair, exhaling slowly. The events of the night played through his mind like a fevered dream - the chase, the cryptic symbols, the box now nestled in his pocket. His wolf instincts had guided him, giving him an edge in the investigation. But those same instincts set him apart from the humans he worked alongside.

William's gaze drifted upward, seeking out the sliver of sky visible between the towering buildings. The moon was hidden behind clouds, but he could feel its pull nonetheless. A part of him longed to answer that call, to shed his human form and run free. Another part recoiled at the thought, fearing discovery and rejection.

"You've got that look again," Jaxon observed, breaking into William's thoughts.

William's eyes snapped back to his partner. "What look?"

"Like you're caught between two worlds," Jaxon said softly. "Must be tough, mate."

William sighed, the weight of his dual nature pressing down on him. "You have no idea. In the human, mundane world, I'm always an outsider, hiding who I really am. And with my own kind... magical kind..." He trailed off, shaking his head.

"You don't quite fit in there either," Jaxon finished for him.

"Exactly. My dedication to human law and order doesn't always sit well with the werewolf pack's or other magical, wilder instincts."

As they stood there in the quiet alley, William felt a renewed sense of purpose wash over him. He straightened up, squaring his shoulders.

"But you know what?" he said, a hint of determination creeping into his voice. "This unique position of mine? It allows me to bridge those two worlds. To protect both humans and supernatural beings alike."

Jaxon clapped him on the shoulder. "And that's why you're the best partner I could ask for. Now, shall we crack open that box and see what all the fuss is about?"

William nodded, a small smile tugging at the corners of his mouth. It was a lonely path, fraught with danger and secrecy, but one he chose willingly. And with allies like Jaxon by his side, he felt ready to face any obstacles that awaited them.

WILLIAM'S HEART POUNDED as he and Jaxon navigated the labyrinth of shadowy streets. Every sense was on high alert, his eyes darting from shadow to shadow, ears straining for the slightest sound of pursuit. The box in his pocket seemed to have a life of its own, its otherworldly energy pulsing against his thigh, urging him forward with an insistent rhythm.

"This way," William whispered, tugging Jaxon's sleeve as he ducked down a narrow alley. The cobblestones were slick beneath their feet, and the air hung heavy with the stench of rotting vegetables and something far less pleasant.

A low-hanging sign creaked in the night breeze, its faded letters barely visible: "The Whistling Kettle." William's lips quirked in a humorless smile. What a quaint name for such a den of secrets and supernatural intrigue.

He approached a nondescript door, its wood weathered and scarred. Three sharp raps, followed by two slow ones. The sound echoed in the quiet alley, making William wince. A panel slid open with a soft scrape, revealing a pair of luminous green eyes that seemed to glow in the darkness.

"Moonlight's shadow falls twice," William murmured, the password feeling foreign on his tongue.

The eyes blinked once, and the door creaked open. William ushered Jaxon inside, casting one last wary glance over his shoulder before stepping into the tavern.

The interior hit him like a physical blow. Thick smoke coiled through the air, carrying a dizzying array of scents – the earthy musk of werewolves, the cloying sweetness of fairy wine, and underneath it all, the metallic tang of fresh blood. Hushed conversations in a dozen languages filled his ears, some familiar, others so alien they made his skin crawl.

William's gaze swept the room, taking in the motley assortment of patrons. A group of dwarves hunched over tankards of ale, their beards braided with glittering gems. In one corner, a pair of elegant noble elves sipped crimson, exquisite wine from crystal goblets. And there, in a shadowy booth...

"Puck," William muttered, nudging Jaxon. "Come on."

They approached the small figure hunched in the corner. Puck, a lesser fae barely larger than a child, twitched nervously at their approach. His gossamer wings fluttered feebly beneath a tattered coat, and his long, nimble fingers drummed an erratic rhythm on the sticky tabletop.

"You're late," Puck hissed as they slid into the booth. His eyes, a swirling mix of gold and green, darted around the room like frightened birds.

William leaned back, affecting a casual air he didn't feel. "Complications. You know how it is in this city."

Jaxon snorted. "Yeah, if by 'complications' you mean nearly getting eaten by a pack of ghouls."

Puck's eyes widened. "Ghouls? In the Upper Quarter? That's... unusual."

"Tell me about it," William growled. "Now, what've you got for me?"

The fae lifted a glass filled with swirling, phosphorescent liquid. It cast an eerie glow across his sharp features. "The blood drinkers are restless. Something's got 'em stirred up like a hive of angry bees."

William's patience wore thin. "Details, Puck. I need details."

Puck leaned in close, his voice barely above a whisper. The scent of wildflowers and ozone clung to him. "There's a name being passed around. Lord Everett Wentworth. Folks speak it like they're afraid he'll appear if they say it too loud."

William's brow furrowed, his mind racing. "Wentworth? The vampire lord? What's he up to?"

"Don't know specifics," Puck admitted, his wings fluttering nervously. "But the word is he's after something big. Ancient magic, is the kind that can reshape ... things... Maybe even on the same level as the Heart of Empathy."

As Puck spoke, William's mind raced, connecting threads of information. The strange symbols at the crime scene, the cloaked figure they'd glimpsed fleeing the area, the mysterious box now nestled in his pocket – could they all be linked to this vampire lord?

"Anything else?" William pressed, leaning forward.

Puck shook his head, downing his glowing drink in one swift gulp. He shuddered, whether, from the drink or fear, William couldn't tell. "That's all I got. And for both our sakes, you never heard it from me."

William nodded, sliding a pouch of coins across the table. The soft clink of metal seemed unnaturally loud in the smoky tavern.

As they rose to leave, Jaxon muttered, "Well, that was suitably cryptic and unhelpful."

William shot him a warning glance. "It's more than we had before. Come on, we need to move."

They made their way to the exit, the weight of this new information settling on William's shoulders like a heavy cloak. As the door closed behind them, he took a deep breath of the night air, tainted though it was.

"So," Jaxon said, his voice low, "what now?"

William's hand unconsciously moved to the box in his pocket. "Now," he said grimly, "we find out what Lord Wentworth wants with ancient magic... and why he's willing to tear the city apart to get it."

WILLIAM'S FOOTSTEPS echoed in the empty hallway as he pushed open the door to his office. Moonlight spilled through the grimy windows, casting long shadows across the cluttered space. He blinked, his eyes adjusting to the dim light as exhaustion tugged at his limbs.

"I should get some sleep," Jaxon mumbled, stifling a yawn and scratching his beard. "Meet up later to compare notes?"

William nodded, his mind still buzzing with the night's revelations. "Good idea. I'll see what I can dig up here."

As Jaxon's footsteps faded, William shrugged off his coat, draping it over a chair already piled high with dusty tomes. The fabric settled with a soft whisper, disturbing a thin layer of dust.

The mysterious box sat on his cluttered desk, its presence magnetic. William's gaze kept drifting back to it as he turned to the towering bookshelves lining the walls. His fingers trailed along the spines, seeking familiar titles.

He pulled down several volumes, their leather bindings protesting with creaks and groans. The musty scent of old paper filled his nostrils as he spread them across his desk. William's heart raced with anticipation as he began to sift through the arcane knowledge within.

"There has to be something here," he muttered, tracing intricate diagrams with a calloused finger. His eyes, a deep blue that appeared almost black in the low light, scanned faded script for any mention of the symbol or the vampire, Lord Everett Wentworth.

The steady ticking of an old clock marked the passage of time. Pages rustled as William delved deeper into his research. His eyes burned, and he rubbed them, smearing ink across his cheek.

"Blast," he grumbled, but pressed on, driven by a growing sense of urgency.

As the night wore on, connections began to form in William's mind like a spider's web. The disappearances plaguing London's supernatural community. The strange markings at the crime scene. Whispers of increased vampire activity. All of it pointed to something far more sinister than isolated incidents.

William leaned back in his chair, running a hand through his disheveled dark hair. He stared at the ceiling, mind racing. "It's all connected, but how?"

The pieces were there, but the full picture remained frustratingly out of reach. His gaze drifted to the box on his desk, its presence a constant reminder of the depths of this mystery.

A heavy realization settled over him, as thick and oppressive as London's infamous fog. This could be bigger than anything he'd faced before. William's shoulders sagged under the weight of it all.

"I can't do this alone, or even with Jaxon's help," he whispered to the empty room. His voice was hoarse from disuse. "I need more help."

William's mind raced through potential allies, people who could navigate the treacherous waters of both human and supernatural worlds. People he could trust with this and who had intricate knowledge of vampire lore. The enormity of the task ahead loomed before him, but a spark of determination ignited in his chest.

"Whatever's brewing beneath London's surface," he said, straightening in his chair, "I'll uncover it..."

WILLIAM BLACKWOOD'S eyes fluttered open as the first rays of sunlight pierced through the grimy office window. He groaned, stretching his aching muscles. The night had been long, but the case demanded his full attention.

"Bloody hell," he muttered, rubbing his eyes. "Another day, another mystery."

He stood, his gaze drawn to the evidence board he'd meticulously assembled. Red strings crisscrossed between newspaper clippings, sketches, and hastily scribbled notes. The magnitude of the case loomed before him, a tangled web of intrigue and danger.

William's blue eyes narrowed as he traced the connections. "This is it," he whispered to himself. "My chance to prove I'm more than just a monster."

The thought sent a surge of energy through his weary body. He paced the room, his footsteps echoing in the quiet office. The disappearances, the strange markings, Lord Wentworth's rumored quest for ancient magic - it all swirled in his mind, pieces of a puzzle he was desperate to solve.

He paused at his desk, his fingers brushing against the small, ornate box. It seemed to pulse with untold secrets, a tangible reminder of the supernatural world he straddled.

"I really am in over my head, and can't do this alone," William admitted aloud. The words felt heavy in the air, a rare acknowledgment of his own limitations.

William's quill scratched against the parchment, leaving inky trails as he scribbled down names. His brow furrowed in concentration, blue eyes darting across the page. The flickering candlelight cast dancing shadows on the worn desk, illuminating the growing list of potential allies.

"Gabriel," he muttered, tapping the quill against his chin. "The Crimson Paw's alpha. Wise old wolf, that one. And Fiona, his mate – her herbal concoctions could prove invaluable."

He paused, a wry smile tugging at the corners of his mouth. "And let's not forget Inspector Graves. A human detective who scoffs at the mere mention of werewolves. What could possibly go wrong?"

William leaned back in his creaking chair, running a hand through his tousled brown hair. His mind raced with possibilities, weighing the strengths and weaknesses of each potential ally.

"Lilly," he mused aloud, adding her name to the list. "Quick-witted and fearless. Elizabeth's sharp tongue could keep the vampires at bay, and Lady Cassandra... well, her connections alone make her worth considering."

As the list grew, so did the familiar thrill in William's chest. This was his element – piecing together the puzzle, assembling a team to bridge the gap between two worlds. He could almost taste the excitement, like electricity in the air before a storm.

"It's a motley crew," he chuckled, setting down the quill. "But if anyone can unravel this mystery and protect the innocent, it's us."

William's eyes gleamed with determination as he surveyed the names before him. Each one represented a thread in the complex tapestry of supernatural London – a world he was determined to protect, no matter the cost.

"Right then," he said, straightening his rumpled shirt. "Time to face the music."

William grabbed his coat, pausing for a moment to steel himself. Whatever challenges lay ahead in his quest to uncover the truth and save the missing people of London, he was ready to face them head-on. With a deep breath, he stepped out into the bustling streets of the Victorian London morning, the weight of two worlds resting on his shoulders.

Unlikely Alliances

The crunch of broken glass beneath William's boots echoed through the abandoned room. Dawn's pale light struggled through the fog, casting eerie shadows across the crime scene. With the police gone, an oppressive silence settled in, making the hairs on the back of his neck stand at attention.

William inhaled deeply, his werewolf senses on high alert. The lingering scent of fear tickled his nostrils, but there was something else—an acrid smell that made him wrinkle his nose. Dark magic. His suspicions were confirmed; this was no ordinary crime.

He knelt beside a strange symbol etched into the floorboards, pulling out his notebook. His pencil danced across the page, capturing every curve and line of the cryptic markings. So engrossed was he in his work that he almost missed the telltale prickle of another presence.

Almost.

In one fluid motion, William spun around, his hand instinctively reaching for his weapon. His eyes locked onto a familiar figure in the doorway, and his lips pulled back in an involuntary snarl.

Thaddeus Ironheart stood there, his weathered face a roadmap of scars. His steel-gray eyes, hard as flint, bore into William with unconcealed contempt.

"Blackwood," Thaddeus growled, his voice like gravel scraping against stone. "Fancy meeting you here."

William straightened, fighting the urge to bare his teeth. Every muscle in his body coiled, ready to spring. "Ironheart," he replied, keeping his voice level. "I could say the same."

The air between them crackled with unspoken hostility. William watched as Thaddeus's hand came to rest on the hilt of a silver dagger at his belt. The gesture wasn't lost on him.

"What's a dog like you doing sniffing around a crime scene?" Thaddeus asked, his lip curling in disdain.

The insult stung, but William refused to take the bait. He took a deep breath, reminding himself of his purpose. "My job," he said coolly. "Or have you forgotten I work with Scotland Yard now?"

Thaddeus snorted, a sound somewhere between amusement and disgust. "As if I'd forget. The day they let your kind help with investigations was the day this city truly went to the dogs."

William's jaw clenched so hard he thought his teeth might crack. He wanted nothing more than to wipe that smug look off Ironheart's face, but information was more valuable than the satisfaction of a fight.

"What brought you here, Ironheart?" William asked, gesturing around the room. "This doesn't seem like your usual hunting ground."

Suspicion was etched into every line of Thaddeus's face. For a moment, William thought he wouldn't answer. Then the vampire hunter spoke, his voice low and ominous.

"That's my business, wolf. But I'll tell you this—there's dark magic at work here. Magic that could tear this city apart if left unchecked."

William's gaze flickered to his notebook, where the strange symbols stared back at him. A chill ran down his spine as he realized just how right Thaddeus might be.

"Care to elaborate?" William pressed, his curiosity overriding his animosity. "Or is sharing information beneath the great Thaddeus Ironheart?"

Thaddeus's eyes narrowed. "Watch your tone, Blackwood. I don't owe you anything."

"No," William agreed, "but we're both here for a reason. Maybe, just maybe, we could actually accomplish something if we worked together."

A bark of laughter escaped Thaddeus. "Work with you? I'd sooner dance with a vampire."

William shrugged, turning back to the symbol on the floor. "Suit yourself. But remember, Ironheart, pride comes before a fall. And in this case, that fall might take all of London with it."

As he knelt to examine the marking more closely, William could feel Thaddeus's eyes boring into his back. He tensed, half-expecting the hunter to attack. Instead, he heard a heavy sigh.

"Fine," Thaddeus grumbled. "What do you make of that symbol?"

William allowed himself a small smile. It wasn't much, but it was a start. Perhaps there was hope for cooperation after all. As he began to share his observations, the first real rays of sunlight broke through the fog outside, illuminating the room in a new light. It was going to be an interesting day indeed.

THE WETNESS OF THE London fog still clung to William's coat as he crouched over the mysterious markings, his keen werewolf senses picking up traces of dark magic. The scent of evil hung in the air, faint but unmistakable.

A sudden rush of footsteps broke his concentration. William's ears twitched, before the vampire hunter even spoke.

"Out of my way, mutt," Thaddeus growled, his voice as rough as gravel. "This is no place for slow amateurs."

William rose slowly, squaring his broad shoulders as he turned to face the hunter. Thaddeus's steel-gray eyes glinted with disdain, his hand resting on the ornate dagger at his hip.

"Funny," William replied, keeping his voice level despite the anger bubbling beneath the surface. "I was about to say the same to you, Ironheart. Last I checked, my PI license gives me every right to be here."

Thaddeus scoffed, his fingers tightening around the dagger's hilt. "A piece of paper doesn't make you qualified. What could a domesticated wolf possibly hope to accomplish here?"

William's eyes flashed for a moment before he reined in his temper. "More than a trigger-happy vampire hunter, that's for certain. Some of us prefer to solve crimes, not create new ones."

Thaddeus's face darkened, a vein pulsing at his temple. "Watch your tongue, wolf. My methods may not be pretty, but they get results. Can you say the same?"

William felt his canines lengthening, a growl building in his chest. He took a deep breath, forcing the wolf down. "Results? Is that what you call leaving a trail of bodies across London? Some of us actually care about protecting both humans and supernaturals."

"Protecting supernaturals?" Thaddeus spat, disgust twisting his features. "They're the ones we need protection from. Or have you forgotten what you become under the full moon?"

The accusation stung, but William held his ground. "I haven't forgotten anything, Ironheart. But unlike you, I don't let my nature dictate my actions."

They glared at each other, the fog swirling around them like a physical manifestation of the tension in the air. Then, almost reluctantly, Thaddeus's gaze flicked to the symbols William had been examining.

"So, what do you make of those markings?" he asked, his tone gruff but tinged with genuine curiosity.

William blinked, caught off guard by the sudden shift. "They're unlike anything I've seen before," he admitted. "But there's a pattern to them, some kind of ritual circle."

Thaddeus nodded grudgingly, his steel-gray eyes narrowing as he studied the ground. "Aye, I noticed that too. And the residue of dark magic?"

"Faint, but present," William confirmed, surprised to find himself agreeing with the hunter. "You picked up on that as well?"

Thaddeus grunted, running a hand through his salt-and-pepper hair. "Course I did. Been hunting long enough to recognize the stench of evil."

As they continued to exchange observations, William realized Thaddeus had noticed details he'd missed - the orientation of the symbols, and traces of ash in specific locations. And from Thaddeus's reluctant nods, it was clear William's keen senses had picked up on things the human hunter couldn't detect.

"Well," William said, a wry smile tugging at his lips, "looks like the mutt and the trigger-happy hunter might actually make a decent team."

Thaddeus snorted, but there was a hint of amusement in his eyes. "Don't push your luck, wolf. We've got work to do."

WILLIAM'S KEEN SENSES tingled as he watched Thaddeus approach the ornate floorboards. The vampire hunter's weathered fingers traced invisible patterns, his brow furrowed in concentration. William's blue eyes narrowed, straining to see what had caught the old man's attention.

"Come here, wolf," Thaddeus muttered, his voice barely above a whisper. "Tell me what you see."

William crouched beside him, his nostrils flaring as he caught the faint scent of old blood. He leaned in closer, squinting at the wooden surface.

"I... I'm not sure," he admitted reluctantly.

Thaddeus clicked his tongue. "Look closer. Faint claw marks, easy to miss if you're not looking for them."

As the words left Thaddeus's mouth, William's eyes widened. There they were, barely perceptible scratches marring the polished wood. He felt a twinge of annoyance at having overlooked such a crucial detail.

"Blast," William growled. "How did I miss that?"

Thaddeus stood, his keen gaze sweeping the room like a hawk searching for prey. "Don't beat yourself up, wolf. Even I almost missed them." His eyes settled on a shadowy corner. "Now, what do you make of this?"

William followed Thaddeus's pointing finger, seeing nothing but dust and cobwebs. He shook his head, frustration mounting.

"Ash residue," Thaddeus explained, a hint of smugness in his voice. "Vampires leave it behind when they move at supernatural speeds."

William's nostrils flared again, this time catching the unmistakable scent. He cursed under his breath, annoyed at his earlier oversight.

"You're right," he admitted grudgingly. "There's been vampire activity here."

Thaddeus raised a bushy eyebrow, his steel-gray eyes glinting with curiosity. "Oh? And what led you to that conclusion, wolf? Besides my expert analysis, of course."

William hesitated, weighing his options. Finally, he decided to share his findings. "I followed a cloaked figure here earlier. There was a strange symbol on the door, and my fae informant shared some... concerning rumors about Lord Wentworth."

As William spoke, he watched Thaddeus's face grow increasingly grave. The vampire hunter's hand returned to his dagger hilt, knuckles white with tension.

"This symbol," Thaddeus interrupted, his voice low and urgent. "Was it a crescent moon pierced by a thorned vine?"

William nodded, surprised. "You've seen it before?"

Thaddeus's eyes darted around the room, as if expecting shadows to come alive at any moment. "Aye, I have. It's the mark of the Thorned Crescent, an ancient vampire clan I thought wiped out centuries ago."

"And Lord Wentworth?" William pressed, feeling a chill run down his spine.

"If he's involved with the Thorned Crescent," Thaddeus muttered, "this is far worse than I feared. We're not dealing with random attacks or a newly turned fledgling. This is organized, calculated... and on a scale I've never encountered before."

Their eyes met, a moment of understanding passing between them. William saw his own concern mirrored in Thaddeus's weathered face.

"We need to pool our resources," William said, surprising himself with the offer.

Thaddeus nodded reluctantly, his lips pressed into a thin line. "Agreed. But don't think this makes us friends, wolf. I still don't trust your kind."

William couldn't help but chuckle, despite the gravity of the situation. "Wouldn't dream of it, old man. Now, shall we get to work before the sun sets and we have bigger problems on our hands?"

Thaddeus grunted in agreement, already moving towards the door. "Aye, let's. And William?" He paused, glancing back. "Watch your back. The night is dark and full of fangs."

THE COBBLESTONE STREET echoed with the distant clatter of horse hooves and the hum of gaslit lamps. William's nostrils flared, catching the scent of rain-soaked earth and something else—fear. It radiated from Thaddeus in waves, a scent he'd never associated with the gruff vampire hunter before.

Suddenly, Thaddeus's calloused hand clamped around William's forearm. "This way," he growled, yanking the werewolf into a shadowy alcove between two looming buildings.

William's back hit the cold brick wall. "What the—"

"Quiet," Thaddeus hissed, his usual stern facade cracking. In the dim light, William could see the hunter's eyes darting left and right, searching for unseen threats.

"Thaddeus, what's going on?" William whispered, unnerved by the man's uncharacteristic behavior.

The vampire hunter's shoulders sagged, as if an invisible weight pressed down upon them. He met William's gaze, and for the first time, the werewolf saw raw vulnerability in those steel-gray eyes.

"Listen, wolf," Thaddeus began, his voice barely above a whisper. "You're in over your head. This isn't some petty supernatural spat or a string of random attacks. There's a conspiracy at play, one that's been festering for centuries."

William's brow furrowed, his amber eyes searching Thaddeus's face. "What do you mean, 'conspiracy'? You're not making sense."

Thaddeus closed his eyes, his face etched with pain. When he opened them again, they were distant, lost in a memory. "The Thorned Crescent," he breathed, the words hanging heavy in the air. "They're a special attack group within the Black Thorns. And they... they took everything from me."

William's chest tightened. He'd never heard Thaddeus speak like this before. The hunter's voice, usually so gruff and commanding, now trembled with suppressed emotion.

"My family, my home," Thaddeus continued, his words coming faster now. "All of it, gone in a single night of blood and fire. I can still hear the screams, still smell the smoke..."

William shifted uncomfortably, unsure how to respond. He cleared his throat. "Is that why you hunt them? The Black Thorns?"

Thaddeus nodded, his eyes refocusing on William. "But they're not just any vampire clan. They're ancient, and powerful beyond measure. And if they're resurfacing now, after all this time..." He trailed off, shaking his head.

A chill ran down William's spine, his wolf instincts bristling. The gravity of the situation began to sink in, far beyond what he'd initially imagined when he'd started investigating the disappearances.

"Thaddeus," William said, his voice low and urgent. "What exactly are we dealing with here?"

The vampire hunter's gaze hardened, resolved to replace the earlier vulnerability. "A force that could reshape the very fabric of our world, wolf. One that sees both humans and supernatural beings as mere pawns in their grand design."

William's throat constricted as the full magnitude of the situation dawned on him. The gravity of Thaddeus's revelation bore down upon his shoulders, more oppressive than any lunar transformation he'd ever experienced.

"What's our next move?" William inquired, his voice scarcely carrying over the muted urban din. The secluded nook they'd ducked into dampened most of the everyday bustle surrounding them, creating an eerie pocket of quiet amidst the city's ceaseless activity.

Thaddeus's eyes bored into him. "That depends on you, wolf. You can walk away now, go back to your simpler cases and relative safety. Or..." He paused, his expression grim. "Or you can join me in this fight. But I warn you, it'll be dangerous. Every step could be your last."

William stood frozen, the choice looming before him. The sensible part of his brain screamed at him to run, to forget everything he'd just heard. But something else, something deeper, whispered of duty and the chance to make a real difference.

He took a deep breath, the scents of the city mingling with the lingering fear and determination emanating from Thaddeus.

WILLIAM'S FINGERS RAKED through his tousled dark hair, his chest tightening as Thaddeus's words sank in. The vampire hunter's revelation hung between them like a fog, thick and suffocating.

"Damn it," William muttered, his blue eyes stormy. "This is bigger than us, isn't it?"

Thaddeus leaned against the wall, his scarred face etched with grim amusement. "What gave it away? The impending doom or the fact we're actually talking without trying to kill each other?"

William's lip curled. "Don't push it, Ironheart. Working together isn't exactly on my list of fantasies."

"Oh, I'm crushed," Thaddeus drawled. "Here I thought all werewolves dreamed of moonlit hunts with a dashing vampire slayer."

"Dashing?" William scoffed. "More like homicidal. Your kind isn't exactly known for asking questions before swinging that silver sword of yours."

Thaddeus's eyes hardened. "And your furry friends are paragons of restraint when the moon's full? Please."

William's hands clenched, claws threatening to emerge. He took a deep breath, forcing them back. "My control isn't the issue here. How do I know you won't compromise everything I stand for?"

"Because without each other, we're dead men walking," Thaddeus growled, pushing off the wall. "The Thorned Crescent will rip through London like it's made of paper. You know it, I know it."

William paced the small open space between the buildings absently avoiding a small puddle of filth as he stomped about on the cobbles beneath his boots. His mind raced, weighing options that all seemed to lead to disaster. Finally, he turned. "Fine. But we need rules. No unnecessary bloodshed, no innocents caught in the crossfire."

Thaddeus rolled his eyes. "This isn't a gentleman's game of whist, Blackwood. Sometimes you need to-"

William snapped, stepping closer to his companion. "Do what exactly?" he demanded. "Turn into the same fiends we're chasing? A boundary exists, Thaddeus. Step over it, and we're just as wicked as our quarry."

Quiet descended, interrupted solely by the faraway clatter of coaches outside the passageway. Thaddeus scrutinized William, his stern expression revealing a mix of exasperation and what could have been admiration.

"Your bleeding heart will get us killed," he muttered, then sighed. "But fine. You have contacts in the shadow world, I've got weapons that'll make a demon cry. We pool our resources and share intel. But when it comes to the fight-"

"We decide together," William cut in. "I'm not your trained hound, Ironheart."

Thaddeus's jaw clenched, a muscle ticking beneath his skin. For a moment, William thought he'd push back. Then, to his surprise, the hunter thrust out his hand.

"Partners, then," Thaddeus grumbled. "God help us both."

William hesitated, eyeing the calloused palm. Everything in him screamed this was madness. But the memory of innocent blood spilled by the Crescent steeled his resolve. He clasped Thaddeus's hand firmly.

"Partners," he agreed, a wry smile tugging at his lips. "Now, shall we toast our impending doom with tea or something stronger? There should be a tavern nearby."

WILLIAM'S EARS PRICKED at the faint creak of a crate and the shuffling of feet on cobblestones outside the backway alcove. His enhanced hearing caught the subtle rhythm of multiple footsteps trying—and failing—to be stealthy. He locked eyes with Thaddeus, tension coiling in his muscles.

"Company," William breathed, barely audible.

Thaddeus moved like a shadow, fingers finding the lantern's knob. With a swift twist, darkness engulfed them in the small space between the old leaning houses. William blinked, his supernatural vision adjusting instantly. He caught the outline of Thaddeus sliding into position beside the corner, a wicked curve of steel materializing in his hand.

William sank into a low stance, his senses heightened to their utmost. The pungent odor of grime mixed with the aroma of recently excavated soil assaulted him initially, followed by the metallic scent of newly spilled blood. His nostrils flared in revulsion.

The initial undead emerged with excruciating sluggishness from beyond the bend. William's eyes fixed upon a trio of silhouettes as they lurched forward. Their motions were erratic and clumsy—unmistakable indications of freshly transformed vampire servants, perhaps mere hours exhumed from their burial sites, still intoxicated by their heightened perceptions and unaccustomed to their amplified muscular prowess.

Without a word, William exploded into action. He lunged, tackling the first thrall with bone-crushing force. They hit the ground hard, the impact driving the stale air from the creature's unused lungs. William's fist connected with its jaw, the satisfying crunch of breaking bone reverberating through his knuckles.

To his right, Thaddeus moved with the fluid grace of a seasoned predator. His blade flashed in the dim light, opening a deep gash across a thrall's arm. The limb hung uselessly at its side as Thaddeus followed up with a vicious kick that sent the creature sprawling into the far wall.

The third thrall snarled, baring needle-sharp fangs as it charged at William. He ducked under wild, flailing arms, allowing Thaddeus to circle behind their attacker. A glance passed between them, a silent strategy forming in an instant. William feinted left, drawing the thrall's attention. It fell for the ruse, leaving its back exposed to Thaddeus's waiting blade, he swiftly parted the undead's spine.

In a matter of heartbeats, it was over. Three incapacitated thralls lay at their feet, groaning weakly.

William stood, chest heaving, and met Thaddeus's steely gaze. A flicker of grudging respect passed between them.

"Not bad... for a dog," Thaddeus muttered, wiping black clotted blood from his blade with a practiced flick.

William snorted, a hint of a smirk tugging at his lips. "You move well for a relic. Those creaky joints holding up alright?"

Thaddeus's eyes narrowed, but there was no real heat behind the glare. They surveyed their handiwork, and the presence of vampire thralls confirmed their worst suspicions.

"I suppose this proves your theory," William admitted, running a hand through his disheveled hair.

Thaddeus nodded grimly. "And demonstrates why we need each other, loathe as I am to admit it." He paused, studying William with a calculating gaze. "Ready to get to work, partner?"

William's eyebrows shot up. "Partner? That's a bit generous, don't you think?"

"Don't let it go to your head," Thaddeus grumbled. "We have a job to do, and I'd rather not end up as some bloodsucker's midnight snack."

"Agreed," William said, his expression hardening. "Let's find out who's pulling these thralls' strings and end this."

WILLIAM CROUCHED BEFORE the first thrall, his blue eyes locking onto the creature's wild gaze. The dank cellar air clung to his skin as he leaned in, voice soft as velvet. "Easy now. We're not here to hurt you."

The vampire thrall's muscles coiled tight, fangs gleaming in the dim light. Its ragged breaths echoed off stone walls.

"That's it," William coaxed, never breaking eye contact. "Just breathe. Tell us what you know, and we can help you."

Behind him, Thaddeus's heavy boots scraped against the floor. The older man's presence loomed like a storm cloud, setting William's teeth on edge.

Slowly, the thrall's shoulders lowered. Its gaze darted between them, less frantic now.

Thaddeus growled, impatience clear in his gruff voice. "Enough coddling. Speak up, or I'll show you how we dealt with your kind in my day."

William shot him a sharp look. "Thaddeus, please—"

But the threat had its intended effect. The thrall's resolve crumbled like wet sand.

"The prophecy," it rasped, words scraping past pointed teeth. "Our master... he seeks the Weaver's Loom."

Thaddeus leaned in, steel-gray eyes narrowing. "What loom?"

Another thrall piped up trying to coordinate its damaged limbs, words tumbling out in a frenzied rush. "A cosmic artifact! It can reshape reality itself, glorious in our master's image!"

William's mind raced, pieces clicking into place. A reality-altering artifact would explain the recent surge in supernatural activity across London. He kept his voice steady, though his heart hammered. "And who, pray tell, is your master?"

The thralls exchanged nervous glances. William could almost taste their fear, acrid and thick. It ran deeper than any threat he or Thaddeus could pose with claw or silver blade.

Thaddeus's patience snapped. He lunged forward, meaty hand closing around one thrall's collar. "Answer him!"

"Lord Everett!" the creature yelped, eyes bulging. "We serve Lord Everett Wentworth!"

William inhaled abruptly. Everett Wentworth – among the most ancient and influential bloodsuckers in the city, renowned for his ties to aristocratic circles. If such a being coveted this relic...

Thaddeus let go of the minion, pivoting toward William with a somber inclination of his head. Their gazes locked, a wordless understanding passing between them. Their contrasting approaches had produced outcomes neither could have accomplished independently.

As they had extracted all possible intelligence from the recently deceased thralls, they swiftly and efficiently terminated their undead state using a silver dagger and consecrated water. William's thoughts raced. He cast a look at Thaddeus, observing the tightness in his companion's jawline. "Well," William remarked sardonically, "I have a single acquaintance at the Yard, Elizabeth. I don't imagine you have any contacts within Scotland Yard who'd give credence to our tales of vampiric nobility and otherworldly looms capable of unleashing catastrophe upon our existence?"

Thaddeus snorted. "Lad, half my friends don't believe in indoor plumbing yet."

William allowed himself a wry chuckle. Their unlikely partnership might just be the key to unraveling this growing threat. They'd need every advantage – and a healthy dose of gallows humor – to face what lay ahead.

HALF AN HOUR LATER, William leaned against his mahogany desk in his study, his muscular arms crossed over his chest. The flickering candlelight cast dancing shadows across his face, highlighting the worry lines etched around his eyes. Across the room, Thaddeus paced like a caged lion, his boots thumping against the worn floorboards.

"Dammit, Blackwood!" Thaddeus exploded, whirling to face William. "We can't just sit here twiddling our thumbs. Every second we waste, Everett's sinking his fangs into another innocent!"

William's jaw clenched, but his voice remained steady. "And charging in half-cocked is a surefire way to get ourselves killed. We need intel, Thaddeus. Solid leads."

Thaddeus's eyes blazed with fury. "Intel? While people are getting attacked in the streets?" He slammed his fist against the wall, rattling a nearby bookshelf.

William pushed off from the desk, his own temper rising. "And how many more will join them if we fail? Think, man! We're not dealing with some common cutthroat. Everett's got centuries of cunning and an army of the undead at his beck and call."

Thaddeus scoffed, his lip curling in disgust. "Cunning? Evil is evil, Blackwood. It needs to be put down, plain and simple."

"Is it really that black and white?" William challenged, taking a step closer. "What about redemption? Second chances?"

"For bloodsuckers?" Thaddeus spat on the floor. "There's no salvation for monsters."

The words hung in the air like a physical blow. William's eyes, usually an amiable tone of blue, flashed with a hint of frosty power – a reminder of the beast that lurked beneath his skin. "And what does that make me, Thaddeus?" he asked, his voice dangerously soft. "A werewolf. Am I beyond redemption too?"

The room fell silent, save for the crackle of the dying fire. Thaddeus's shoulders sagged, the fight draining out of him. "You're... different," he muttered, unable to meet William's gaze.

"Because you know me," William pressed, seizing the moment. "What if others deserve that same chance? What if there's more gray in this world than just black and white?"

Thaddeus ran a hand through his aging black, with salt-and-pepper hair, frustration etched in every line of his weathered face. "Christ,

Blackwood. While we're having a bloody philosophy debate, Cursed Everett's out there plotting his next move."

William nodded, conceding the point. "You're right. We need action. But smart action, not a suicide mission."

Their eyes locked, and a grudging respect passed between them. Thaddeus sighed, the sound heavy with resignation. "Alright then, genius. What's your grand plan?"

A hint of a smile tugged at William's lips. "We play to our strengths. Your encyclopedic knowledge of vampire lore, my investigative skills. We track Everett's movements, gather allies who can stomach working with a werewolf, and then – when we're good and ready – we strike."

Thaddeus considered for a long moment, then gave a slow nod. "A compromise. I suppose I can work with that. But if I see an opening to take that bastard's head off, I'm taking it."

"Fair enough," William chuckled. "Now, shall we get to work? These vampires won't slay themselves."

As they bent over maps and began outlining their strategy, William felt a glimmer of hope. This unlikely partnership – a grizzled vampire hunter and a reluctant werewolf – might just be London's best defense against the gathering darkness.

THE FIRST RAYS OF SUNLIGHT crept through the windows of William's study, casting long shadows across the polished wooden floor. William caught Thaddeus's eye, a wry smile tugging at the corner of his mouth. The irony of their situation wasn't lost on him.

"A werewolf and a vampire hunter working together," William mused, his voice tinged with amusement. "Who'd have thought?"

Thaddeus grunted, but the steel-gray eyes that met William's held a glimmer of humor. "Strange times make for strange bedfellows, Blackwood."

William's fingers paused on the fabric of his sleeve, the cool metal of his cufflink pressing against his skin. "Indeed," he said, his gaze drifting to the bustling London street beyond the window. "I never imagined I'd be sharing information with someone who's dedicated their life to hunting supernatural creatures."

A heavy sigh escaped Thaddeus, his broad shoulders slumping slightly beneath his worn leather coat. "And I never thought I'd trust a werewolf with... well, anything." He met William's gaze, a flicker of uncertainty crossing his weathered features. "Perhaps I've been too quick to judge in the past."

William nodded, feeling the weight of that admission settle between them. "We've both had our preconceptions challenged," he said softly. "It seems this threat is bigger than our old rivalries."

"Agreed," Thaddeus said, his voice gruff but sincere. A hint of a smile played at the corners of his mouth. "Though don't expect me to start howling at the moon with you."

William chuckled, the sound rich and warm in the quiet room. "And I won't be joining you for any vampire staking parties," he quipped back.

As they stepped out into the bustling London street, the cacophony of horse hooves, carriage wheels, and chattering pedestrians enveloped them. William inhaled deeply, the scents of the city – smoke, horses, and humanity – mingling with the earthy smell of the grizzled hunter beside him. A strange sense of camaraderie settled over him, born of necessity and forged in the face of a greater evil.

Thaddeus cleared his throat, his eyes scanning the crowded street. "Well, Blackwood, I'll follow up on those vampire nests in the East End," he said, his voice low. "You'll look into the mystical angle, maybe talk to Jaxon or Lady Cassandra?"

William nodded, his mind already racing with possibilities. "I'll consult with some contacts about the Weaver's Loom," he replied. "We'll meet back here at sundown?"

"Sundown it is," Thaddeus agreed. He hesitated for a moment, then extended his hand, rough and calloused from years of wielding weapons. "Good hunting, werewolf."

William grasped it firmly, feeling the strength in the hunter's grip. "And to you, hunter."

As they parted ways, William couldn't help but marvel at how quickly the world could change. The weight of his pocket watch seemed to remind him of the passage of time. Yesterday, he would have considered Thaddeus an enemy. Today, this gruff, battle-worn man might be the key to saving London from an unimaginable threat.

William's heightened senses picked up Thaddeus's steady heartbeat fading into the crowd. He shook his head, a wry smile playing on his lips. Life, it seemed, had a way of surprising even the most jaded of supernatural creatures.

WILLIAM STEPPED OUT onto the cobblestone street, his boots clicking against the worn stones. A shiver raced down his spine, and he tugged his coat tighter around him. The weight of their discovery pressed on his mind, far heavier than any supernatural threat he'd faced in his years as an investigator.

His eyes darted from rooftop to rooftop, a habit ingrained by years of vigilance. A flicker of movement caught his attention. There, on the edge of a nearby building, a cloaked figure watched them. William blinked, and in that instant, the watcher vanished like morning mist.

"Thaddeus," he called out, but his companion was too far ahead to hear. William hesitated, torn between pursuing the mysterious observer and catching up to Thaddeus. He decided against chasing shadows, not wanting to add to their already mounting concerns.

Thaddeus, meanwhile, found his gaze drawn to the ground. Among the worn cobblestones, intricate symbols had been etched with painstaking precision. They bore a striking resemblance to the markings at the crime scene, yet these were more elaborate, more sinister.

His fingers twitched, itching to trace the lines, to decipher their meaning. But he resisted, aware of the dangers such arcane knowledge could bring. "Bloody hell," he muttered under his breath, "what have we stumbled into?"

William finally caught up, his brow furrowed with concern. "You look like you've seen a ghost, Thaddeus. What's wrong?"

Thaddeus glanced up, noting the distracted look in William's eyes. He considered sharing his discovery but thought better of it. "Nothing," he lied, "just... thinking about our next move."

William raised an eyebrow, unconvinced. "Right. And I'm the Queen of England."

Thaddeus snorted, a hint of a smile tugging at his lips. "You'd look dreadful in a crown, my friend."

As they walked side by side, the air between them seemed thick with unspoken words and shared apprehension. Their newfound alliance, forged in the face of an overwhelming threat, felt both fragile and vital.

"We should part ways here," Thaddeus said, his voice low. "Meet back as agreed upon tonight?"

William inclined his head, his gaze sweeping over the throng surrounding them. "Watch yourself, Thaddeus. I've got a hunch we're more entangled than we initially thought."

Thaddeus gave William's shoulder a firm squeeze. "You can say that again, old chap. We're certainly wading into murky waters, aren't we?" With those words, he vanished into the bustling morning masses, abandoning William to his private musings.

As William watched his friend disappear, the weight of their impending task settled on his shoulders like a lead cloak. He took a deep breath, steeling himself for what was to come. "Into the breach once more," he murmured, before setting off in the opposite direction, the bustling streets of London swallowing him whole.

The Vampire Lord's Ambition

L ord Everett Wentworth's study pulsed with an eerie energy. Candlelight danced across the room, casting long shadows that seemed to writhe with a life of their own. The vampire lord sat hunched over his mahogany desk, his pale fingers tracing the yellowed pages of an ancient manuscript.

"Fascinating," he murmured, his dark eyes gleaming with excitement. "The Weaver's Loom... it's all here."

The air around him crackled with power, making the hairs on the back of his neck stand on end. He leaned in closer, his nose nearly touching the fragile parchment.

A soft knock at the door broke his concentration. "Enter," he called, not bothering to look up.

The door creaked open, and a young servant stepped in, carrying a silver tray. The moment he crossed the threshold, the supernatural aura hit him like a physical force. He stumbled, his hands shaking as he tried to steady the tray.

Lord Wentworth's head snapped up, his eyes narrowing. "Careful, boy," he hissed.

The servant swallowed hard, his face pale with fear. "M-my apologies, my lord," he stammered, inching forward.

As he set the tray down, a drop of crimson liquid sloshed over the rim of the crystal goblet landing on the tray. Lord Wentworth's nostrils flared, catching the coppery scent of blood.

"Your clumsiness tries my patience," he said, his voice soft but laced with menace.

The servant's eyes widened in terror. "F-forgive me, my lord. It won't happen again."

Lord Wentworth waved a dismissive hand. "See that it doesn't. Now leave me."

The servant bowed low and backed out of the room, his footsteps barely audible on the plush carpet. As the door closed, Lord Wentworth allowed himself a small smile of triumph.

He leaned back in his chair, running a hand through his raven-black hair. "The setback at the hidden chamber was... unfortunate," he mused aloud. "But this..." He tapped the manuscript. "This changes everything."

His dark eyes gleamed with renewed determination. The path to ultimate power lay before him, and nothing would stand in his way.

LORD EVERETT WENTWORTH'S pale fingers traced the faded ink on the ancient manuscript, his dark eyes narrowing as he focused on a particular passage. The parchment crackled beneath his touch, its age-worn surface revealing secrets long hidden from mortal eyes.

"The Weaver's Loom," he whispered, savoring each syllable as if tasting a fine wine. "Ms. Jenny's loom... a tool to rewrite the very fabric of reality."

He leaned back in his high-backed leather chair, allowing the weight of this revelation to settle over him. Wentworth had known of the loom's existence for centuries, had pursued whispers and rumors across continents. But this... this was different. This manuscript held details he'd never encountered before.

"Well, well," he mused, a hint of excitement creeping into his usually controlled voice. "It seems our dear Ms. Jenny has been holding out on us all."

The prophecy unfolded before him, each line painting a vivid picture of power beyond imagination. Wentworth's lips curled into a smile, revealing the tips of his fangs. His mind raced with possibilities, each more tantalizing than the last.

He rose from his seat, unable to contain the energy surging through his immortal frame. Pacing the study, his footsteps muffled by the thick Persian rug, Wentworth allowed himself to dream.

"A world reshaped according to my desires," he said, his voice low and filled with dark promise. "Vampires ruling openly, no longer confined to the shadows. And I, Lord Everett Wentworth, standing at the pinnacle of this new order."

The magnitude of the discovery sent a shiver of anticipation through him. He paused by the window, gazing out at the fog-shrouded London streets below. How different they would look when he wielded the loom's power.

"At last," he murmured, pressing a hand against the cool glass, "the key to everything."

Wentworth returned to the desk, his fingers drumming against the manuscript's weathered pages. The prophecy spoke of challenges, of trials to overcome before one could claim the loom's power. But such obstacles were mere trifles to a being of his age and cunning.

"Challenges, indeed... What tasty morsels for little old me," he scoffed, a wry smile playing across his lips. "As if anything could stand in my way now."

The setback in the hidden chamber no longer seemed so insurmountable. This new information, this prophecy, would guide his path forward. Wentworth's dark eyes gleamed with renewed determination.

"The world will tremble," he said, his voice barely above a whisper yet filled with unshakeable conviction. "And I shall remake it in my image."

He closed the manuscript with a gentle touch, almost reverent in its care. Wentworth's gaze swept across his study, taking in the shelves of arcane tomes and mystical artifacts. Soon, they would all pale in comparison to the power he would wield.

"Ms. Jenny," he mused, a hint of amusement coloring his tone, "I do believe it's time we had a little chat about your loom."

CANDLELIGHT FLICKERED, casting eerie shadows across the room's dark corners. He paused, his pale fingers drumming against the polished surface of his mahogany desk.

"Come," he commanded, his voice barely above a whisper.

One by one, they emerged from the darkness: Tilitha, her raven hair cascading over shoulders draped in crimson silk; Marcus, his hulking frame filling the doorway; golden eyes gleaming with barely contained violence; and Lady Moiragwynn, lithe and graceful, her silver hair a stark contrast to her youthful features.

Wentworth's gaze swept over his assembled lieutenants, a predatory smile playing at the corners of his mouth. "My faithful servants," he purred, "I trust you're all... hungry for change?"

Marcus chuckled, a low rumble that sent shivers down the spines of the others. "Always, Master."

Wentworth began to pace, and each step was measured and deliberated. The candlelight caught the sharp angles of his face, accentuating the otherworldly pallor of his skin. "For centuries, we've lurked in the shadows, content with the scraps of humanity," he mused. "But no longer."

Tilitha leaned forward, curiosity burning in her obsidian eyes. "What do you mean, Master?"

A triumphant gleam lit Wentworth's ice-blue eyes. "I've discovered something extraordinary, my dears. A tool that will elevate us from predators to gods."

The room fell silent, save for the soft crackle of candle wicks. Moiragwynn's brow furrowed. "Gods? Surely you don't mean—"

"I mean exactly that," Wentworth interrupted, his voice sharp. "The power to reshape reality itself."

A collective gasp rippled through the group. Marcus clenched his fists, barely containing his excitement. "How do we obtain this power, Master?"

Wentworth's lips curled into a cruel smile. "Through fear, my dear Marcus. Through suffering." He locked eyes with each of his lieutenants in turn. "I need you to expand our hunting grounds. No more skulking in alleys, preying on the destitute and forgotten. We require... quality victims."

Tilitha's eyes widened. "The risks—"

"Are nothing compared to the rewards," Wentworth cut in. He glided towards her, cupping her chin in his hand. "Imagine it, Tilitha. No more hiding. No more cowering from the sun. We would be unstoppable."

She swallowed hard, torn between desire and trepidation. "And if we fail?"

Wentworth's grip tightened, his nails digging into her porcelain skin. "Then pray you don't live to regret it."

He released her and turned to address the group. "Go forth, my children. Sow terror in the hearts of the worthy. Bring me their fear, their anguish, their despair." His eyes blazed with fanatical intensity. "And I shall forge it into the key that unlocks our destiny."

As his lieutenants filed out, each lost in their own thoughts of power and peril, Wentworth returned to his desk. He traced his fingers over an ancient tome, its cover adorned with eldritch symbols.

"Soon," he whispered to the empty room. "Very soon."

THE LOOM OF MS. JENNY

THE CRACKLE OF PARCHMENT filled the dimly lit study as Wentworth unfurled an intricate map of London across his polished mahogany desk. His pale fingers smoothed out the creases, revealing a sprawling web of streets and alleys. The vampire's lieutenants crowded around, their eyes glinting with a mix of curiosity and hunger.

Wentworth's lips curled into a smirk. "Gentlemen, ladies," he purred, his aristocratic accent dripping with anticipation. "Behold our playground."

His index finger traced the inky line of the Thames. The assembled vampires leaned in, hanging on his every word.

"Now, pay attention," Wentworth commanded, tapping specific locations. "These areas are ripe for the picking."

He indicated the docks. "Here, desperate souls practically throw themselves at us." His finger slid to another spot. "The opium dens - addicts too lost in their haze to notice a little blood loss." Finally, he circled an affluent neighborhood. "And here, where the rich and complacent sleep, unaware of the monsters at their door."

Gladys, a striking redhead, licked her lips. "Oh, I do love the taste of privilege," she purred.

Wentworth's ice-blue eyes locked onto hers. "Patience, my dear. We must tread carefully."

He straightened, surveying his minions. "The human authorities may be blind, but they're not completely useless. And let's not forget our... furry friends."

Mortimer, tall and gaunt with eyes like frozen chips, sneered. "The mongrels grow bolder by the day."

"Indeed," Wentworth nodded. "And those blasted fae... we can't afford to draw their attention. Not yet."

He turned to Mortimer. "You'll oversee our operations in the East End. Your talent for melting into shadows will be invaluable there."

A cruel smile played at the corners of Mortimer's thin lips. "It will be my pleasure, sir."

"Gladys," Wentworth continued, "your charm has ensnared many a foolish mortal. I want you to infiltrate the upper crust. Find us some juicy targets among the nobility."

The redhead's green eyes sparkled with malicious glee. "Consider it done, darling."

As Wentworth assigned roles to each lieutenant, his carefully cultivated facade began to slip. The predator within clawed its way to the surface, eager for the hunt to begin. His eyes blazed with an unholy light, and his voice took on a guttural quality.

"Remember," he growled, gripping the edge of the desk so hard the wood creaked. "We are not mere animals, driven by base hunger. We are the apex predators, and London is our hunting ground."

The assembled vampires nodded, their own eyes gleaming with bloodlust. The air in the study crackled with dark anticipation as they prepared to unleash their reign of terror upon the unsuspecting city.

THE DANK AIR CLUNG to Wentworth's skin as he descended the winding staircase, each step echoing off the cold stone walls. His nostrils flared at the acrid scent of decay mingled with the electric tang of ancient magic.

As he entered the vast circular ritual chamber, the flickering torchlight cast his shadow across the faces of his gathered acolytes. Their eyes, wide with a mixture of awe and trepidation, followed his every move.

Wentworth's lips curled into a thin smile. "Shall we begin?" he asked, his voice barely above a whisper.

The chamber burst into activity. Chalk scraped against rough stone as the acolytes etched intricate symbols onto the floor. Wentworth's keen gaze darted from one to another, scrutinizing every line and curve.

"Steady now," he hissed, noticing an acolyte's trembling hand. "One misplaced stroke could be our undoing."

The young man swallowed hard, steadying his grip on the chalk. "Yes, Master Wentworth," he mumbled, sweat beading on his brow.

At the chamber's edges, more followers worked with feverish intensity. The air filled with the pungent aroma of crushed herbs and the soft clink of glass vials.

Wentworth prowled among them, inspecting their work with critical eyes. He paused, lifting a twisted piece of metal that seemed to devour the torchlight. With reverent care, he placed it within the chalk circle.

"This artifact," he explained, his voice carrying easily in the hushed chamber, "is the key to unlocking our prize. Ms. Jenny's loom has eluded us for centuries, but tonight, we change that."

An acolyte nearby couldn't contain her curiosity. "Master, how can you be certain this will work?"

Wentworth fixed her with a piercing stare. "Doubt has no place here. Faith in our cause is paramount."

As the final preparations neared completion, the atmosphere shifted palpably. The air grew thick and heavy, laden with malevolent energy. Torches sputtered and danced, casting grotesque shadows across the walls.

Wentworth stood at the heart of it all, barely containing his excitement. Centuries of patience, of meticulous planning, had led to this moment. He could feel the power building around him, a dark promise whispering in his ear.

"At last," he murmured, more to himself than anyone else. "The fruits of our labor are within reach."

An expectant hush fell over the chamber as Wentworth raised his arms, ready to begin the ritual that would change everything.

WENTWORTH'S EYELIDS fluttered closed as the ritual began, the droning chants of his acolytes fading to a distant hum. His mind drifted, memories surfacing like bubbles in a murky pond.

He saw himself as a young nobleman, swagger in his step as he strode through the halls of his family's estate. The scent of polished wood and expensive perfumes tickled his nostrils. His human self laughed, the sound echoing off marble walls.

"Another brandy, Jeeves!" he called, voice dripping with entitlement.

The scene shifted abruptly. Searing pain erupted in his neck as fangs pierced flesh. Wentworth gasped, reliving the agony of transformation. He felt his humanity slipping away, replaced by an icy immortality.

"What... what's happening to me?" he croaked, his voice barely recognizable.

The world sharpened, colors intensifying as vampire eyes replaced mortal ones. Everything looked different now - crisper, colder, full of untapped potential.

Centuries flashed by in a dizzying blur. Wentworth glimpsed himself crossing oceans, scaling mountains, devouring knowledge like a man starved. He pulled strings from the shadows, orchestrating the rise and fall of empires.

"Dance, my little puppets," he murmured, a cruel smile playing on his lips.

Then came the moment that changed everything. In a musty Prague library, dust motes dancing in shafts of moonlight, his fingers trembled as they caressed an ancient tome. The prophecy leaped from the page, searing itself into his mind.

The Weaver's Loom - an artifact of unimaginable power.

Wentworth's breath caught in his throat. "With this," he whispered, "I could reshape the very fabric of reality."

Ambition surged through him like wildfire. He envisioned a world remade in his image, vampires ruling openly with him as their immortal king.

His path crystalized in that instant. Nothing else mattered but the Loom. Rivals fell before him, alliances crumbled, and entire bloodlines were manipulated - all stepping stones on his relentless march toward destiny.

Wentworth's eyes snapped open, crimson irises blazing in the gloom of the ritual chamber. Dark energy pulsed around him, mirroring the intensity of his desire.

"Soon," he breathed, fangs glinting in the flickering candlelight. "Soon, the world will be mine to shape as I see fit."

A wicked smile curved his lips. The sacrifices he'd made, the blood he'd spilled - it would all be worth it in the end. The Loom was within his grasp, and with it, ultimate power.

THE AIR CRACKLED WITH dark energy as Wentworth's voice rose above the chants of his acolytes. Sweat beaded on his brow, his eyes glowing with an eerie light as he felt the veil between worlds grow thin.

Suddenly, the magical currents shifted. The carefully controlled energies began to fluctuate wildly, like a storm-tossed ship on a raging sea. Wentworth's brow furrowed, his fingers trembling as he struggled to maintain his grip on the spell.

"Focus, you fools!" he snarled at his followers, spittle flying from his lips. But his command was drowned out by a deafening roar that shook the very foundations of the chamber.

The air before him shimmered like a heat haze, and visions began to flicker into existence. Wentworth's eyes widened, his breath catching in his throat as he saw glimpses of unfamiliar figures moving through London's shadowy streets.

A werewolf, lean and alert, prowled through a narrow alley. Its blue eyes gleamed in the darkness, muscles rippling beneath its silver-gray fur. Beside the beast walked a man with hard, steel-gray eyes and a crossbow at his hip - a vampire hunter. The unlikely pair moved with purpose, their steps in perfect sync.

Wentworth's fists clenched, nails digging into his palms. "No," he whispered, his voice hoarse. "This cannot be."

As the vision faded, leaving Wentworth seething, he turned to his lieutenants. They stood frozen in shock, their faces pale and drawn in the flickering candlelight.

"Find them," he hissed, his voice dripping with venom. "I want every scrap of information you can gather on this wolf and hunter. Their names, their haunts, their weaknesses - everything."

His minions nodded eagerly, scurrying from the chamber like rats fleeing a sinking ship.

Wentworth paced the room, his footsteps echoing off the stone walls. His mind raced, thoughts tumbling over one another like leaves in a storm. "This changes everything," he muttered, running a hand through his disheveled hair. "A werewolf and a hunter, working together? Impossible."

He paused, staring at the intricate symbols etched into the floor. "I've come too far," he growled, his voice low and dangerous. "Sacrificed too much. I won't let some mongrel and a mortal with delusions of heroism interfere."

Wentworth's eyes narrowed, a cruel smile twisting his lips. "They must be eliminated," he said, his voice barely above a whisper. "And quickly, before they become a true obstacle. London will be mine, no matter the cost."

THE LOOM OF MS. JENNY

LORD EVERETT WENTWORTH burst into his study, his usual grace abandoned. The heavy oak door slammed behind him with a resounding thud. He strode to the fireplace, his reflection in the ornate mirror above revealing a face twisted with rage.

"Damn it all!" he snarled, running a hand through his raven-black hair. The flickering flames cast eerie shadows across his pale features, accentuating the steel in his gray eyes.

Wentworth's mind raced, replaying the scene he'd witnessed earlier. A werewolf and a vampire hunter, working together. The very thought made his stomach churn.

"Centuries of work," he muttered, pacing back and forth. "All hanging by a thread because of this... this abomination of an alliance."

He paused before a massive map of London was pinned to the wall. His long, elegant fingers traced the intricate network of streets and alleys. Each touch sent a spark of possibility through his mind.

"I could simply eliminate them both," Wentworth mused aloud. But even as the words left his lips, he shook his head. "No, too messy. Too obvious. I need something more... refined."

A cruel smile played across his lips as a more devious plan took shape. He turned to his desk, pulling out a sheet of parchment and a quill.

"Why dirty my own hands," he chuckled softly, "when I can make them destroy each other?"

The scratch of quill on parchment filled the room as Wentworth began to write. His elegant script flowed across the page, weaving a tapestry of lies and half-truths.

"A whisper here about the hunter's true intentions," he murmured. "A rumor there about the werewolf's past betrayals. How delightfully easy it will be to play on their inherent mistrust."

But Wentworth was nothing if not thorough. He pulled out another sheet, sketching out contingency plans. His gray eyes glittered with cold calculation as he detailed potential traps and ambushes.

"And if manipulation fails," he said to the empty room, "we move to more... direct methods."

As the night wore on, Wentworth's frustration gave way to a grim determination. He stood, stretching his tall frame, and walked to the window. The gas lamps of London flickered in the distance, a reminder of the world he sought to control.

"Let them think they've gained the upper hand," he said softly. "It will make their fall all the more satisfying."

With a final glance at his handiwork spread across the desk, Lord Everett Wentworth allowed himself a small, victorious smile. This setback was merely an opportunity to prove why he had survived and thrived for so long. He would adapt, overcome, and ultimately prevail.

THE MAHOGANY DOOR OF Wentworth's study creaked open, admitting a stream of men with furrowed brows and twitching fingers. The vampire lord sat behind his imposing desk, his pale fingers steepled beneath his chin. A smirk played at the corners of his bloodless lips as he surveyed his lieutenants.

"Gentlemen," Wentworth purred, his voice as smooth as aged whiskey, "our moment has arrived."

He rose, his movements fluid and predatory. The candlelight caught the glint in his obsidian eyes as he circled the room.

"I require your utmost discretion and skill," he continued. "Every whisper in a dark alley, every furtive glance across a crowded room - I want to know about it all."

One of the men, a burly fellow with a scar across his cheek, cleared his throat. "Beggin' your pardon, m'lord, but what exactly are we lookin' for?"

Wentworth's smile widened, revealing the barest hint of fang. "An excellent question, Mr. Hobbs."

He glided to a nearby cabinet, withdrawing a stack of sealed envelopes. The wax seals bore the imprint of a twisted tree - Wentworth's personal sigil.

"Within these, you'll find your specific assignments," he explained, distributing the envelopes. "Your primary targets are the werewolf and the hunter. I want to know their strengths, their weaknesses, their favorite bloody breakfast if need be."

A nervous titter rippled through the group. Wentworth's eyes narrowed, silencing them instantly.

"This is no laughing matter, gentlemen. Our very survival may hinge on this information."

As his agents filed out, murmuring amongst themselves, Wentworth turned his attention to a weathered tome on his desk. Its cover was etched with symbols that seemed to writhe in the flickering candlelight.

"Now," he murmured, tracing the symbols with a long, pale finger, "for the true prize."

Hours passed as Wentworth pored over the cryptic text, deciphering clues to the loom's components. Each revelation sent a thrill of excitement through his cold, dead veins.

"Fascinating," he breathed, scribbling notes furiously. "To think, such power has been hidden in plain sight all this time."

He summoned more agents, this time tasking them with scouring London's occult underbelly for the rare artifacts he needed.

"Spare no expense," he instructed a wiry man with darting eyes. "And remember, discretion is paramount. We cannot afford to alert our... competitors."

Across London, the supernatural community buzzed with activity. In smoky opium dens and hidden speakeasies, creatures of the night whispered of a growing power.

"Have you heard?" a goblin hissed to his fairy companion. "The old bat's on the move. Says he's found something big."

The fairy snorted, her gossamer wings fluttering nervously. "Wentworth's always claiming he's found something big. Remember the incident with the cursed chamber pot?"

But despite the skepticism, alliances were formed and broken with dizzying speed. Everyone wanted to be on the winning side when the dust settled.

Meanwhile, William and Thaddeus continued their investigation, unaware of the web tightening around them. In a dingy tavern that reeked of stale beer and desperation, William met with a trembling informant.

"Here," the man whispered, pressing a scrap of paper into William's hand. His eyes darted nervously, scanning the room for potential eavesdroppers. "Be careful with this. Something big's brewing, and powerful folks are on the move."

William's brow furrowed as he examined the note. "What do you mean? Who's involved?"

But the informant had already melted into the crowd, leaving William alone at the table with his questions.

Across town, Thaddeus found himself in a similar situation. He had a low-level vampire pinned against a grimy alley wall with a wooden stake, and the creature's fangs bared in a desperate snarl.

"Talk," Thaddeus growled, pressing his silver-tipped oak stake against the vampire's chest. "What's got all you bloodsuckers in such a tizzy lately?"

The vampire's red eyes widened in fear. "I-I don't know much," he stammered. "Just that there's been more activity than usual. Lots of secret meetings, folks disappearing..."

Thaddeus released his grip after thrusting the stake home, letting the vampire withering slump to the ground. "Disappearing, you say? Interesting coincidence, that."

As he walked away, Thaddeus couldn't shake the feeling that he and William were on the verge of something big. The pieces were there, tantalizingly close, but the full picture remained frustratingly out of reach.

Little did they know, their every move was being watched by Wentworth's ever-growing network of spies. The vampire lord smiled to himself as reports flooded in, each one bringing him one step closer to his ultimate goal.

"Soon," he murmured, running a finger along the spine of the ancient tome. "Soon, the power will be mine, and this city will tremble at my feet."

LORD EVERETT WENTWORTH stood at the window of his study, his tall frame casting a long shadow across the plush carpet. The twinkling lights of London sprawled before him, a glittering tapestry of gas lamps and candles. His lips curled into a smirk, dark eyes gleaming with anticipation.

"Soon," he murmured, his voice barely above a whisper. "Soon, it will all be mine."

He ran a pale hand through his raven-black hair, savoring the moment. Centuries of careful planning have led to this. The loom, the key to reshaping reality itself, was finally within his grasp.

Wentworth's gaze swept across the shadowy streets below. Rats scurried along the gutters, and cats prowled the alleyways. He chuckled softly, imagining the chaos that would soon engulf them all.

"Come, my little pawns," he purred. "Dance for me."

His long fingers tapped a rhythmic pattern on the windowsill. Out there, somewhere in the labyrinth of London's streets, the werewolf and the hunter fumbled in the dark. Unaware of the storm about to break upon them.

"Let them come," Wentworth said, his voice dripping with amusement. "They'll make for an entertaining diversion."

Across the city, William and Thaddeus pressed on with their investigation. Gas lamps cast flickering shadows as they moved through the narrow streets, following leads that seemed to vanish like smoke.

William paused, his nose twitching. He frowned, a low growl rumbling in his chest.

Thaddeus glanced at his partner, hand instinctively moving to the silver-plated revolver at his hip. "What is it?" he asked, voice tense.

"Not sure," William replied, his golden eyes scanning the darkness. "But there's a pattern here we're not seeing. It's like... like we're being herded."

Thaddeus nodded grimly. "I've had that feeling too. Like we're rats in a maze."

"Charming analogy," William snorted. "Thanks for that."

They pressed on, unaware of the eyes that followed their every move. In the shadows, figures melted away, hurrying to report back to their master.

In his study, Wentworth turned from the window, a look of supreme confidence etched on his aristocratic features. He strode to a nearby chess set, picking up the black king.

"The pieces are in motion," he mused, rolling the piece between his fingers. "And the game has begun."

He set the king down with a decisive click. London would soon bear witness to a clash that would shake the very foundations of its world. And Everett Wentworth would be there, pulling the strings, orchestrating the chaos.

A slow, predatory smile spread across his face. "Let the hunt begin."

Grasping at Straws

William hunched over his desk, his fingers tracing the edges of ancient parchments. The office around him was a testament to organized chaos - stacks of papers swayed like drunken sailors, threatening to capsize at the slightest breeze. Arcane artifacts winked in the dim light, their mysterious energies pulsing softly amidst the clutter.

Tick. Tick. Tick. The old clock on the wall counted down the seconds, its steady rhythm a constant companion to William's racing thoughts. His hazel eyes darted from one document to another, searching for connections in the sea of information before him.

The door creaked open, a sound so familiar it barely registered in William's consciousness. Olivia glided in, her presence as quiet as a whisper. She navigated the labyrinth of supernatural oddities with the grace of a dancer, her auburn hair catching the faint lamplight.

"Tea, love?" Olivia's soft voice broke through William's concentration. She leaned in, pressing a gentle kiss to his stubbled cheek.

William blinked, momentarily disoriented. "Hmm? Oh, yes. Tea would be... nice," he mumbled, his mind still tangled in the web of clues spread before him.

Olivia's emerald eyes sparkled with understanding. "Still chasing that elusive lead?" she asked, her fingers ghosting over his tense shoulders.

"It's here, Liv. I can feel it," William replied, frustration coloring his words. "Like trying to catch smoke with bare hands."

She squeezed his shoulder gently. "You'll crack it. You always do." With a final reassuring pat, Olivia slipped out of the room, the door clicking softly behind her.

William barely registered her departure. He rubbed his temples, feeling the weight of unsolved mysteries pressing down on him. The cluttered room mirrored his mind - overwhelmed by information, yet struggling to form a coherent picture.

"What am I missing?" he muttered to himself, eyes scanning the documents once more. The artifacts around him seemed to whisper secrets, just beyond his grasp. William leaned back in his chair, letting out a deep sigh. The hunt for answers continued, each tick of the clock a reminder of the mysteries that still lay ahead.

WILLIAM, BARELY VISIBLE beneath a sea of papers. His piercing blue eyes darted from one piece of evidence to another, desperately seeking connections. Sketches of gruesome crime scenes jostled for space with hastily scrawled notes, each one a potential key to unlocking the mystery.

He reached for a spool of red string, his fingers trembling slightly as he unraveled it. "Come on, you bastards," he muttered, stretching the thread between two seemingly unrelated clues pinned to the corkboard. "Show me what you're hiding."

Stepping back, William ran a hand through his unkempt brown hair. The web of strings and papers before him looked more like the work of a madman than a seasoned detective. Frustration bubbled up inside him, threatening to boil over.

"Bloody hell," he growled, his gaze falling on a set of notes from his conversation with Thaddeus. The vampire hunter's insights, as much as it pained him to admit, had provided valuable leads. "That smug git might actually be onto something."

William's heightened senses picked up on details others would miss. The faint scent of decay clung to a victim's clothing, making his nose wrinkle. An almost imperceptible pattern in the body placements nagged at the edges of his mind. Yet the bigger picture remained stubbornly out of focus.

He slumped into his chair, the leather creaking in protest. A wave of inadequacy washed over him, threatening to drown him in self-doubt. "Some supernatural guardian I am," he said bitterly, his voice barely above a whisper. "Can't even solve a simple string of disappearances."

The weight of unsolved cases pressed down on him like a physical force. William closed his eyes, he drew a long breath. The recognizable aromas of aged documents, writing ink, and Olivia's tea permeated his senses, anchoring him to reality.

As his eyelids lifted, an object snagged his gaze. A magically produced image from an incident site, which he'd scrutinized countless times, abruptly unveiled a hidden detail. There, obscured within the murky backdrop, lurked an odd emblem.

William leaned in, his nose nearly touching the glossy surface. "Well, well," he murmured, a spark of excitement igniting in his chest. "Hello... What have we here?"

His fingers traced the outline of the symbol, mind racing with possibilities. For the first time in days, a genuine smile tugged at the corners of his mouth. "Maybe this old dog isn't out of tricks just yet."

WILLIAM BLACKWOOD'S fingers trembled as he smoothed the wrinkles from his worn vest. The sharp rap at the door sent his heart racing, a mix of anticipation and dread coursing through his veins. Inhaling deeply, he navigated the maze of stacked books and scattered papers that littered his cramped office.

As he swung open the creaky door, William's keen eyes took in every detail of the man before him. Impeccably tailored suit, polished shoes, but the haunted look in his eyes spoke volumes.

"Mr. Blackwood?" The stranger's voice quavered. "I'm Edmund Hartley. I... I need your help finding my daughter."

William's throat tightened. Another lost soul, another desperate plea. "Please, come in," he murmured, gesturing towards a battered armchair. "Can I offer you some tea?"

Hartley shook his head, sinking into the chair. "No, thank you. I just... I need to find her."

William perched on the edge of his desk, notebook in hand. "Tell me everything, Mr. Hartley. Leave nothing out, no matter how insignificant it might seem."

As Hartley recounted his daughter's disappearance, William's senses sharpened. The faint scent of fear clung to the man like a shroud. His hands trembled as he spoke, voice cracking on certain words. William's pen flew across the page, capturing every detail.

"Mr. Hartley," William began, leaning forward, "I want you to know that I'm uniquely qualified to handle this case." He paused, choosing his next words carefully. "My methods may seem... unconventional, but I assure you, they're highly effective."

Hartley's brow furrowed. "Unconventional how, exactly?"

William's stomach churned. This was always the tricky part. "Well, you see, I specialize in cases that often have... supernatural elements."

The change in Hartley's demeanor was instant. His eyes narrowed, lips pressing into a thin line. William pressed on, desperate to make him understand.

"I know it sounds far-fetched, but I've solved dozens of cases like this. There are things in this world, Mr. Hartley, that defy conventional explanation. And sometimes, those things are responsible for disappearances like your daughter's."

Hartley stood abruptly, chair scraping against the floorboards. "Mr. Blackwood," he spat, "I came here seeking a serious investigator, not some... charlatan peddling ghost stories!"

William's chest tightened. "Sir, please, if you'd just listen-"

"No, I've heard quite enough of these crackpot theories," Hartley snapped, striding towards the door. "Good day, Mr. Blackwood. I'll find someone who takes this seriously."

The slam of the door echoed through the cluttered office. William slumped in his chair, the familiar ache of rejection settling in his bones. He ran a hand through his unkempt hair, gaze drifting to the corkboard on the wall.

Newspaper clippings, illustrations, and scrawled notes covered every inch. Evidence of the supernatural world he knew existed, hidden just beneath the surface of everyday life. But in that moment, surrounded by the detritus of his investigations, William felt more alone than ever.

"They never believe," he whispered to the empty room. "Not until it's too late."

"Maybe a stroll by Scotland Yard and Elizabeth can shine some light on my thoughts..."

WILLIAM'S CANE TAPPED a staccato rhythm on the worn floorboards as he entered Scotland Yard. The familiar scents assaulted his senses: musty papers, nervous sweat, and stale coffee. He wrinkled his nose, fighting the urge to sneeze.

Conversations hushed as he passed, replaced by not-so-subtle whispers.

"There goes that Blackwood fellow," a gruff voice muttered.

"Odd one, ain't he?" another replied.

"Heard he believes in ghosts and werewolves," a third chimed in with a snicker.

William's jaw clenched. He squared his shoulders, willing himself to ignore the gossip. The weight of their stares pressed down on him, making his skin crawl.

At the records department, a thin clerk peered at him over wire-rimmed spectacles. His lips curled in barely concealed disdain.

"Mr. Blackwood," the clerk drawled. "What can I do for you today?"

William leaned on his cane, meeting the clerk's gaze. "I need access to the files on the recent disappearances."

The clerk's eyebrows shot up. "Those are active investigations, sir. I'm afraid I can't-"

"I'm working with Inspector Graves," William interjected. It wasn't exactly a lie, but it wasn't the whole truth either. He felt a twinge of guilt but pushed it aside.

"Be that as it may," the clerk sniffed, "regulations clearly state-"

William's frustration mounted. He could smell the clerk's smugness, sharp and acrid. The man's heartbeat quickened, a rapid thump-thump that grated on William's nerves.

"Surely there must be some public information you can provide?" William pressed, struggling to keep his voice level.

The clerk's lips thinned. "I'm sorry, Mr. Blackwood, but rules are rules."

William pinched the bridge of his nose. The whispers around him grew louder, pressing in like a physical weight. He tried a different approach.

"Is Elizabeth available? She's usually quite helpful in these matters."

A flicker of something - annoyance? jealousy? - passed over the clerk's face. "Miss Hawthorne is indisposed and not in a position to assist you today."

William's shoulders sagged. He'd hoped Elizabeth's friendliness might open a few doors, but it seemed even that avenue was closed to him.

"I see," he said, his voice tight. "Thank you for your time."

As he turned to leave, snippets of conversation reached his ears, making his skin crawl.

"Wasting our time again," someone muttered.

"Why do they even let him in here?" another voice added.

William quickened his pace, desperate to escape the suffocating atmosphere of mistrust and ridicule. Once outside, he leaned against the cool stone of the building, gulping in deep breaths of smog-filled London air.

The visit had yielded nothing but frustration and a deeper sense of isolation. William ran a hand through his dark hair, his mind racing. How could he hope to protect a city that saw him as an outsider at best, a lunatic at worst? The gap between his world and theirs seemed to yawn wider with each passing day.

He straightened, adjusting his coat. There had to be another way to get the information he needed. As he set off down the street, determination glinted in his frosty blue eyes. He would find the truth, with or without Scotland Yard's help.

WILLIAM'S CANE SWORD struck the cobblestones with a dull thud, echoing his weariness as he trudged through London's grimy streets. The weight of the day's fruitless investigations bore down on him, each step a reminder of his failures.

He paused, leaning against a soot-stained wall in Whitechapel. The stench of desperation and decay assaulted his nostrils, mixing with the acrid smoke from nearby factories. Exhaustion seeped into his bones, and he closed his eyes, allowing himself a moment of respite.

"Oi, watch it!" a gruff voice called out.

William's eyes snapped open as a group of dock workers stumbled past, their laughter grating on his already frayed nerves.

"Did ya 'ear about ol' Tom?" one of them slurred. "Says 'e saw a bleedin' monster down by the river!"

"Monsters?" another scoffed. "You've had too much gin, mate!"

Their words faded as they disappeared into the gathering twilight, but they left William with a familiar ache in his chest. Once, he would have eagerly pursued such rumors. Now, they only served as bitter reminders of his shortcomings.

His gaze fell on a crumpled poster nearby, its edges curling in the damp air. A child's face stared back at him, wide-eyed and innocent. The word "MISSING" loomed above in bold, accusing letters.

"Damn it all," William muttered, his throat tightening. He thought of the families waiting for answers he couldn't provide, their hope dwindling with each passing day.

The day's events replayed in his mind, a parade of dead ends and disappointments. The fishmonger at the docks, his story crumbling under scrutiny. The contradictory accounts at the boarding house. The abandoned warehouse with its cryptic symbols offered no new insights.

William's hand clenched around his cane sword, knuckles white with frustration. "I'm London's guardian," he whispered to himself, the words tasting bitter on his tongue. "Its protector against the supernatural. And yet..."

He trailed off, unable to finish the thought. The weight of his responsibility pressed down on him, threatening to crush his spirit. William straightened, squaring his shoulders against the burden. He couldn't give up, not while innocents were in danger.

With a deep breath, he pushed off from the wall and continued down the narrow alley. The shadows seemed to lengthen around him, but William pressed on. He was no closer to unraveling the mystery than when he'd begun, but he would keep searching. It was his duty, his calling.

As night fell over London, William disappeared into the gloom, a solitary figure battling against the encroaching darkness. The city's guardian, weary but undefeated, continued his relentless pursuit of the truth.

WILLIAM SANK INTO HIS leather chair, wincing as the ancient wood creaked beneath him. The dim office swam with dancing shadows, cast by the flickering gaslights. He pressed his palms against his eyes, feeling the weight of exhaustion in every bone.

A soft knock at the door pulled him from his misery. "Come in," he called, his voice rough with fatigue.

Olivia stepped inside, her copper hair gleaming in the low light. "You look terrible," she said, a hint of concern in her green eyes.

William managed a weak chuckle. "Your bedside manner needs work, my dear."

She perched on the edge of his desk, her skirts rustling. "Perhaps. But my observational skills are impeccable. What's troubling you?"

He gestured vaguely at the papers strewn across his desk. "This case. It's... complex."

Olivia's brow furrowed. "Have you considered reaching out to Thaddeus?"

William's jaw clenched. "I'd rather not."

"Pride goeth before a fall, William," she said softly.

He sighed, running a hand through his dark hair. "I know. But-"

"But nothing," Olivia interrupted. "Lives are at stake. Use every resource at your disposal."

William's gaze drifted to the 'Think orb' on his desk. The crystalline sphere seemed to pulse with potential, an invention that could bridge impossible distances in an instant.

Olivia followed his gaze. "Ah, the orb. Marvelous piece of work, if I do say so myself."

"Indeed," William murmured, his fingers hovering near the device.

Olivia stood, smoothing her skirts. "I should get back to my workbench. But William?" She waited until he met her eyes. "Don't let stubbornness cloud your judgment."

As the door closed behind her, William's attention returned to the orb. His hand inched closer, then jerked back. "Damn it all," he muttered.

The faces of the missing flashed through his mind, their silent pleas echoing in the quiet office. Could he really let his ego stand in the way of finding them?

His eyes fell on the mysterious box recovered from the crime scene. It sat on his desk, its intricate patterns seeming to shift in the low light. William's fingers brushed its surface, feeling the thrum of hidden power within.

This case stretched far beyond the mundane, delving into realms where even he, London's supernatural guardian, felt out of his depth.

The Think orb winked at him, as if mocking his indecision. William took a deep breath, steeling himself. Pride be damned. He had a job to do.

WILLIAM'S EYELIDS DROOPED as he hunched over his desk, the flickering gaslight casting eerie shadows across the cramped room. His head bobbed once, twice, and then he slumped forward, his cheek pressed against the cool, polished wood.

Darkness swallowed him whole. The acrid stench of coal smoke filled his nostrils as he found himself standing on a fog-shrouded London street. Ghostly figures moved around him, their features blurred and indistinct. William squinted, his heart racing as he realized these were the missing people he'd been searching for.

Their hollow eyes locked onto him, silent pleas etched across their hazy faces. William tried to move, to reach out, but his legs felt like lead weights. He opened his mouth to call out, but no sound came.

The world shifted, melting away like candle wax. A searing pain ripped through William's body. His bones cracked and reshaped, fur sprouting from his skin as his face elongated into a lupine muzzle. Horror gripped him as he realized he was transforming into his werewolf form, but something was terribly wrong.

He had no control. His newly formed paws, tipped with razor-sharp claws, carried him through London's winding streets. The scent of fear permeated the air, driving him forward with a primal hunger he couldn't resist. In his mind, William screamed, but the beast paid no heed.

"William! Wake up, mate!"

William's eyes snapped open, a strangled gasp escaping his lips as he nearly toppled from his chair. His heart hammered against his ribs, sweat beading on his brow. Jaxon stood beside him, concern etched across his face, one hand on William's shoulder.

"Blimey, you look like you've seen a ghost," Jaxon said, his grip on William's shoulder tightening slightly. "Olivia sent me to check on you. Said you've been working yourself to the bone."

William ran a shaky hand through his disheveled brown hair, his blue eyes wild. "It was... it was just a nightmare," he muttered, more to himself than to Jaxon.

"Must've been a right nasty one," Jaxon replied, pulling up a chair. "Want to talk about it?"

William hesitated, the remnants of the dream clinging to him like cobwebs. He could still taste the fear, feel the loss of control. "I... I dreamt I was turning into the wolf," he said quietly. "But I couldn't control it. I was hunting... something. Or someone."

Jaxon's expression softened. "It's just a dream, Will. You've got a handle on the wolf now, remember?"

"Do I?" William asked, his voice barely above a whisper. "What if I lose control? What if I fail them, Jax? All those missing people..."

Jaxon leaned forward, his spectacles sliding down his nose as he fixed William with an earnest gaze. The flickering lamplight caught the concern etched in the creases around his eyes.

"Hey now," he said, his voice soft but firm. "You're not in this alone, you daft git."

William blinked, surprised by the intensity in Jaxon's tone. The nightmare's tendrils still clung to the edges of his mind, threatening to pull him back into the darkness.

Jaxon continued, "We're all here to help, alright? You, me, Olivia - we're a team."

A wry chuckle escaped Jaxon's lips. "Elizabeth and Lilly... well, you know how Lilly is... Even that git Thaddeus is on our side."

William's shoulders relaxed a fraction, the tension slowly ebbing away. He nodded, unable to find words just yet. The remnants of fear clung to his skin like a cold, damp cloth. Sweat beaded on his forehead, and he wiped it away with a trembling hand.

But Jaxon's words had ignited something within him. A small flame of hope flickered to life in his chest, its warmth spreading through his chilled body. He wasn't alone in this fight. His friends stood beside him, ready to face whatever darkness lay ahead.

William took a deep breath, inhaling the scent of old books and leather that permeated the room. He met Jaxon's gaze, silently conveying his gratitude. The corners of his mouth twitched, not quite a smile, but a ghost of one.

"You're right," William said, his voice hoarse. "I... I forget sometimes. That I have you all."

Jaxon grinned, reaching out to clasp William's shoulder. "That's what I'm here for, mate. To remind you when that thick skull of yours forgets."

A genuine chuckle escaped William's lips, surprising even himself. "Thick skull, is it? Rich coming from you, Jax."

As they shared a moment of levity, William felt the last tendrils of the nightmare loosening their grip. The beast that haunted his dreams still lurked in the shadows, but with his friends by his side, maybe - just maybe - they stood a chance of keeping it at bay.

THE FIRST LIGHT OF dawn crept through the office window, painting the room in a soft, golden hue. William blinked, his eyes struggling to focus on the scattered papers before him. He ran his hands over his face, feeling the rough stubble beneath his palms.

"Bloody hell," he muttered, his voice hoarse from hours of silence.

A detail caught his eye, something he'd overlooked before. William's heart quickened as he snatched up a map of London. With trembling hands, he marked each disappearance on the weathered parchment. The quill scratched softly against the paper, unnaturally loud in the quiet room.

As he placed the final mark, William stepped back. His breath caught in his throat. A pattern emerged, subtle but distinct. It was like a sinister constellation etched across the city, a perfect circle of vanished souls.

The discovery jolted him awake, chasing away the lingering tendrils of his nightmare. He dove back into his research, pulling dusty tomes from shelves and rifling through stacks of notes.

"There's got to be a connection," William murmured, his eyes darting between the map and an ancient text on StainedSteam. The musty smell of old books filled his nostrils as he flipped through brittle pages.

Across the room, Jaxon sat yawning in a plush armchair near the fireplace. The warm glow of the dying embers cast flickering shadows across his face as he studied a thick volume on vampire migrations by ship.

"Find anything interesting?" William called out, not looking up from his work.

Jaxon stretched, his joints popping audibly. "Nothing but centuries of seasick bloodsuckers. You?"

William's lips quirked into a half-smile. "Maybe. Come take a look at this."

Jaxon ambled over, peering over William's shoulder at the map. His eyes widened as he took in the circular pattern. "Well, I'll be damned," he whispered.

William nodded, excitement building in his chest. "It's not much, but it's a start. We need to cross-reference this with historical records, see if there's any mention of similar occurrences in London's past."

They worked tirelessly, piecing together fragments of supernatural lore. The room grew brighter as the sun climbed higher, but neither man paid it any mind. They were lost in the thrill of the hunt, chasing down every lead, no matter how small.

Though the full meaning of the pattern remained elusive, William felt the rush of a breakthrough coursing through his veins. He'd stumbled onto something important, he was certain of it. This small victory, after days of dead ends, rekindled the fire in his belly.

Jaxon's eyes danced with amusement as he surveyed the chaos around them. Books lay scattered across the floor, their pages fluttering in the gentle breeze from the open window. Stacks of papers teetered precariously on every available surface, threatening to topple at the slightest disturbance.

He couldn't help but chuckle, the sound low and warm in his throat. "You know, William," he said, his voice tinged with playful sarcasm, "I'm beginning to think my unique perspective might actually be good for something."

As he spoke, Jaxon ran a hand through his already disheveled hair, making it stand up in wild tufts. The gesture was absent-minded, a habit born of countless hours spent poring over dusty tomes and ancient manuscripts.

William looked up from the book he was hunched over, his brow furrowed in concentration. "Oh? And what might that be?" he asked, curiosity piquing his interest despite his focus on the task at hand.

Jaxon's lips quirked into a lopsided grin. "Well, for starters, I can see over this mountain of paperwork you've created." He gestured dramatically at the chaos surrounding them. "And I'm thinking that maybe, just maybe, you should let Ms. Potts do her job in here sometimes. You know, before we're buried alive under an avalanche of academic pursuits."

William's eyes widened in mock offense, but the corners of his mouth twitched, betraying his amusement. "Are you suggesting that I'm incapable of maintaining an organized workspace?"

"Suggesting?" Jaxon laughed, picking up a stray piece of paper and waving it like a signal flag. "My dear William, I'm stating it outright. This isn't a study; it's a paper labyrinth!"

Jaxon snorted, clapping him on the shoulder. "You mean being a half-breed freak of nature has its perks? Who would've thought?"

William chuckled, shaking his head. "Watch it, you old goat. This freak of nature might just crack this case wide open."

As they shared a moment of levity, William couldn't help but feel a surge of hope. Perhaps his ability to straddle the line between human and supernatural would allow him to see connections others might miss. And just maybe, it would be enough to unravel the mystery that had consumed them for so long.

"Alright, enough joking around," William said, his voice taking on a more serious tone. "Let's get back to work. We've got a city to save, after all."

Jaxon nodded, his expression sobering. "Right you are. Though I must say, saving the world is much more enjoyable with a bit of banter thrown in."

As they settled back into their research, William couldn't help but smile to himself. Despite the gravity of their task, he was grateful for Jaxon's presence. The man's wit and humor kept him grounded, preventing him from losing himself entirely in the dark mysteries they sought to unravel.

WILLIAM STOOD BEFORE the tarnished mirror in his office, his reflection a stark reminder of his dual nature. The early morning light filtered through the dusty windows, casting long shadows across his face. Deep lines etched into his forehead spoke of sleepless nights and relentless worries.

He leaned closer, his piercing blue eyes searching his own gaze for answers. "What am I?" The whisper escaped his lips, barely audible even to his own sensitive ears.

As he watched, his reflection seemed to shimmer and shift. One moment, he saw the man - the detective, the protector of London, with his neatly trimmed beard and carefully combed hair. The next, he glimpsed the wolf - wild, untamed, with gleaming fangs and fur the color of midnight. The two images blurred and merged, a visual representation of the constant struggle within him.

William's hand clenched into a fist, his knuckles turning white. "I'm neither fully human nor fully werewolf. Where do I belong?" The question hung in the air, unanswered, as heavy as the fog that clung to London's streets.

He thought of the humans he sought to protect, imagining their faces contorted in fear if they ever discovered his true nature. Then he considered the supernatural beings, their eyes narrowed with suspicion, never fully accepting him as one of their own.

A low growl rumbled in his chest, frustration and longing intertwined. He pressed his palm against the cool glass, feeling the smooth surface beneath his calloused skin.

The door to his study creaked open, and Jaxon's familiar scent wafted in. William turned to see his friend struggling with a large, leafy monstera plant.

"Blimey, William," Jaxon grunted, maneuvering the pot through the doorway. "You could use a bit of green in here. It's like a bloody mausoleum."

William couldn't help but chuckle. "And you thought a jungle plant was the solution?"

Olivia's voice chimed in from behind Jaxon. "It was my idea, actually. Something to liven up the place."

As they bickered good-naturedly about the plant's placement, William felt a small smile tugging at his lips. These were his people, accepting him without question.

Ms. Potts appeared in the doorway, her round face flushed from the kitchen's heat. "Begging your pardon, sirs and madam, but there's food ready for those who feel peckish."

"Ah, Ms. Potts, you're a treasure," Jaxon said, patting his stomach. "I'm famished."

As his friends filed out, chattering about breakfast, William turned back to the mirror. The circular pattern he'd discovered on the map flashed in his mind, and suddenly, he saw the connection.

"Like the city itself, I'm a blend of the ordinary and the extraordinary," he murmured, his voice gaining strength. "My strength lies not in division, but in unity."

For the first time in months, William felt a sense of peace settle over him. He straightened his shoulders, meeting his own gaze with newfound determination.

"This case needs someone who can walk in both worlds," he declared to his reflection. "And that's exactly what I am."

With a final nod to himself, William turned away from the mirror. The scent of freshly baked bread and strong tea beckoned, and with it, the promise of a new day and a renewed sense of purpose. He strode out of his study, ready to face whatever challenges lay ahead, both man and wolf united in one form.

WILLIAM STARED INTO the mirror, his hazel eyes reflecting a mix of determination and weariness. He ran a hand through his tousled brown hair, exhaling deeply.

"Enough brooding," he muttered, turning away from his reflection. A surge of energy propelled him towards his desk, each step causing the old floorboards to groan in protest.

He yanked open a drawer, fingers closing around a battered leather notebook. The familiar texture brought a hint of a smile to his lips. Flipping it open, he inhaled the musty scent of aged paper, memories of past cases flooding his mind.

"Right then," William said, gripping his pen. "Time to call in some favors."

As he began to write, a frown creased his brow. "Blast it all," he growled, tapping the pen against the page. "Where in blazes are Elizabeth and Lilly? It's not like them to be out of touch for so long."

He shook his head, pushing the worry aside for now. "Focus, William," he chided himself. "One problem at a time."

The scratch of pen on paper filled the room as he jotted down names. "Thaddeus," he murmured, picturing the grizzled vampire hunter's scarred face. "Better stock up on stakes and silver, old friend."

He hesitated before adding the next name. "Gabriel - Crimson Paw alpha." William chuckled. "Hope you're in a cooperative mood, you overgrown furball."

As he wrote, scenes from past adventures flickered through his mind. Each name carried the weight of shared perils and hard-won trust.

"Madam Esmeralda," he said, recalling the fortune teller's enigmatic smirk. "Time to peer into that crystal ball of yours."

His pen paused over the next name. "And Jaxon, you cantankerous old coot." William grinned, imagining the gruff detective's reaction to being dragged into another supernatural case.

A flicker of movement caught his eye. William's gaze drifted to a small, ornate mirror hanging in a shadowy corner. For a moment, the glass seemed to ripple, and he could almost swear he saw a familiar face within its depths.

"Even you, Lilly," he whispered, adding his sister's name to the list. Her mastery of the arcane arts could be the key to unraveling this mystery. "Where are you, little sister?"

Leaning back in his chair, William surveyed the names before him. Each one represented a unique piece of London's hidden world, a realm he'd navigated alone for far too long.

He let out a rueful laugh. "Bloody hell, I've been a right fool, haven't I? Trying to be the lone wolf when the pack's strength was always there."

Standing, William stretched, his muscles protesting after hours at the desk. The list of names seemed to pulse with potential, each one a thread in a vast tapestry of knowledge and abilities.

"This is how we'll crack the case," he said, excitement creeping into his voice. "Not through brute force or solitary brilliance, but by weaving together our collective wisdom."

With renewed purpose, he reached for his coat. The familiar weight settled on his shoulders like armor, readying him for the challenges ahead.

As he prepared to leave, his fingers brushed against the mysterious box in his pocket. Its presence sent a shiver down his spine, a stark reminder of the high stakes and lurking dangers.

William paused at the door, his hand on the knob. He glanced back at the list of names, a wry smile playing at the corners of his mouth.

"Well, my friends," he said to the empty room, "let's see what trouble we can stir up together, shall we?"

William adjusted his collar and took a deep breath, steeling himself for the night ahead. As he reached for the doorknob, Ms. Potts' voice called out from the kitchen.

"Mr. Blackwood, are you heading out?"

He paused, turning to face the plump, gray-haired housekeeper. "Indeed I am, Ms. Potts. Duty calls."

She wiped her hands on her apron, a knowing smile on her face. "Well then, have a good evening on the town. And if you happen to pass by the market, we could use some fresh vegetables."

William nodded, a hint of warmth in his usually stern expression. "I'll see what I can do."

With that, he stepped out into the gas-lit streets of London. The cool night air filled his lungs, carrying with it the scent of coal smoke and damp stone. Cobblestones clicked beneath his polished boots as he set off, each step echoing in the quiet street.

His mind raced with possibilities. Tonight marked the beginning of something bigger than himself. He would start building the network that would help him unravel the mystery of the disappearances.

The fog rolled in, thick and mysterious, wrapping around street lamps and muffling distant sounds. William pulled his coat tighter, feeling the reassuring weight of his revolver against his side.

"The game's afoot," he muttered, his breath visible in the chilly air. A passerby gave him an odd look, but William paid no mind. His piercing blue eyes scanned the misty streets, searching for familiar faces or potential allies.

As he disappeared into the fog-shrouded night, a grim smile played on his lips. "And this time," he thought, determination coursing through him, "I'm not playing alone."

The gas lamps flickered, casting long shadows as William melted into the London night, ready to face whatever challenges lay ahead.

Breaking the Isolation

William's fingers traced the cool glass of his office window, leaving ghostly imprints as he gazed at the London streets below. Gas lamps flickered to life, their warm glow battling the encroaching dusk. The cobblestones echoed with the clip-clop of hooves and the rumble of carriage wheels.

He pressed his forehead against the pane, closing his eyes. "What have I become?" he whispered, his breath fogging the glass.

Jaxon's hearty laugh echoed in his memory. "Come now, Will! You can't solve every mystery alone," his friend had once said. Elizabeth's gentle smile flashed before him, her kind eyes filled with concern. Cassandra's fierce determination, Gabriel's unwavering loyalty, and his sister Lilly's unconditional love – all pushed aside in his quest for solitude.

The faces of potential clients blurred together, their pleas for help fading into white noise. And then there was Thaddeus, his recent companion, whose presence both intrigued and unsettled him.

William's dark hair fell into his eyes as he stepped back from the window. "Bloody fool," he muttered, running a hand through the unruly strands.

As he watched, the city's rhythm seemed to shift. The chaos of humanity began to reveal hidden patterns. A flower seller with a bright yellow bonnet nodded conspiratorially to a soot-stained chimney sweep. A constable in a crisp black uniform exchanged meaningful glances with a cloaked figure lurking in a shadowy alley.

"How blind I've been," William said, his voice barely above a whisper. "All this time..."

His fingers tightened on the windowsill, knuckles turning white. How many leads had slipped through his grasp? How many potential allies had he coldly turned away? The protective walls he'd built over years of secrecy now felt like a prison of his own making.

William spun away from the window, surveying his cluttered office. Case files lay scattered across every surface, each representing a piece of the puzzle he'd stubbornly tried to solve alone. The weight of his solitude pressed down on him, threatening to crush his spirit.

"To move forward," he said aloud, "I must break free." The words hung in the air, both liberating and terrifying.

He picked up a file, thumbing through its pages. "It won't be easy," he mused. "Years of habit don't vanish overnight."

William's gaze drifted back to the window, to the city alive with possibility. A surge of determination coursed through him, straightening his shoulders.

"I've been London's shadow guardian for too long," he declared to the empty room. "It's time to step into the light." He paused, a wry smile tugging at his lips. "Consequences be damned."

With renewed purpose, William strode to his desk. He pulled out a fresh sheet of paper and dipped his pen in ink. It was time to reach out, to rebuild the bridges he'd so carefully burned.

As he began to write, his hand trembled slightly. "Dear Gabriel," he murmured, the words feeling foreign on his tongue. "I hope this letter finds you well. I find myself in need of your expertise..."

William paused, chuckling softly. "He'll think I've gone mad," he said to himself. "Or worse, that I've been replaced by some doppelganger."

But as he continued writing, the weight of isolation began to lift. Each word felt like a step towards a new future, one where he wasn't alone in his battles. For the first time in years, a cautious hope bloomed in his chest.

"Perhaps," William mused, glancing at the darkening sky outside, "it's time to let others into my world of shadows and secrets." He dipped his pen once more, ready to face whatever consequences his newfound openness might bring.

WILLIAM'S FINGERS TREMBLED as he stuffed his notes and the enigmatic box from the crime scene into his worn leather satchel. The weight of his decision settled on his shoulders like a heavy cloak. His stomach churned with a potent cocktail of anticipation and nerves.

He inhaled deeply, steadying himself before reaching for the doorknob. As he stepped into the hallway, Olivia's emerald eyes met his, brimming with concern.

"Ready for this?" she asked softly, her slender fingers intertwining with his.

William managed a weak smile. "As I'll ever be, I suppose."

They descended the creaky stairs together, each step seeming to whisper encouragement. At the bottom, William fumbled with his keys, hyper-aware of every sensation around him.

"You know," Olivia mused, "I half expect these stairs to start giving us advice any day now."

William chuckled despite himself. "Stranger things have happened, my dear."

As he locked the door, the scent of Mrs. Finch's lavender sachets wafted from next door, mingling with an earthy, primal aroma. William's nostrils flared. A werewolf had passed by recently – a fact he'd have willfully ignored mere days ago.

They stepped onto the bustling street, awash in the golden hues of late afternoon. A group of children darted past, their laughter tinged with an otherworldly melody that marked them as changelings.

"I used to think they just had particularly musical parents," William muttered, shaking his head.

Near the corner, a woman with eyes as green as spring leaves haggled with a fruit vendor. The fading sunlight caught her gaze, and William's breath hitched.

"Olivia," he whispered, "I believe that's a dryad."

Olivia squeezed his hand. "Welcome back to the world, William."

"Good evening, Mr. Blackwood!" called Mr. Thornberry from his tobacco shop across the street.

William raised a hand in greeting, his eyes drawn to the faint shimmer of protective runes etched into the shop's doorframe. How had he never noticed them before?

As they made their way toward Jaxon's residence, guilt gnawed at William's insides. The box in his satchel seemed to pulse with energy, a constant reminder of his willful blindness.

"I can hear you thinking from here," Olivia said, nudging him gently. "What's troubling you?"

William sighed. "How many people have I failed, Olivia? In my stubborn insistence on separation?"

"You can't change the past," she replied, her green eyes softening. "But you're here now, and that's what matters."

Her words bolstered his resolve, and William quickened his pace. They'd wasted too much time already.

Jaxon's townhouse loomed ahead, windows aglow with warm lamplight. William paused at the gate, his hand hovering over the latch.

"Second thoughts?" Olivia asked, arching an eyebrow.

William shook his head. "Old habits die hard, I'm afraid."

"Then let's kill them together," she said with a grin, placing her hand over his.

They pushed the gate open in unison, stepping onto the path that would lead them back into the world they'd left behind. As they approached the front door, William felt a curious mix of trepidation and exhilaration coursing through his veins.

"Whatever happens," he said, turning to Olivia, "I'm glad you're here with me."

She smiled, her emerald eyes sparkling in the fading light. "Always, William. Now, shall we see what mysteries await us?"

With a deep breath, William raised his hand and knocked, ready to embrace the extraordinary once more.

WILLIAM'S HAND HOVERED over the brass knocker, his knuckles white with tension. The scent of old leather and parchment wafted through the cracks in the door, stirring memories of late-night research sessions and heated debates. He took a deep breath, his chest rising and falling visibly.

Olivia nudged him gently. "Come on, Will. It's just Jaxon. What are you waiting for?"

He glanced at her, a wry smile tugging at his lips. "You've never seen the inside of this place. It's... something else."

"Oh, please. I've known Jaxon for years. How bad could it be?"

William chuckled, then rapped twice on the door. The sound echoed ominously.

After a moment, the door creaked open, revealing a cluttered interior that seemed to defy the laws of physics. Books teetered in precarious stacks, their spines a kaleidoscope of faded colors and gilded lettering. Mystical artifacts peeked out from between tomes, their purpose as enigmatic as their origins.

Olivia's jaw dropped. "Good lord," she whispered. "It's like a bookshop exploded in here."

"William, my boy!" Jaxon's voice boomed from somewhere within the chaos. "Come in, come in!"

William stepped inside, careful not to disturb the delicate balance of knowledge surrounding him. The familiar scent enveloped him, bringing an unexpected sense of comfort. Olivia followed, her eyes wide as she took in the spectacle.

Jaxon emerged from behind a towering bookshelf, his curly graying hair wild and his glasses slightly askew. Despite the disorder around him, his brown eyes twinkled with a serene wisdom that belied his eccentric appearance.

"It's been too long," Jaxon said, clasping William's hand warmly. His gaze shifted to Olivia, and his smile widened. "And Olivia! What a delightful surprise. First time in the old curiosity shop, eh?"

Olivia nodded, still looking around in wonder. "It's... certainly something, Jaxon. How do you find anything in here?"

Jaxon tapped his temple. "It's all up here, my dear. Organized chaos, I assure you."

William felt a lump form in his throat. The contrast between Jaxon's calm demeanor and the chaotic shop struck him, as a visual representation of the balance he'd been struggling to achieve in his own life.

"I need your help, Jaxon," William admitted, the words coming easier than he'd expected. "And to be honest... I might need the rest of the gang as well. There's a case, as you well know... and I think I'm in well over my head."

Jaxon's bushy eyebrows rose, but he nodded sagely. "Well then, let's sit and discuss it properly. I'll put on some tea."

As they settled into worn armchairs, surrounded by the accumulated wisdom of centuries, William felt a sense of homecoming he hadn't experienced in a long time. The weight of his solitude began to lift, replaced by the comforting presence of trusted friends and allies.

Olivia leaned forward, her green eyes bright with curiosity. "So, Will, what's this case that's got you so rattled?"

William sighed, running a hand through his dark hair. "It's... complicated. But I'm glad you're both here. I think I'm going to need all the help I can get."

WILLIAM'S FINGERS CURLED around the delicate porcelain, warmth seeping into his palms. He lifted the teacup to his nose, inhaling deeply. The rich aroma of Ceylon tea danced with the musty scent of leather-bound books, creating an oddly comforting cocoon around him. He took a careful sip, savoring the bold flavor as it coated his tongue.

"It all began with the disappearances," he said, his voice barely above a whisper. William's gaze flicked between Jaxon and Olivia, gauging their reactions. "At first, they seemed random. A banker vanishing from his locked office. A street urchin melting into the shadows of an alley. But then..." He paused, his brow furrowing. "I saw it. A pattern."

Jaxon leaned forward, the dim lamplight catching the silver threads in his beard. His eyes, sharp and alert, fixed on William. "What kind of pattern are we talking about, old chap?"

William set his cup down with a soft clink. "Circular," he replied, fishing a folded map from his coat pocket. The paper crinkled as he spread it across the cluttered table, revealing a series of angry red marks. "Each disappearance... here, here, and here. All equidistant points around the city." His finger traced the pattern. "And then there's this... peculiar box we discovered at one of the scenes." Jaxon nods remembering the crime scene.

Olivia's emerald eyes narrowed, a crease forming between her brows. "A box? What's so remarkable about it?"

William ran a hand through his disheveled hair, exhaling slowly. "That's the rub. I can sense something... off about it. Otherworldly, even. But I can't quite put my finger on what."

As William continued his explanation, he felt a weight lifting from his shoulders. Jaxon and Olivia listened intently, peppering him with questions that made him pause, forcing him to reconsider aspects of the case he'd overlooked.

"Have you considered the timing?" Jaxon mused, stroking his beard thoughtfully. "Any correlation with lunar cycles or other celestial events?"

William blinked, surprised he hadn't thought of that. "I... no, I haven't. That's brilliant, Jaxon. Why didn't I think of that?"

Olivia leaned closer, her green eyes sparkling with curiosity. The scent of lavender wafted from her auburn hair. "What about the victims themselves? Any commonalities beyond their locations?"

As they talked, William felt the fog in his mind clearing. Connections formed, puzzle pieces sliding into place. He realized how much he'd missed this - the back-and-forth, the collective wisdom of trusted friends. For too long, he'd isolated himself, trying to shoulder the burden alone.

"I've been a right fool," he admitted softly, setting down his empty teacup. The porcelain clinked against the saucer. "I thought I could crack this case on my own, but I've been stumbling about in the dark like a drunk in a maze."

Olivia reached out, her warm hand settling on his forearm. "You're not alone, Will. We're here for you - all of us."

Jaxon nodded, a warm smile crinkling the corners of his eyes. "Indeed, my boy. Two heads are better than one, and three? Well, we're practically a think tank now, aren't we?" He chuckled, the sound rich and comforting. "Now, let's see what we can make of this mystery together, shall we? I have a feeling we're in for quite the adventure."

JAXON'S WEATHERED HANDS cradled the delicate teacup as he set it down on the saucer with a soft clink. His hazel eyes, framed by a web of wrinkles, sparkled with a mixture of hard-earned wisdom and youthful mischief. He leaned back in his chair, the leather creaking softly beneath him.

"William, my dear friend," he began, his voice a rich baritone that filled the room, "I've listened to your tale, and I must say, you've been carrying quite the burden."

William's shoulders sagged, as if Jaxon's words had made the weight he bore suddenly tangible. He ran a hand through his dark hair, disheveling it further. Beside him, Olivia reached out, her slender fingers brushing his arm in a gesture of silent support.

"Be true to yourself, William," Jaxon urged, leaning forward. The movement caused the gaslight to catch the silver threads in his hair. "Seek those who understand our world."

The words hit William like a physical blow, causing him to inhale sharply. It was as if Jaxon had reached into his mind and plucked out the very thoughts that had been swirling there, giving them form and substance.

"You're right," William admitted, his voice barely above a whisper. He glanced at Olivia, her emerald eyes filled with concern. "I've been pushing everyone away, thinking it was for the best."

Jaxon's lips curved into a gentle smile, the corners of his eyes crinkling. "Building a network of allies isn't just about solving cases, my friend. It's about your own well-being too. This life we lead, straddling two worlds, can be isolating. But it doesn't have to be."

As Jaxon spoke, William felt a spark of hope ignite within him. It was small, fragile, but undeniably there. He straightened in his chair, his blue eyes brightening for the first time in what felt like ages.

"There are others in London's supernatural community who could be valuable allies," Jaxon continued, gesturing with his hand as if painting a picture in the air. "Some you've avoided in the past, I suspect, to maintain your cover. But perhaps it's time to reconsider that approach."

William nodded slowly, his mind already racing with possibilities. The fae he'd dismissed as too unpredictable, their ethereal beauty masking ancient power. The witches whose abilities he'd been wary of, their knowledge of arcane arts both fascinating and terrifying. Even the vampires who weren't aligned with Wentworth - they all held potential as allies.

"You're suggesting a complete change in how I operate," William said, a mix of excitement and trepidation coloring his voice.

Jaxon's eyes twinkled, reminding William of starlight on a clear night. "Indeed I am. And not just in your work, William. In your life too. It's time to embrace all aspects of who you are, and to surround yourself with those who can truly understand and support you."

Olivia squeezed William's hand, her touch warm and reassuring. "He's right, you know," she said softly. "You don't have to face this alone anymore."

William looked from Olivia to Jaxon, feeling a surge of gratitude for these two people who had somehow wormed their way past his defenses. For the first time in years, he allowed himself to imagine a future where he wasn't constantly looking over his shoulder, where he could be both protector and protected.

"I suppose," he said with a wry smile, "it's time I learned to play well with others."

Jaxon chuckled, the sound was rich and warm. "That's the spirit, my boy. Now, shall we discuss strategy over another cup of tea?"

WILLIAM'S HAND TREMBLED slightly as he reached into his coat, fingers closing around the ornate box he'd discovered at the crime scene. The weight of it felt significant, like a key to unlocking a greater mystery. He placed it gingerly on Jaxon's cluttered desk, shoving aside a teetering stack of ancient tomes.

"Olivia, take a look at this," he said, his voice low and intense. His blue eyes flickered with a mix of excitement and apprehension. "I've never encountered anything quite like it."

Jaxon leaned forward, his spectacles sliding down his nose as he peered at the box. His weathered hands hovered over its surface, not quite touching, as if afraid it might vanish. "Good heavens," he breathed. "The craftsmanship is... exquisite."

Olivia stepped closer, her emerald eyes scanning the intricate engravings that covered every inch of the box. Her brow furrowed in concentration. "There's a faint magical aura surrounding it," she observed, her voice barely above a whisper. "Can you sense it, William?"

William nodded, watching as Jaxon's fingers traced the air just above the box's lid. The older man's face was a mask of intense focus, the lines around his eyes deepening.

"These symbols," Jaxon muttered, tapping a particular engraving. "I've seen them before, in ancient vampire lore. This one here... It represents eternal life. And this..." His finger moved to another symbol. "Blood sacrifice."

William felt a jolt of excitement course through him, making his heart race. "Vampire lore? Are you certain, Jaxon?"

The older man nodded, his gaze never leaving the box. "Quite certain, my boy. In fact, if I'm not mistaken, these particular symbols are associated with some of London's oldest and most powerful vampire families."

Olivia gasped softly, her hand flying to her mouth. "That would explain the connection to the missing persons cases," she said, her voice tight with worry. "But why? What could they possibly want with those poor people?"

"Food..."

William's mind raced with possibilities, each more terrifying than the last. The pieces of the puzzle were starting to fall into place, revealing a picture far more complex and dangerous than he'd initially imagined.

"This changes everything," he said, straightening up and running a hand through his dark hair. "If we're dealing with ancient vampire families, we'll need to tread very carefully. One wrong move and we could end up as their next victims."

Jaxon looked up at William, a glint of excitement in his eyes despite the gravity of the situation. "Indeed, my boy. But think of the implications! This could be the key to unraveling the entire mystery. We could be on the brink of exposing a centuries-old conspiracy!"

"Or on the brink of getting ourselves killed," Olivia muttered, but there was a spark of determination in her emerald eyes.

As they continued to discuss the potential ramifications of their discovery, William felt a renewed sense of purpose coursing through him. The weight of the investigation that had been crushing him earlier now felt like a thrilling challenge to be conquered.

"Well," he said, a wry smile tugging at his lips, "I suppose this means we won't be getting much sleep for the foreseeable future. Who's up for a spot of vampire hunting?"

Jaxon chuckled, the sound warm and reassuring in the tense atmosphere. "My dear boy, at my age, sleep is overrated anyway. Let's get to work."

WILLIAM LEANED AGAINST Jaxon's cluttered desk, his fingers tracing the intricate patterns on the ornate box. The weight of it seemed to pulse with hidden secrets, sending a shiver down his spine. He glanced at Olivia and Jaxon, their presence a comforting anchor in the sea of uncertainty.

"Right," William said, grabbing a nearby piece of parchment. "We need to make a list. Anyone who might know something about these vampire families or the missing persons."

Jaxon stroked his beard, his eyes twinkling behind his spectacles. "I've got a few tricks up my sleeve. Madame Zara, for one. That old bird's visions are eerily spot-on."

Olivia's emerald eyes lit up. "Oh! What about Silas? That elf's nuttier than a fruitcake, but his gossip network is second to none."

William's quill scratched across the parchment, each name a spark of hope. "We should rope in Gabriel too. The Crimson Paw pack might've caught a whiff of something."

"Brilliant!" Jaxon exclaimed, snapping his fingers. "And Lady Cassandra Trevelyan. Her family's been neck-deep in London's supernatural muck for centuries."

As they brainstormed, William marveled at the web of connections unfolding before him. Lilly, Elizabeth – each name added to the list was a potential key to unlocking the mystery.

Jaxon adjusted his spectacles, a mischievous glint in his eye. "I'll smooth things over where needed. Some of these folks are jumpier than a cat in a room full of rocking chairs when it comes to newcomers."

Olivia nodded, her auburn hair catching the lamplight. "I've got a few tricks up my sleeve too. It's amazing how much ground we can cover when we put our heads together."

William felt a warmth blooming in his chest as he looked at his companions. This sense of camaraderie was intoxicating, a stark contrast to the lonely nights he'd spent hunched over clues in his dimly lit study.

"I can't believe I've been trying to go it alone all this time," he admitted, shaking his head. "This... this feels different. Better."

Jaxon clapped him on the shoulder, his weathered face creasing into a knowing smile. "That's the magic of teamwork, my boy. No man is an island, especially not in our line of work. Now, shall we start hunting down these leads, or are we going to stand around gawking at each other all night?"

William couldn't help but chuckle. For the first time in months, he felt a genuine spark of optimism. With these two by his side, perhaps they stood a chance of unraveling this tangled web of mysteries after all.

THE LONDON TWILIGHT cast long shadows across the opulent study, its rich mahogany furnishings a stark contrast to the tension that hung in the air. Jaxon leaned back in his leather chair, his keen hazel eyes studying William with a mixture of concern and understanding. The silence stretched between them, broken only by the soft ticking of an antique clock.

"William," Jaxon finally spoke, his voice gentle but firm. "I can't help but notice how you tense up every time we discuss your... unique abilities. It's like watching a spring coil tighter and tighter."

William's shoulders stiffened, his hand moving almost unconsciously to touch the wolfsbane pendant that hung around his neck. The cool metal seemed to burn against his skin, a constant reminder of the secret he carried.

"It's necessary caution, Jaxon," William replied, his voice low and controlled. "You know the risks."

Jaxon raised an eyebrow, leaning forward slightly. "Do I? Or do I know the risks you've convinced yourself exist?"

The question hung in the air, heavy with implication. William felt his chest tighten, anxiety coiling in his gut like a serpent. He took a deep breath, trying to steady himself.

"What are you suggesting?" William asked, his voice barely above a whisper.

Jaxon leaned forward, resting his elbows on his knees. His gaze never wavered from William's face. "I'm suggesting that perhaps it's time to reconsider how tightly you're holding onto this secret. Not to shout it from the rooftops, mind you, but to be more open with those you trust."

William began to pace, his footsteps silent on the thick Persian carpet. The familiar action helped to calm his racing thoughts. "And risk exposure? Risk everything I've built?"

"Or gain allies who understand you fully," Jaxon countered, his voice soft but insistent. "Allies who could support you in ways you've never allowed before."

The words struck William like a physical blow. He paused by the window, staring out at the London skyline without really seeing it. The city lights twinkled like stars, oblivious to the turmoil within him.

"I've spent so long hiding," William admitted, his voice barely audible. "I've only let Olivia in, and even then, only to a degree. I'm not sure I know how to do anything else."

Jaxon rose from his chair, joining William at the window. The reflection of their faces overlapped in the glass – Jaxon's open, earnest expression a stark contrast to William's guarded features.

"It doesn't have to be all or nothing, William," Jaxon said softly. "Small steps. Trusted confidants. But imagine the freedom of not having to constantly guard every word, every action. Imagine being able to breathe freely for once."

As William considered Jaxon's words, he felt a weight he hadn't even realized he'd been carrying begin to lift. The idea of being fully known, fully accepted, was both terrifying and exhilarating. It was like standing on the edge of a precipice, uncertain whether the fall would lead to flight or destruction.

"Perhaps," William said slowly, turning to face his friend, "it's time I stopped running from myself."

Jaxon's face broke into a warm smile. "That, my friend, might be the bravest thing you've ever said."

WILLIAM STUMBLED OUT of Jaxon's shop, his eyes squinting against the sudden assault of London's midday sun. The cobblestones beneath his feet thrummed with an energy he'd long ignored—the pulsing heartbeat of StainedSteam.

StainedSteam, the lifeblood of London's hidden supernatural world, coursed through the city's veins. It was an intricate network of magical energy, invisible to most, but now painfully apparent to William's newly reawakened senses.

"Well, that was... enlightening," Olivia remarked, falling into step beside him. The sunlight caught her Chestnut hair, setting it ablaze with copper highlights. Her green eyes sparkled with a mix of curiosity and concern.

William ran a hand through his disheveled hair, his mind whirling. "It's like I've been sleepwalking for a long time, Liv. Bloody hell, how did I miss all this?"

As they navigated the bustling street, London seemed to come alive around William. Colors were brighter, sounds sharper, and the air itself seemed to crackle with hidden power.

A group of pedestrians brushed past them. William's gaze locked onto a woman with eyes that glowed an impossible shade of violet.

"Liv," he whispered, gripping her arm. "Did you see that?"

She frowned, scanning the crowd. "See what?"

"The pixie. Disguised as a human. Right there, with the violet eyes."

Olivia's eyebrows shot up. "You can spot them now? Just like that?"

William nodded, his attention already captured by a man whose shadow seemed to writhe and twist of its own accord. "And that one... I'd bet my last shilling he's a lesser demon."

"Blimey," Olivia breathed, her green eyes wide. "It's like you've got new eyes."

They paused in front of a quaint shop, its wooden sign adorned with intricate carvings. To the average Londoner, they'd appear as mere decoration, but William's newfound sight revealed their true nature.

"Look at those symbols," he murmured, tracing the air in front of the sign. "They're warding off evil. Ancient runes of protection."

Olivia squinted, tilting her head. "All I see are some fancy swirls. You're not having me on, are you?"

William chuckled, a sound tinged with wonder and disbelief. "I wish I was, Liv. This is... it's incredible."

As they continued down the street, William's senses sharpened with each step. A flower vendor's cart wafted a mix of familiar roses and something... otherworldly. The melody from a street musician's violin carried undertones that resonated with the magical frequencies humming through the air.

"Can you hear that?" William asked, gesturing towards the musician.

Olivia cocked her head, listening intently. "It's lovely, but... oh! There's something else, isn't there? Like a hidden harmony."

William nodded, a smile tugging at his lips. "Exactly. It's like... like hearing colors or seeing music. Does that make any sense?"

"Not a lick," Olivia grinned. "But I'm starting to get used to that feeling."

Turning a corner, they spotted a sleek black cat perched on a windowsill. Its golden eyes locked with William's, and he felt a jolt of recognition course through him.

"That's no ordinary cat," he whispered, unable to look away.

The feline blinked slowly, as if acknowledging his newfound awareness, before melting into the shadows with unnatural grace.

Olivia tugged at his sleeve. "William? You've gone all quiet. What is it?"

He shook his head, overwhelmed by the cascade of sensations and revelations. "I always thought I was protecting both worlds, but now... It's like I'm seeing London for the first time. The supernatural isn't just hiding in dark corners. It's everywhere, Liv. Woven into the very fabric of the city."

Olivia squeezed his hand, her touch grounding him amidst the whirlwind of new perceptions. "Well, partner, looks like we've got our work cut out for us."

William nodded, his blue eyes scanning the street with newfound wonder and determination. "Indeed we do, Olivia. Indeed we do." He paused, a wry smile playing on his lips. "Though I must say, I never expected my midlife crisis to involve seeing pixies on my morning commute."

Olivia laughed, the sound bright against the backdrop of London's hidden symphony. "Come on, then. Let's see what other surprises this new world of yours has in store for us."

As they walked on, William couldn't shake the feeling that he was seeing not just London, but himself, with new eyes. The city he thought he knew was now a tapestry of magic and mystery, waiting to be unraveled.

AS NIGHT FELL OVER London, William and Olivia returned to his townhouse, their footsteps echoing on the cobblestone streets. William's mind buzzed with new ideas and possibilities, the city's hidden world still fresh in his memory.

Entering his study, William approached the evidence board with renewed determination. The red strings connecting various clues seemed to pulse with newfound significance. He saw connections he'd missed before, patterns emerging from the chaos of information.

"It's all coming together," he murmured, tracing a line between two photographs.

The weight of isolation that had burdened him for so long began to lift, replaced by a sense of purpose and belonging. William knew that to solve this case and find acceptance, he must embrace both sides of his nature - the rational detective and the supernatural guardian.

As he turned from the board, William caught sight of Ms. Potts, his loyal housemaid, tidying up nearby. A wave of gratitude washed over him.

"Ms. Potts," he called out, his voice warm. "I can't thank you enough for your dedication. Your support means more than you know."

The older woman blinked in surprise, a pleased smile spreading across her face. "Why, Mr. Blackwood, it's my pleasure. Though I must say, you're in quite the mood this evening."

William chuckled, feeling lighter than he had in years. "Indeed I am, Ms. Potts. Indeed I am."

As Ms. Potts bustled away, William's gaze fell on Olivia, who was gravitating towards her workshop just a room away. Her chestnut hair caught the lamplight, and a surge of affection filled his chest.

With a mischievous grin, William crossed the room in a few quick strides. "And where do you think you're going, my dear?" he teased, his voice low and playful.

Before Olivia could respond, William swept her into his arms, eliciting a surprised laugh from her. "William!" she exclaimed, her green eyes sparkling with delight.

"I believe you deserve a proper thank you for your support today," William said, carrying her toward their bedroom. "And I intend to deliver it thoroughly."

Olivia wrapped her arms around his neck, her smile radiant. "Well, who am I to argue with such logic?"

As William carried Olivia across the threshold of their bedroom, he felt more alive and focused than he had in a very long time. The challenges ahead no longer seemed insurmountable. With Olivia by his side and a growing network of allies, he was ready to face whatever mysteries London had in store.

Crossing the Threshold

William's eyes snapped open, his heart pounding as a kaleidoscope of colors suddenly flooded his dimly lit office. The 'Think Orb', Isaac's peculiar invention, pulsed with frantic energy on his desk. Rainbow hues danced across the walls, casting long, eerie shadows in the pale light of dawn.

A crackling voice, tinged with panic, filled the air. "William! It's Isaac. Elizabeth and Lilly are missing!"

William bolted upright, sleep evaporating as adrenaline surged through his veins. He gripped the edge of his desk, knuckles turning white. "What? When? How?"

"They didn't show up for our meeting," Isaac's words tumbled out in a rush. "Last seen near the docks. Something about investigating disappearances."

The words hit William like a punch to the gut. His mind raced, connecting dots he'd previously overlooked. The case he'd been working on had suddenly become intensely personal.

"Bloody hell," William muttered, running a hand through his disheveled hair. "When exactly, Isaac?"

"Yesterday afternoon. I've been trying to reach you all night."

William cursed under his breath, guilt gnawing at him. He'd been so wrapped up in his own investigations, that he'd missed the signs of danger closing in around his friends.

As he shrugged on his coat, the fabric rough against his skin, William's fingers closed around the familiar weight of his cane sword. The metal was cool to the touch, a stark contrast to the warmth of fear spreading through his chest.

"I'm on my way, Isaac," William said, his voice tight with determination. He paused, then added, "We'll find them. I promise."

"Just... hurry, William," Isaac replied, his voice fading as the orb's light dimmed.

Left alone in the quiet of his office, William took a deep breath. The silence was deceptive. In his mind, a storm was brewing, filled with possible scenarios and potential leads. As he strode towards the door, each step echoed with purpose.

"Hold on, Elizabeth. Hold on, Lilly," he whispered to the empty room. "I'm coming."

WILLIAM'S HEART POUNDED as he tore through London's labyrinthine streets. The city's early morning fog clung to his skin, dampening his clothes and hair. His heightened senses picked up every detail: the acrid smell of coal smoke, the distant rumble of carriages, the muffled voices of shopkeepers preparing for the day.

"The docks," he muttered, Elizabeth's words echoing in his mind. "What did you find there, Lizzie?"

He vaulted over a low wall, landing with inhuman grace on the cobblestones beyond. A nearby worker was startled, dropping his toolbox with a clatter.

"Oi! Watch where you're going, mate!" the man shouted.

William barely registered the words, his focus laser-sharp on his destination. He ducked into a narrow alley, the brick walls pressing close on either side. The scent of rotting fish and seawater grew stronger, guiding him toward the waterfront.

Lilly's voice whispered in his memory: "Those symbols, Will. They're not just decorative. I've seen them before, on old sailors' arms."

He emerged onto a wider street, weaving between early morning carts and pedestrians. A flash of amber caught his eye – his own reflection in a shop window. William's eyes glowed with an inner fire, betraying the wolf that simmered just beneath the surface.

"Damn it all," he growled, no longer caring about concealment. "Hold on, girls. I'm coming."

The docks loomed ahead, a forest of masts and rigging shrouded in mist. William's nostrils flared, catching a faint whiff of Elizabeth's lavender perfume on the breeze. His ears pricked at the sound of lapping waves and creaking timber.

He paused at the edge of the harbor, scanning the scene before him. Dockhands moved with purpose, loading and unloading ships. But something felt off – an undercurrent of tension that made the hairs on the back of his neck stand up.

"Where are you?" William whispered, his eyes darting from ship to ship. "Give me a sign, anything."

A distant scream pierced the air, barely audible to human ears. But to William, it might as well have been a cannon blast. His muscles bunched, the wolf inside him howling for release.

"Hold on," he snarled, launching himself forward with inhuman speed. "I'm coming for you both. And God help anyone who stands in my way."

WILLIAM'S BOOTS CLATTERED on the worn cobblestones as he approached the docks. The cacophony of smells and sounds hit him like a wall, nearly staggering him. He inhaled deeply, tasting the salty tang of the Thames on his tongue, mingled with the pungent odor of fish and the acrid stench of industrial waste.

He paused, his keen eyes scanning the scene before him. Dock workers shuffled about, their movements sluggish in the pale light of dawn. Fishermen's voices carried across the water, gruff and tired.

"Oi, Tom! Pass us that net, will ya?"

"Right-o, coming your way!"

To the untrained eye, it was just another morning at the docks. But William was far from untrained.

His nostrils flared as a familiar scent reached him – the delicate floral notes of Elizabeth's favorite perfume. Relief flooded through him, his tense shoulders relaxing for a brief moment. "She was here," he murmured to himself, hope flickering in his chest.

But then another smell hit him, and his stomach churned. The cloying, sickly-sweet odor of decay. Necromancy.

William's heart sank, his mind racing with the implications. He'd encountered that smell before, during investigations involving vampires and other undead creatures. His jaw clenched, a low growl rumbling in his chest.

"Bloody hell," he muttered, running a hand through his dark hair. "What have you gotten yourself into, Elizabeth?"

Steeling himself, William began to move through the docks. His eyes darted from face to face, searching for any sign of his missing friends or anything out of the ordinary. The intertwined scents of Elizabeth's perfume and the necromantic magic guided him, growing stronger with each step.

As he walked, William's mind raced. This wasn't just a simple kidnapping or disappearance. The presence of necromancy meant something far more sinister was at play.

"Excuse me," he called out to a nearby dock worker, his voice tight with barely contained worry. "Have you seen a woman pass through here? Red hair like fire, green eyes, probably in a hurry?"

The worker shook his head, eyeing William suspiciously. "Ain't seen no ladies 'round here, guv. This ain't no place for 'em."

William nodded, forcing a smile. "Right, of course. Thank you."

He pressed on, his senses on high alert. The smell of decay grew stronger, making his nose wrinkle in disgust. "Come on, Elizabeth," he whispered. "Where are you?"

As he rounded a corner, a flicker of movement caught his eye. William froze, his hand instinctively moving to the cane sword at his hip. Something was off about that shadow, something unnatural.

"Well," he said under his breath, a grim smile tugging at his lips. "Looks like I've found my first clue. Let's see where this leads us, shall we?"

WILLIAM'S NOSTRILS flared as he followed the scent trail, his heart hammering against his ribs. The maze of warehouses loomed around him, their weathered brick walls seeming to close in with each step. The odors grew stronger, a nauseating cocktail of Elizabeth's delicate jasmine perfume, the sickly-sweet stench of necromancy, and something else - something wild and dangerous that made the hairs on the back of his neck stand up.

He skidded around a corner, his boots scraping against the cobblestones. The sight before him made him freeze, his breath catching in his throat. The secluded area behind the warehouses was a scene of chaos and violence.

"Bloody hell," William muttered, his eyes widening as he took in the carnage.

Overturned crates littered the ground, their contents strewn across the cobblestones like discarded toys. Shards of glass glinted in the weak morning light, the remnants of shattered bottles catching the sun's rays. Deep scuff marks scarred the ground, telling a silent tale of a desperate struggle.

William's keen eyes swept the scene, cataloging every detail with the precision of a seasoned investigator. His gaze landed on a dark spot on the ground, and his stomach clenched painfully.

"No, no, no," he whispered, crouching down to examine it closely.

The metallic scent hit him like a punch to the gut. Blood. Elizabeth's blood. The realization sent a chill down his spine, and he had to fight the urge to retch.

The acrid stench of vampire minions assaulted his nostrils, stronger here than before. It clung to the air like a foul miasma, mixing with the coppery tang of blood and the lingering traces of Elizabeth's perfume. William's hands clenched into fists, his nails digging crescents into his palms.

As he stood, surveying the scene once more, worry for Elizabeth and Lilly intensified. It twisted in his gut like a knife, sharp and unrelenting. The evidence before him painted a clear picture - this was no random attack.

"Damn it all," William growled, running a hand through his hair in frustration. "This is organized. Multiple vampires, well-coordinated. Who the hell are we dealing with?"

He paced the area, his mind racing. The stakes had just been raised astronomically. This was no longer just about disappearances. He was up against a formidable enemy, one that had now taken two people he cared about.

William's jaw clenched tight, determination hardening his features. "I'll find you," he promised the empty air, his voice low and dangerous. "Both of you. And heaven help whoever's behind this when I do."

WILLIAM'S FROSTY BLUE eyes swept across the chaos, his gaze as keen as a bird of prey. The stench of vampire minions hung in the air, thick and acrid. He wrinkled his nose, fighting the urge to gag. Something caught his attention, out of place among the carnage.

He stepped closer to the wall, his boots crunching on debris. "Bloody hell," he muttered, leaning in for a better look.

There, scrawled in what could only be blood, was a message that sent a chill down his spine:

"Ms. Jenny's loom awaits its master."

William's face hovered inches from the crimson letters. The metallic tang of blood mixed with the vampire stench, creating a nauseating cocktail that made his stomach lurch.

"What in God's name..." he breathed. He ran a hand through his dark hair, leaving it disheveled.

Ms. Jenny's loom. The phrase nagged at him, like an itch just out of reach. Fragments of hushed conversations in dimly lit taverns and shadowy alleyways surfaced in his mind.

"Supernatural beings and their bloody tall tales," William grumbled, shaking his head. But doubt crept in, unwelcome and persistent.

He'd dismissed the whispers as folklore, another fantastical story in London's sea of myths. Now, those whispers took on a sinister new weight.

"Bollocks," William swore softly. He turned, addressing the empty room. "This is no longer just about missing persons or vampire turf wars, is it?"

The loom was real, and it sat at the heart of this expanding mystery. William's mind raced, trying to connect the disappearances, the vampire attack, and now this enigmatic artifact.

"What are you playing at?" he asked the silence. "And who's pulling the strings?"

The cryptic message hinted at a plot far more intricate and dangerous than he'd imagined. This wasn't just about London's supernatural underworld anymore. This threatened to upend everything.

William's jaw clenched, muscles working beneath his skin. The case had evolved, branching into realms of ancient magic and forgotten lore he'd scarcely dared believe existed.

"Right then," he said, squaring his shoulders. "Time to dig deeper into this city's occult underbelly. Find out what this loom really is, and who's so keen on becoming its master."

As he turned to leave, William cast one last glance at the blood-scrawled message. A shiver ran through him as the true scope of what he faced sank in. This was no longer just an investigation. This was war.

WILLIAM'S PIERCING blue eyes swept across the docks, searching for any overlooked clues. The salty air filled his nostrils as he scrutinized every shadow and crevice. A nervous cough broke his concentration.

He turned to see a scrawny dock worker approaching, his weathered cap clutched in trembling hands. The man's eyes darted about, fear etched across his gaunt face.

"You the detective?" the worker asked, his voice barely above a whisper.

William nodded, softening his stern expression. "I am. Did you witness something?"

The worker's Adam's apple bobbed as he swallowed hard. "I... I saw them take two ladies. But it wasn't natural, sir. Not natural at all."

William's brow furrowed. "Tell me everything you saw. Don't leave out any details, no matter how strange they might seem."

The worker's story tumbled out in a confused jumble. "It was David, the Beggar King, and his lot. They confronted the ladies, but then... then things got scary. The shadows, they... they moved."

"Moved?" William prompted, his mind racing.

The man nodded vigorously. "Like smoke, they were. And their eyes... God help me, their eyes..." He shuddered. "Empty. Like there was no one home."

William's suspicions about vampire involvement solidified, but something nagged at him. "These shadows," he probed gently, "how exactly did they move?"

The worker's face contorted in concentration. "It was like... like they weren't bound by anything. They flowed over walls, under carts. I've never seen anything like it."

William's heart raced. This level of fluid movement was beyond even vampiric capabilities. What were they truly dealing with?

"Did you see where they took the ladies?" William asked, his voice low and urgent.

The worker shook his head. "They vanished into the night. But I heard one of the ladies cry out. She had a posh accent, like them fancy folk up in Mayfair."

William's mind whirled with possibilities. "Thank you," he said, reaching into his pocket. "Your information is invaluable." He pressed a coin into the worker's hand.

As the man muttered grateful words of thanks and scurried away, William stared out at the murky waters of the Thames. The mystery had only deepened, the extent of their foes' abilities growing more terrifying and unknown. He clenched his fists, determination etched across his face. Whatever these creatures were, he would find them, and he would bring those ladies home.

WILLIAM'S HEART POUNDED as he absorbed the dock worker's words. His mind raced, connecting invisible threads between seemingly unrelated events. The pieces of the puzzle, once scattered, now clicked into place with terrifying clarity.

"Bloody hell," he muttered, running a hand through his dark hair. "It's not random at all, is it?"

The dock worker, a weathered man with salt-and-pepper stubble, shifted uneasily. "What d'you mean, sir?" He said in clear confusion.

William's piercing blue eyes met the man's nervous gaze. "Elizabeth and Lilly's abduction. It's part of something bigger, isn't it?"

He pulled out his worn leather notebook, its pages filled with scribbled notes and diagrams. As he flipped through it, the other disappearances he'd investigated took on a sinister new light. Patterns emerged from the chaos, like constellations revealing themselves in the night sky.

"Ms. Jenny's loom," William whispered, the words from the cryptic message echoing in his mind. A chill ran down his spine as the implications hit him in full force.

The dock worker cleared his throat. "You alright, sir? You've gone pale as a ghost."

William barely heard him. His mind was reeling with the enormity of what he'd uncovered. This wasn't about vampires satisfying their bloodlust or expanding their hunting grounds. No, this was something far more insidious, he could feel it in his bones.

He clenched his fists, feeling the weight of his revolver in his coat pocket. Anger and determination coursed through him like fire in his veins.

"Elizabeth and Lilly," he said, his voice low and intense. "They're not just victims. They're pawns in some twisted game."

The dock worker took a step back, clearly unnerved by William's intensity. "I... I don't understand, sir."

William's gaze snapped back to the man. "No, I suppose you wouldn't... Nevertheless, you've helped more than you know." He reached into his pocket and pulled out a coin, flipping it to the worker. "Thank you for your time."

As the man scurried away, clutching his payment, William turned his attention back to the docks. The shadows seemed to writhe and twist, hiding untold dangers in their depths. But he was no longer fumbling in the dark. He had a direction, a purpose.

"Right then," he muttered to himself, straightening his coat. "Time to change the rules of this game."

With renewed resolve, William set off into the night. The cobblestones echoed beneath his boots, each step taking him deeper into a world of secrets and danger. But he was ready. Ready to face whatever came next, ready to save his friends, and ready to protect the city he called home.

As he disappeared into the fog-shrouded streets, one thought burned in his mind: The game had changed, and so had the stakes. But William Blackwood was ready to play.

WILLIAM'S BOOTS CLICKED against the polished wooden floor as he paced before the crackling fireplace. The dancing flames cast flickering shadows across his furrowed brow, mirroring the turmoil within. His mind raced, grappling with the weight of his recent discoveries.

From the nearby room, the rhythmic clanking of Olivia's tools on her workbench filtered through the walls. Ms. Potts' cheerful humming drifted up from the kitchen below, a stark contrast to the gravity of his thoughts. William ran a hand through his hair, the familiar sounds both comforting and distracting.

"Blast it all," he muttered, coming to a halt before his desk. His eyes fell on the carefully penned note resting atop a stack of papers. One name stood out in bold ink: Thaddeus Ironheart.

William's jaw clenched as he recalled their last encounter. The vampire hunter's gruff voice echoed in his memory, laced with disdain. "You're out of your depth, Blackwood. Leave the real hunting to professionals."

He could still feel the sting of those words, the barely concealed sneer on Thaddeus' weathered face. But now, with Elizabeth and Lilly's lives hanging in the balance, those petty grievances seemed as insubstantial as smoke.

William's fingers hovered over the inkwell, indecision gnawing at him. Pride whispered that he could handle this alone, but reason knew better. Thaddeus' expertise in vampire lore and combat skills could be the edge they needed to unravel this twisted plot and save his friends.

"Damn it all," William growled, snatching up the note. He strode to the window, throwing it open with a bang. The cool London air rushed in, carrying with it the sounds and smells of the bustling street below.

"Pug!" he called out, spotting one of the street urchins loitering nearby. The boy's head snapped up, a grin spreading across his dirt-smudged face. "Got a job for me, guv'nor?"

William nodded, holding up the folded note. "I need this delivered to Thaddeus Ironheart. You know his usual haunts?"

Pug's eyes widened. "The vampire 'unter? Blimey, that's a right dangerous errand, that is."

"Double pay," William said firmly, tossing down a coin. "And there's more where that came from if you're quick about it."

As Pug scampered off, note clutched tightly in his grimy fist, William leaned against the windowsill. The gravity of the situation settled over him like a heavy cloak. How much had changed since he and Thaddeus had last crossed paths. The stakes were higher now, more personal. The fate of London's supernatural world - and the lives of those he cared about - hung in the balance.

William closed his eyes, picturing Elizabeth's warm smile, and Lilly's mischievous grin. For them, he would swallow his pride. For the city he had sworn to protect, he would face whatever came next.

"Let's hope the old bastard still knows how to fight," William murmured, a wry smile tugging at his lips. He turned back to his study, ready to prepare for whatever Thaddeus' response might bring. The battle ahead would require every ounce of skill and cunning they could muster – and perhaps, just perhaps, the beginnings of an unlikely alliance.

WILLIAM'S FOOTSTEPS echoed on the hard wooden planks and smooth cobbles in the small yard as he returned to the docks, the day's earlier events replaying in his mind. The salty breeze carried a lingering taint of dark magic, sending a chill down his spine.

"Focus," he muttered, closing his eyes and taking a deep breath. Every detail mattered.

Crouching down, William pulled on a pair of thin leather gloves. He carefully collected dried blood samples, the dark flakes stark against the weathered wood. As he sealed each vial with a cork stopper, a familiar scent caught his attention.

"Elizabeth," he whispered, recognizing her perfume mingled with the coppery tang of blood. His heart clenched, worry for his friend gnawing at him.

Shaking off the emotion, William turned to the magical sigil etched into the planks. He produced a piece of parchment and charcoal from his coat pocket, his movements practiced and precise as he made a rubbing of the sigil.

"What secrets are you hiding?" he murmured, meticulously tracing each intricate symbol. The charcoal scratched softly against the parchment, capturing every curve and line.

A nearby scrawl caught his eye – a cryptic message that made his brow furrow. William flipped open his leather-bound notebook, jotting down the exact wording.

"Every word could be the key," he reminded himself, his quill scratching across the page.

As William surveyed the scene, a glint of white caught his eye. He moved closer, spotting a torn piece of fabric caught on a rusty nail.

Gently, he removed it, bringing it to his nose. A faint, unfamiliar scent clung to the cloth – the kidnappers' trace.

"Got you," William said, a grim smile tugging at his lips as he carefully wrapped the fabric in a clean handkerchief.

His keen eyes darted around, searching for anything else out of place. A discarded button winked in the dim light, and William pocketed it with a satisfied nod.

"Every touch leaves a trace," he mused, knowing the button might carry valuable evidence.

As William worked, his mind raced. Each piece of physical evidence, every lingering magical trace, could be the key to finding Elizabeth and Lilly. The weight of the expanding mystery pressed down on him, but he steeled his resolve.

"I'll find you," he promised the empty docks, his voice barely above a whisper. "Whatever it takes."

William knew the challenges ahead would be formidable. He'd need every resource at his disposal, every ally he could trust. But as he gathered his evidence and prepared to leave, a fierce determination burned in his eyes.

"Time to get to work," he said, striding purposefully away from the crime scene. The hunt was on, and William wouldn't rest until he uncovered the truth behind these sinister events and brought his friends home safely.

HIS FOOTWEAR ECHOED on the cobbled street as he marched from the harbor, every footfall reflecting his fresh resolve. The salty breeze swirled about him, yanking at his jacket and tousling his locks, yet he scarcely noticed. His thoughts raced, assembling bits of proof like an intricate jigsaw.

"This isn't just another case," he muttered to himself, his breath visible in the chilly air. "It's personal now."

The doubts that had plagued him earlier evaporated, replaced by an iron resolve that settled in his chest. Elizabeth and Lilly weren't just names on paper anymore – they were flesh and blood, friends and family in dire peril.

As William navigated the labyrinthine streets of London, the familiar cityscape morphed before his eyes. The gas lamps cast long, eerie shadows that danced and flickered, revealing glimpses of a world hidden beneath the surface. Alleyways that once seemed ordinary now held the potential for supernatural threats lurking in every corner.

He caught sight of his reflection in a shop window and paused, startled by what he saw. The man staring back at him looked different – harder, more focused. The weight of responsibility etched deep lines in his face, but there was an unmistakable fire burning in his eyes.

"You've changed, old boy," William whispered to his reflection. "But so has the game."

His mind raced with plans and strategies as he continued his journey. He mentally cataloged his resources, considering how each ally could contribute to the rescue mission. The network he'd been hesitant to build now seemed like a lifeline in the darkness.

As he approached the meeting point with Thaddeus, William clenched his fists, his knuckles turning white. "I'll do whatever it takes," he vowed silently. "Whatever it takes to bring them home."

The city pulsed around him, oblivious to the unseen war unfolding in its midst. But William was acutely aware of every shadow, every whisper on the wind. He was no longer just London's supernatural guardian – he was a hunter, and the predators who dared to strike at his friends were now his prey.

"They think they can hide in the darkness," William growled, his eyes scanning the streets. "But they don't know what true darkness is. Not yet."

With each step, his resolve hardened. The dark forces threatening London had made a grave mistake in targeting those close to him, and William was determined to make them pay dearly for their error.

Enemies and Allies

The converted church loomed before William, its gothic spires piercing the twilight sky. Gargoyles perched on the eaves, their stone eyes seeming to track his every move.

He paused at the foot of the steps, nostrils flaring. The faint scent of holy water and silver tickled his enhanced senses. Vampire hunter, through and through.

Pride warred with desperation in William's chest. Elizabeth and Lilly's faces flashed in his mind, their fate pushing him forward. He clenched his jaw and climbed the steps.

William's hand hovered over the heavy oak door. "Bloody hell," he muttered, then rapped his knuckles against the wood.

The knock reverberated through the building. No turning back now.

His keen ears caught the rustle of movement inside, followed by determined footsteps. William's muscles coiled, centuries of survival instinct battling his need for help.

The lock clicked. Hinges creaked. Thaddeus's stern face appeared in the gap, his blue eyes widening in surprise.

"Blackwood?" Thaddeus's voice held a mix of shock and wariness. "What in God's name are you doing here?"

William swallowed hard, tasting ash. "Thaddeus, I... I need your help." The words felt like gravel in his throat. "Elizabeth and Lilly have been taken."

Thaddeus's gaze sharpened, assessing. Silence stretched between them, taut as a bowstring.

Finally, Thaddeus stepped back. "Come in. Tell me everything."

William hesitated at the threshold. The weight of wards and protective spells prickled against his skin as he entered.

Inside, the church was a far cry from its ornate exterior. Bare walls lined with weapons and ancient tomes. A desk cluttered with maps and silver-tipped stakes.

"Nice place," William said dryly. "Very... homey."

Thaddeus snorted. "Didn't exactly decorate with vampires in mind." He gestured to a chair. "Sit. Start from the beginning."

William sank into the offered seat, the gravity of the situation settling over him like a shroud. He took a deep breath and began to speak.

WILLIAM'S HEART POUNDED like a steam engine as he hammered on Thaddeus's door. Sweat beaded on his forehead, his usually immaculate attire now rumpled and stained. The night air felt thick, and oppressive, clinging to his skin like a damp shroud.

"Who in blazes is making that infernal racket?" Thaddeus's gruff voice boomed from within.

William swallowed hard, his throat dry as sandpaper. "It's William! Please, Thaddeus, I need your help!"

The door creaked open, revealing Thaddeus's towering frame. His steel-gray eyes narrowed, taking in William's disheveled state. The scent of gunpowder and leather wafted out from behind him.

"Good God, man," Thaddeus growled. "You look like you've been dragged through hell backward."

William pushed past him, stumbling into the cluttered room. His blue eyes were wild, darting around the arsenal of weapons and arcane artifacts. "Elizabeth and Lilly," he gasped, "they're gone. Taken. There was blood, Thaddeus. Blood..."

Thaddeus's weathered face hardened, a flicker of concern passing over his features at the mention of Lilly's name. "Slow down, William. Take a breath and tell me what happened."

William ran a trembling hand through his tousled dark hair. "They were investigating near the docks. I found signs of a struggle. Elizabeth's blood, Thaddeus. I'd know it anywhere." His voice cracked, the memory of crimson stains on cobblestones flashing before his eyes.

Thaddeus's thick eyebrows furrowed, creating deep furrows in his forehead. "And Lilly?"

"No trace," William replied, his blue eyes clouding with worry. "But there was a message. Something about a loom and its master. I'm certain it's connected to the other disappearances we've been investigating."

Thaddeus's jaw clenched, his hand unconsciously moving to the hilt of the dagger at his hip. The air between them crackled with tension, each second stretching into an eternity.

William watched Thaddeus intently, trying to read the man's thoughts. The vampire hunter's face was a mask of concentration, but his eyes betrayed a hint of unease.

"This loom," Thaddeus finally broke the silence, "it's not the first time I've heard whispers of such a thing." He ran a calloused hand through his salt-and-pepper hair, a rare display of uncertainty. "If it's what I think it is, we're dealing with powers beyond our usual fare."

William leaned in, his voice low and urgent. "Thaddeus, I suspect this abduction is connected to the vampire activity we've been tracking. The timing, the location – it can't be a coincidence."

Thaddeus fixed William with a piercing gaze. "You're absolutely sure about what you saw?"

William nodded, his jaw set with determination. "I wouldn't be here if I wasn't certain. We need to work together on this. Elizabeth and Lilly's lives may depend on it."

Thaddeus held William's gaze for a long moment, searching for any sign of deception. Finding none, he let out a heavy sigh. "Well, then," he growled, "I suppose we'd better get to work. Though I warn you, partnering with me isn't for the faint of heart."

A ghost of a smile flickered across William's face. "I'll take my chances. After all, what's a little danger between friends?"

Thaddeus snorted. "Friends? Don't push your luck, pretty boy. Now, help me with these books. We've got a long night ahead of us."

As they began pulling dusty tomes from the shelves, William felt a glimmer of hope. This unlikely alliance was taking shape, born of necessity and a shared goal.

"I hope you're ready for a crash course in the occult," Thaddeus growled, hefting a massive leather-bound volume onto the table.

William's lips tightened into a thin line. "We'll find them, Thaddeus. We have to."

Thaddeus glanced up, his steel-gray eyes meeting William's blue ones. "Aye, that we will. And heaven help whoever's taken them when we do."

The flickering candlelight cast long shadows across the room as the two men bent over the ancient texts, the ticking of a nearby clock marking the passage of precious time. Outside, the fog-shrouded streets of London held their secrets, waiting for dawn to break.

WILLIAM'S HANDS TREMBLED as he spread the evidence across Thaddeus's cluttered desk. The metallic scent of blood samples hung in the air, a grim reminder of the danger Elizabeth and Lilly faced. Crime scene illustrations, stark and haunting, covered the worn wood surface.

"The dock worker's testimony," William said, his voice low and urgent, "it changes everything." He tapped a finger on one of the illustrations. "He described creatures with supernatural speed and dead eyes. But their movement... it was odd, not typical for vampires."

Thaddeus leaned in, his expert gaze catching details William had missed. The older man's weathered face creased in concentration as he studied the images. Suddenly, he jabbed a finger at a shadow in one of the illustrations, barely visible to the untrained eye.

"There," Thaddeus muttered. "That's not a vampire's shadow. It's something... different."

William felt a mix of relief and unease at Thaddeus's observation. He took a deep breath, the musty air of the office filling his lungs. "There's more," he said, his heart racing. "I found a cryptic message at the scene. It mentioned Ms. Jenny's loom and its master."

The change in Thaddeus was immediate and dramatic. His eyes widened, a flicker of recognition and fear passing through them. The gruff vampire hunter seemed to pale, his usual stoic demeanor cracking like thin ice.

"Ms. Jenny's loom?" Thaddeus whispered, his voice hoarse. "Are you certain that's what it said?"

William nodded, watching Thaddeus carefully. "You've heard of it before?"

Thaddeus turned away, running a hand through his graying hair. The tension in the room thickened, the air growing heavy with unspoken dread. When he turned back to William, his face was grim, the lines around his eyes deeper than ever.

"If it's what I think it is," Thaddeus said slowly, each word weighted with significance, "we're dealing with something far more dangerous than vampires or werewolves. This artifact... it's not just powerful, it's reality-altering."

William felt a chill run down his spine, his mind reeling at the implications. "Reality-altering?" he echoed, his voice barely above a whisper. "What does that even mean, is it like do you know more about it?"

Thaddeus sank into his chair, the wood creaking under his weight. "It means, my boy, that the rules we thought we knew might not apply anymore. We're in uncharted territory now."

The gravity of the situation settled over them both, the realization that they were facing a threat beyond their usual scope was something William had suspected and heard from his other companions. William's gaze drifted back to the evidence spread before them, each piece now seeming more ominous than before.

"Oh," was all he could manage, the single syllable hanging in the air like a death knell.

THADDEUS WHIRLED AROUND, his coattails swishing through the air. William's eyes followed the vampire hunter's purposeful strides to a cabinet nestled in the room's shadowy corner. The wooden structure stood out, its intricate carvings a stark contrast to the otherwise sparse furnishings.

"What's he up to now?" William muttered under his breath, leaning forward in his chair.

Thaddeus's nimble fingers danced over a series of locks, each one more complex than the last. Click. Click. Click. The sounds echoed in the tense silence, setting William's teeth on edge. With a final turn of an ornate key, the cabinet creaked open, revealing its secrets.

William's breath caught as Thaddeus withdrew an ancient tome. The leather binding was cracked and worn, like the face of a weathered sailor. As Thaddeus laid it on the desk, a musty scent wafted through the air. William wrinkled his nose, imagining the book's pages whispering forgotten tales.

"This," Thaddeus said, his voice barely audible, "is the true nature of Ms. Jenny's loom."

William leaned in, curiosity overriding his usual caution. "A book? That's what all the fuss is about?"

Thaddeus shot him a withering look. "Not just any book, William."

With reverent care, Thaddeus opened the tome. The pages crackled like dry leaves, covered in spidery script and diagrams that made William's head spin. His eyes widened as he took in illustrations of an impossibly complex weaving device.

"Good Lord," William breathed, "What am I looking at?"

Thaddeus's finger traced a line of text, his brow furrowed in concentration. "The loom is no ordinary artifact. It's a mythical object of immense power, capable of weaving the very fabric of reality itself."

William felt his stomach drop. "Weaving reality? That's... that's impossible, surely?"

"Impossible?" Thaddeus scoffed. "After everything you've seen, you still cling to that word?"

William ran a hand through his hair, his mind reeling. "Fair point. But how does it work?"

Thaddeus's expression darkened, his eyes glinting like polished obsidian in the dim light. "The how doesn't matter. What matters is that dark forces have sought this loom for centuries. Its location was lost to time... until now, it seems."

The gravity of the situation settled over William like a lead weight. He thought of Elizabeth, her fiery red hair and emerald eyes flashing in his mind, and little Lilly with her curious gaze. Both were caught up in something far more dangerous than they had imagined.

"This stinks of the Empaths all over again," William groaned, massaging his temples. "Why can't we ever stumble upon a nice, simple case of petty theft?"

Thaddeus ignored the quip, his voice grim as he continued, "If the vampires gain control of the loom, the consequences would be catastrophic. They could reshape the world to their liking, bending reality to serve their twisted desires."

William listened in horrified fascination, the full scope of the case unfolding before him. What had started as a series of mysterious disappearances had grown into a threat that could unravel the very fabric of existence.

"Well," William said, attempting to inject some levity into his voice, "I suppose this means our evening plans are canceled?"

Thaddeus's lips twitched in what might have been the ghost of a smile. "Indeed. We have work to do, my friend. The fate of reality itself may depend on it."

As they bent over the ancient tome, William couldn't shake the feeling that they were standing on the precipice of something far greater and more terrifying than anything they had faced before. The loom's secrets lay before them, waiting to be unraveled.

WILLIAM'S HEART POUNDED as Thaddeus's words sank in. He turned back to the ancient tome on the desk, its yellowed pages seeming to throb with hidden secrets. The flickering candlelight cast eerie shadows across the room, dancing on the walls like restless spirits.

"The pattern," William muttered, his voice barely audible. He ran a hand through his dark hair, his blue eyes darting across the map spread before them. "Look, Thaddeus. The disappearances... they form a perfect circle around the city."

Thaddeus leaned in, his sharp steel-gray eyes narrowing as he studied the map. "A ritual circle, perhaps?" he mused, stroking his salt-and-pepper beard.

William nodded, feeling the pieces click into place like a macabre puzzle. "And the increased vampire activity... they're not just feeding. They're searching for something."

"Or someone," Thaddeus added grimly. He tapped a finger on the tome's worn cover. "The loom requires a specific individual to activate it, according to the prophecies."

Their eyes met, a shared look of dawning horror passing between them. William felt a chill crawl up his spine, making the hairs on the back of his neck stand on end.

"Elizabeth and Lilly," he said, his voice tight with worry. He began to pace, his footsteps echoing in the cluttered study. "They must have stumbled onto something crucial in their investigations."

Thaddeus nodded, his expression grave. "Making them prime targets for whoever is behind this madness."

William stopped abruptly, spinning to face his companion. "The cryptic message at the docks... 'The master of the loom shall rise.' It's all connected, isn't it?"

"A coordinated effort," Thaddeus agreed, his voice low and ominous. "Likely spanning centuries, waiting for the right moment to strike." He paused, a sardonic smile tugging at his lips. "And here we thought we were merely dealing with a few rogue vampires."

As they spoke, the full scope of the conspiracy began to unfold before them like a poisonous flower. William felt a weight settling on his shoulders, the responsibility of what they'd uncovered pressing down on him like a physical force.

"This is far greater than we imagined," he said, his voice barely above a whisper. He slumped into a nearby chair, the leather creaking beneath him.

Thaddeus closed the ancient tome with a soft thud, a cloud of dust rising from its pages. "Indeed," he said, his tone somber. "We're facing a threat that could reshape the very nature of our world." He fixed William with a piercing stare. "The question is, are we prepared to face it?"

William met Thaddeus's gaze, seeing his own determination reflected in the vampire hunter's eyes. The gravity of their situation hung heavy in the air between them, thick as London fog.

"We have to be," William said, straightening his shoulders. "The fate of London - perhaps the entire world - now rests in our hands." He managed a wry smile. "No pressure, eh?"

Thaddeus chuckled darkly. "Just another day in our line of work, my friend." He reached for his coat, shrugging it on with practiced ease. "Now, shall we go save the world?"

William stood, a newfound resolve burning in his chest. "Lead the way, old man," he said, a hint of fondness in his voice. "Let's hope we're not too late."

As they left the study, William cast one last glance at the tome on the desk. Whatever dark forces were at work, he and Thaddeus would face them head-on. The fate of everything they held dear depended on it.

WILLIAM'S FOOTSTEPS echoed through the room, each thud matching the frantic beat of his heart. His fingers twitched, itching to act, to move, to do something. The scent of old books and polished wood filled his nostrils, but he couldn't focus on it. All he could think about was Elizabeth and Lilly, their faces swimming before his eyes.

Tick. Tock. Tick. Tock.

The grandfather clock in the hall seemed to mock him, each second another moment wasted. William spun around, his blue eyes wild with urgency.

"Damn it, Thaddeus! We can't just sit here!" he growled, his voice raw with emotion. "Every second we waste, they're in more danger!"

Thaddeus leaned against a bookshelf, his steel-gray eyes sharp and calculating. To anyone else, he might have looked relaxed, but William could see the tension in his shoulders, the slight furrow of his brow.

"And rushing in like a bull in a china shop will get us all killed," Thaddeus replied, his voice level but firm. "We need a plan, William. Information. Strategy."

William raked a hand through his dark hair, tugging at the roots in frustration. "Information?" he spat. "While we're gathering bloody information, they could be—" He couldn't finish the sentence, his throat closing up at the thought.

Thaddeus pushed off from the bookshelf, taking a step towards William. "I know you're worried," he said, his tone softening slightly. "But we're no use to anyone if we end up dead."

The words hit William like a physical blow. He turned away, his hands clenching into fists at his sides. He could feel his claws pricking at his palms, the wolf inside him howling to be let loose.

"You don't understand," William said, his voice low and dangerous. "They're not just my friends, Thaddeus. They're my pack. My family. I can't—I won't—stand by while they're in danger."

A flash of something—anger? Pain?—crossed Thaddeus' face. "You think I don't understand loss?" he asked, his voice sharp. "I've lived for centuries, Blackwood. I've lost more friends than you can imagine. Don't lecture me about inaction and its consequences."

The air in the room grew thick with tension, old hurts, and deep-seated prejudices bubbling to the surface. William opened his mouth to argue, but something in Thaddeus' eyes made him pause. Behind the vampire hunter's stoic exterior, he saw a flicker of genuine concern.

William took a deep breath, forcing the wolf back down. "Alright," he said, his voice steadier now. "What do you suggest we do?"

Thaddeus' eyes softened slightly, a hint of approval in their depths. "We start by organizing what we know," he said, gesturing to the pile of books and maps on the nearby table. "The ritual circle, the increase in vampire activity, the prophecy—there's a pattern here, we just need to find it."

As they pored over the information, William felt his detective instincts kick in. His sharp mind picked up on details others might miss, while Thaddeus' centuries of experience with vampire lore filled in the gaps.

"Look here," William said, pointing to a map of London. "These attacks, they're not random. They're forming a pattern, almost like—"

"A summoning circle," Thaddeus finished, his eyes widening. "Clever bastards."

William nodded, a grim smile on his face. "We know where they'll strike next," he said. "We can set a trap."

Thaddeus leaned back, a thoughtful expression on his face. "It's risky," he said. "But it might be our best shot."

As they hashed out the details of their plan, William felt a spark of hope in his chest. They were an unlikely pair—a werewolf detective and a vampire hunter—but together, they might just have a chance.

"We'll need to move fast," Thaddeus said, his eyes keen. "Your wolf senses will be crucial in tracking them down."

William nodded. "And your knowledge of vampire weaknesses will give us the edge we need in a fight."

As they finalized their strategy, William realized that their initial clash had transformed into something stronger. Their differences weren't a weakness—they were the foundation of a powerful alliance.

"Ready to save our friends and stop an apocalypse?" William asked, a hint of his old humor returning.

Thaddeus' lips quirked in a small smile. "Just another Tuesday in London, wouldn't you say?"

With a shared nod of determination, they gathered their weapons and headed out into the night. The hunt was on.

WILLIAM STARED AT THE outstretched hand before him, his heart pounding in his chest. The room seemed to close in around him as he contemplated the weight of this moment. With a deep breath, he grasped Thaddeus' hand firmly.

The vampire hunter's grip was like iron, calloused and unyielding. William could feel the strength born from years of relentless pursuit etched into every line of Thaddeus' palm. As their eyes met, an unspoken understanding passed between them.

"I suppose we have no choice but to work together," William said, his voice low and tinged with reluctance.

Thaddeus nodded, a wry smile tugging at the corner of his mouth. "Strange bedfellows indeed. But desperate times call for desperate measures."

They released their grip, and William flexed his fingers, still feeling the phantom pressure of Thaddeus' handshake.

"We'll need backup," William admitted, running a hand through his dark hair. "Jaxon, Olivia, Gabriel, and Connor – they're our best bet for covering more ground."

Thaddeus grunted in agreement. "The more eyes we have on the streets, the better our chances of finding Elizabeth and Lilly."

An uncomfortable silence settled over them, broken only by the soft ticking of a nearby clock. Thaddeus cleared his throat.

"Well then, let's get you properly armed," he said, striding towards an ornate cabinet.

William watched as Thaddeus unlocked the dark wooden doors, adorned with intricate protective symbols that seemed to shimmer in the dim light. The vampire hunter reached inside, revealing an arsenal that made William's eyes widen.

Thaddeus turned, a quiver in his hands. "Silver-tipped crossbow bolts," he explained, holding them out to William. "And this," he added, presenting a gleaming dagger, "is infused with holy water. It won't kill a vampire outright, but it'll slow the bastards down."

William took the weapons, their unfamiliar weight both comforting and unsettling. He tested the balance of the dagger, its blade catching the light.

"I can track them through the city," William offered, his voice quiet but confident. "My senses are... enhanced, especially at night."

Thaddeus raised an eyebrow, a flicker of respect crossing his weathered features. "Is that so? And what about your connections in London's underbelly?"

William met his gaze steadily. "I've cultivated relationships with various... entities in the supernatural community. If anything unusual has happened involving Elizabeth and Lilly, someone will have seen or heard something."

As they continued their preparations, William found himself studying Thaddeus. The vampire hunter moved with practiced efficiency, every action speaking of years of experience. Despite his distaste for Thaddeus' methods, William couldn't help but admire his skill.

Thaddeus, too, seemed to be reassessing William. The initial contempt in his eyes had given way to a cautious curiosity.

"How precise is this tracking ability of yours?" Thaddeus asked suddenly, pausing in his work.

William considered the question. "Under good conditions, I can follow a scent for miles. And I can hear heartbeats from a considerable distance."

Thaddeus' eyebrows shot up. "Well, I'll be damned," he muttered. "That could be invaluable."

As they finished their preparations, a heavy silence fell over the room. The enormity of their task loomed before them, and William felt the weight of it settle on his shoulders.

"I suppose we should get started," he said, adjusting the quiver on his back.

Thaddeus nodded, his face grim. "Indeed. The night won't wait for us, and neither will our quarry."

As they headed for the door, William couldn't shake the feeling that this unlikely alliance would change everything. For better or worse, their fates were now intertwined in the hunt that lay ahead.

WILLIAM'S CALLOUSED finger traced a winding path through London's streets on the map spread across Thaddeus's weathered oak desk. The parchment crinkled beneath his touch, its edges curling from age and use. Thaddeus loomed beside him, his silver-streaked beard twitching as he furrowed his brow in concentration.

"These tunnels," William murmured, tapping a spot on the map. The ink there was faded, barely visible in the flickering candlelight. "Several disappearances recently. Could be our best lead."

Thaddeus stroked his beard, the coarse hairs rustling against his palm. "Aye," he growled, his voice low and gravelly. "Vampires love such places. Dark as pitch, damp as a witch's... well, you get the idea. Plenty of nooks and crannies to hide their foul deeds."

A sharp rap at the door shattered the silence. William's muscles coiled, his hand flying to the cane sword at his belt. The metal was cool against his palm, a comforting weight. Thaddeus raised a weathered hand, padding silently to the door on feet that belied his bulk.

"Who goes there?" he barked, his voice carrying the authority of years spent battling the supernatural.

"It's us, you old bear," came Jaxon's familiar drawl. "We got your message, William. Thought you might need some help."

Relief washed over William like a cool breeze. He exhaled slowly as Thaddeus threw open the door, revealing their allies. Jaxon sauntered in first, a cocky grin on his face. Olivia followed, her emerald eyes scanning the room with practiced efficiency. Gabriel ducked through the doorway, his imposing frame filling the space, while Connor brought up the rear, closing the door with a soft click.

Olivia's gaze locked onto William, concern etched in the slight furrow of her brow. "Elizabeth and Lilly," she said, her voice tight. "What's happened, William?"

William's throat constricted as he recounted the situation, watching their expressions morph from worry to steely determination. The weight of their concern pressed down on him, a reminder of the stakes they faced.

"We're with you, brother," Gabriel rumbled, his deep voice seeming to vibrate the very floorboards. "Whatever it takes."

Connor nodded, his massive frame casting long shadows in the candlelight. "Just point us in the right direction," he grunted, cracking his knuckles with anticipation.

As they huddled around the map, William felt a spark of hope ignite in his chest. With these formidable allies by his side, their chances had improved dramatically. He allowed himself a small, grim smile.

"Right then," Thaddeus growled, addressing the group. His eyes glinted with barely contained excitement. "We believe Elizabeth and Lilly's disappearance is tied to this loom - a right nasty piece of work that could twist reality like a pretzel. We're starting our hunt in these godforsaken tunnels."

Jaxon leaned in, his sharp eyes studying the map intently. "I've heard whispers about those tunnels," he muttered a hint of awe in his voice. "There's old magic down there, older than London itself. The kind like the Heart of Empathy, a power that makes your teeth itch and your hair stand on end."

William nodded, grateful for Jaxon's insight. "That fits with what we've pieced together," he said, running a hand through his hair. "The

145

loom's history seems to be tangled up with London's oldest, darkest secrets."

As they continued to strategize, the air in the room grew thick with tension and possibility. William felt a cautious optimism blooming within him, like the first rays of dawn after a long, dark night. For the first time since learning of Elizabeth and Lilly's disappearance, he dared to hope. They had a real chance now - a chance to rescue them and stop whatever malevolent forces were at work in the shadows of their beloved city.

THE NARROW STAIRCASE groaned under Thaddeus's heavy boots, each step echoing like a heartbeat in William's ears. He could feel the worn stone beneath his feet, almost as if it were sighing in protest. The soft clink of gear and hushed whispers from his companions filled the air, a stark contrast to the oppressive silence that surrounded them.

As they descended, William's nose twitched. The air grew thick with a blend of scents - aged wood, rusted metal, and something else. Something acrid and pungent that he couldn't quite place. It reminded him of smoldering embers on a damp night, a memory that sent a shiver down his spine.

At the bottom, Thaddeus grasped the iron handle of a heavy oak door. The metal creaked in protest as he pushed it open, and warm, golden light spilled out, washing over their faces.

William's breath caught in his throat as he took in the sight before him. His eyes, wide with wonder, darted from wall to wall.

"Blimey," Connor whispered beside him, his voice barely audible.

The room was a treasure trove of weaponry. Crossbows with gleaming stocks hung next to swords that shimmered like liquid moonlight. Vials of holy water, filled with an almost ethereal liquid, cast dancing shadows on the walls in the flickering torchlight.

William's hand instinctively tightened around his cane sword, the familiar weight comforting. The silver lion's head embossed on its hilt seemed to glow in response, as if sensing the gravity of the moment.

Thaddeus's gruff voice cut through the awed silence. "Right then, let's get you lot properly equipped. We've not got all night." His eyes gleamed with pride as he strode through the room, his long, dark coat billowing behind him like a cape.

With the precision of a maestro, Thaddeus plucked items from the walls. "Silver-tipped bolts, Connor," he said, handing over a quiver. "Aim for the heart or head. Miss, and you'll just be buying yourself a world of hurt."

Connor's freckled face set in determination as he accepted the quiver. The leather creaked as he slung it over his shoulder. "Got it. Heart or head, or I'm answering to you. No pressure, right?"

Olivia, her curly honey-blonde hair tied back in a practical knot, hefted a compact crossbow. She tested its weight, a grim smile playing on her lips. "Nice balance," she murmured, glancing at Thaddeus for approval.

Meanwhile, Jaxon examined a set of throwing knives with scholarly intensity. The razor-sharp edges glinted wickedly in the torchlight, casting tiny, malevolent sparks into the shadows.

Thaddeus stopped in front of William, pressing a small, delicate vial into his palm. "Concentrated garlic essence. Won't drop them in their tracks, but it'll give you a moment's breathing room. Their eyes will water something fierce."

William's fingers closed around the vial, its coolness seeping into his skin. "Useful," he murmured, tucking it into his coat pocket. The weight settled next to his sword, a comforting presence. "Though, from experience, I've found their sense of smell isn't quite as...refined, shall we say, as a werewolf's. Might be an angle worth exploring."

Thaddeus's eyebrow arched, a hint of respect creeping into his gruff tone. "Good thinking, lad. Any other...wolfish insights you care to share?"

William's gaze drifted to the others, now all armed and watching with a mix of curiosity and wariness. He cleared his throat. "Just that their group dynamics can be...exploited, if you know what to look for. The usual hierarchy. If we can identify—"

Gabriel, leaning against a nearby rack of swords, his dark eyes glinting with interest, cut in, "You mean, like a military chain of command?"

William nodded, a ghost of a smile touching his lips. "Exactly. Disrupt the chain, and you create chaos. In the chaos, we find our opening."

"Clever," Olivia chimed in, her green eyes narrowing thoughtfully. "But how do we spot the leaders in the heat of battle?"

William turned to her, his expression serious. "Look for the ones giving orders, or the ones others defer to. They'll likely be better equipped, too."

Thaddeus's gruff expression softened slightly, a nod of approval accompanying his words. "Alright, enough chatter. Let's gear up and get moving. We've got a long night ahead, and not a lot of time for theorizing."

As they made their final preparations, William couldn't help but feel a mix of anticipation and dread. The weight of the garlic vial in his pocket and the familiar grip of his cane sword were reassuring, but he knew the dangers that lay ahead. With one last glance at his companions, he steeled himself for the night to come.

THE FIRST RAYS OF DAWN painted the sky in soft hues of pink and gold, casting long shadows across the cobblestone streets. William stood at the threshold of Thaddeus's home, his heart pounding with anticipation. He glanced at his companions, their faces a mix of determination and apprehension.

"This is it," William murmured, his blue eyes fixed on the illustration of Elizabeth and Lilly in his hand. He traced their faces with his thumb, his jaw clenching. "We're coming for you," he whispered.

Thaddeus methodically checked his weapons, the familiar weight of each piece grounding him. He looked up, catching William's gaze. "Ready?" he asked, his voice low and steady.

William nodded, tucking the illustration safely into his coat pocket. "As I'll ever be."

"Hold on," Jaxon interjected, his curiosity getting the better of him. "You mentioned a stop before we dive into this underworld business. Care to elaborate?"

Thaddeus's lips quirked into a half-smile. "The Troll Market," he said, relishing the mix of surprise and confusion on their faces. "I have... connections there. They've offered us access to some rather potent weapons."

Gabriel's green eyes narrowed, his brow furrowing. "The Troll Market? I've heard whispers. It's not exactly a friendly neighborhood tea party."

"Aw, come on, Gabe!" Connor grinned, his red hair catching the early morning light. "Where's your sense of adventure? I've always wanted to try their famous rock cakes!"

Olivia rolled her eyes, but couldn't suppress a smile. "Connor, please. We're not here for a culinary tour."

"Shame," Connor replied with a wink. "I hear troll cuisine is quite the experience."

Thaddeus cleared his throat, drawing their attention. "Focus, everyone. The Troll Market isn't a place for jokes or distractions. Keep your wits about you."

As they stepped out into the awakening city, William felt a surge of determination. The weight of their mission settled on his shoulders, but he stood tall. "Let's go," he said, his voice steady. "Elizabeth and Lilly are waiting."

They moved as one, melting into the shadows of the narrow streets. The sounds of the city stirring to life surrounded them – the clop of horse hooves, the distant whistle of a steam engine, the calls of early morning vendors. But for William and his companions, there was only the path ahead and the promise of what awaited them in the mysterious Troll Market.

No More Games

William's enhanced senses tingled as he trailed Thaddeus through the maze-like alleys. The air buzzed with magic, thick with the sweet scent of faerie dust and the soft murmur of incantations. Each breath reminded him of the supernatural world he'd tried so hard to forget.

"Watch your step," Thaddeus warned, his voice low. "These cobblestones have a mind of their own."

William nodded, his eyes scanning the narrow streets. Familiar troll architecture loomed overhead, stirring memories of past visits to the market. A pang of nostalgia hit him, unexpected and bittersweet.

Jaxon walked beside him, hazel eyes wide with childlike wonder. "Blimey," he whispered, "I'd forgotten how bloody marvelous this place is. Look at that, Will!" He pointed to a shop window filled with glowing potions.

"Language, Jaxon," Olivia chided gently, but her own green eyes sparkled with excitement. Her hand brushed against William's, sending a jolt through him. "It never gets old, does it?" she murmured.

William shook his head, a small smile tugging at his lips. "No, it doesn't."

Behind them, Gabriel and Connor brought up the rear, their heads swiveling to take in the sights. William could hear Connor's excited whispers, and rapid-fire observations about every magical trinket they passed.

"Oi, Gabe," Connor hissed, "d'you reckon that's a real dragon egg?"

Gabriel snorted. "Doubt it. Probably just a fancy paperweight."

As they delved deeper into the city's shadowy underbelly, William felt a twinge of regret. How much had he missed in his desperate quest for normalcy? Each turn revealed another layer of the hidden realm he'd long been a part of but had chosen to ignore.

The muffled roar of a troll argument echoed from somewhere ahead. William couldn't help but chuckle. Some things never changed.

Thaddeus led them down a particularly narrow alley, the walls pressing in on either side. William's nostrils flared, catching a whiff of something ancient and powerful. His skin prickled with anticipation.

Suddenly, Thaddeus stopped. He pressed his palm against a seemingly ordinary brick, and a faint glow emanated from beneath his hand. The wall shimmered and parted, revealing a massive hidden passageway.

"Blimey," Jaxon breathed again, earning an eye-roll from Olivia.

The passage opened onto a square, dominated by a towering gate set into a wall that seemed to stretch endlessly in both directions. Heavily armed troll guards stood at attention, their eyes scanning the newcomers with suspicion.

Thaddeus turned to face them, a rare smile playing on his lips. "Welcome," he said softly, "to the true heart of supernatural London. The gate to the Troll Market."

William exchanged glances with his companions. He saw the mix of excitement and familiarity in their eyes, mirroring his own emotions. They'd all been here before, but somehow, this visit felt different. More significant.

As they approached the gate, William couldn't shake the feeling that this journey into the Troll Market would change everything. He took a deep breath, steeling himself for whatever lay ahead.

"Well," he said, his voice barely above a whisper, "shall we?"

Olivia squeezed his hand. "Together," she replied.

And with that, they stepped forward, ready to face the wonders and dangers of the Troll Market once more.

THE LOOM OF MS. JENNY

WILLIAM'S FINGERS TREMBLED as they curled around the hilt of his cane sword. The cool metal bit into his clammy palm, a stark contrast to the nervous heat radiating from his body. He drew in a sharp breath, the crisp morning air stinging his cheeks. Invisible currents of arcane energy danced across his skin, raising goosebumps in their wake.

His eyes darted from shadow to shadow, muscles coiled tight like springs. Every rustle of leaves, every whisper of wind, set his nerves on edge. Beside him, Jaxon fidgeted with the strap of his satchel, while Gabriel's hand rested on the pommel of his sword. Connor stood slightly apart, his keen eyes scanning the perimeter.

"Steady now," Thaddeus murmured, his gravelly voice barely above a whisper. The professor's gnarled hands wove intricate patterns in the air, leaving trails of golden sparks that faded like dying fireflies. Waves of magical energy pulsed outward, making William's skin crawl.

"You alright there, William?" Olivia's voice cut through his racing thoughts. "You look like you've seen a ghost."

William turned, meeting her piercing emerald gaze. He found himself anchored by the unwavering focus in her eyes. "Just the usual pre-market jitters," he replied, forcing a wry smile. "Nothing a good cup of mead won't fix."

Olivia's lips quirked upward, but her body remained tense, ready to spring into action at a moment's notice. "Let's hope that's all we'll need to worry about today."

Jaxon chuckled nervously. "Knowing our luck, we'll be running from a horde of angry pixies before noon."

"Quiet," Gabriel hissed, his eyes narrowing. "We're approaching the gate."

As they drew closer, William blinked hard, unsure if his eyes were playing tricks on him. The gate's intricate carvings seemed to come alive, trolls and magical creatures dancing across its surface in subtle, mesmerizing movements.

"Is it just me," William whispered, "or are those carvings... moving?"

Thaddeus grunted, a hint of amusement in his voice. "Welcome to the threshold, lad. Where reality starts to bend."

Connor whistled low. "Now that's a sight I'll never get used to."

The cobblestones beneath their feet glistened with morning dew, each step producing a soft echo in the quiet street. In the distance, William could hear the faint stirrings of the city awakening, but here, in this liminal space, an eerie stillness reigned.

As they reached the threshold, William exchanged glances with his companions. Thaddeus's eyes glimmered with barely contained excitement, a stark contrast to his usual gruff demeanor. Olivia met William's gaze, her emerald eyes filled with determination. Jaxon looked pale but resolute, while Gabriel's hand tightened on his sword hilt.

"Well," William said, taking a deep breath and tasting the tang of magic on his tongue, "shall we?"

Thaddeus nodded, his beard twitching with a suppressed smile. "After you, young man. Age before beauty, and all that."

Olivia rolled her eyes. "If we wait for you two to sort out who's going first, we'll be here till sunset."

"Ladies first, then?" Connor suggested with a grin.

"Oh no," Olivia shot back, "I'm not falling for that one. We go together or not at all."

WILLIAM'S HEART RACED as they neared the Troll Market's entrance. The familiar stone archway loomed ahead, but something felt off. His ears pricked at the rising din of gruff voices and hurried footsteps.

As they got closer, chaos erupted before their eyes. Massive troll guards, their skin like weathered cliff faces, waved their tree trunk arms wildly. Gone was their usual stoic demeanor, replaced by a nervous energy that made William's skin prickle.

"Blimey," he muttered, his gaze darting between the agitated guards. "What's got their knickers in a twist?"

A young woman clutched a wicker basket overflowing with herbs, her face a mix of confusion and anger. "But I need these for my potions!" she cried, her voice rising above the commotion. A troll, his features etched with concern, gently but firmly steered her away from the entrance.

"I'm sorry, miss," the troll rumbled, "but orders are orders. No one in or out today."

William watched as an elderly man in flowing robes approached the entrance. His weathered face fell as a guard turned him away. The man's shoulders slumped, his eyes downcast as he shuffled back towards the bustling London streets.

Beside him, Olivia's emerald eyes narrowed, her frown deepening as she surveyed the scene. "Something's not right," she murmured, tension evident in her voice. "I've never seen them this agitated."

Thaddeus adjusted his spectacles, the lenses catching the morning light. His bushy eyebrows knitted together as he observed the unusual spectacle. "Most irregular, indeed," he muttered, stroking his beard thoughtfully. "Perhaps we should inquire about the nature of this disturbance?"

William felt the wolf within him stir, responding to the anxiety that hung thick in the air. His fingers tightened around his cane sword, ready for anything. "Good idea, Thaddeus," he said, his voice low. "But let's tread carefully. No telling what's got everyone so riled up."

As they approached the nearest guard, William plastered on his most charming smile. "Pardon me, good sir," he called out, "but might we trouble you for a moment of your time? We're rather curious about the commotion."

The troll guard turned, his craggy features softening slightly at William's polite tone. "It's not safe," he grunted, glancing nervously over his shoulder. "Market's closed until further notice. Best be on your way."

Olivia stepped forward, her green eyes flashing with determination. "We understand your concern," she said smoothly, "but surely you can give us some idea of what's happening? We're regulars here, after all."

The guard hesitated, his massive frame shifting uncomfortably. "Well," he rumbled, leaning in closer, "word is there's been some sort of magical disturbance inside. Nasty business, from what I hear. Boss doesn't want anyone getting hurt."

William exchanged a meaningful glance with his companions. Whatever was happening inside the Troll Market, it was clear their day had just gotten a lot more interesting – and potentially dangerous.

WILLIAM'S EARS TWITCHED, his heightened senses picking up fragments of hushed conversations swirling around them. The low, gravelly voices of the trolls painted a clearer picture of the unfolding situation with each snippet.

"Emergency meeting called," one troll growled, his voice barely above a whisper.

Another rumbled, fear lacing his words, "Something's wrong. Really wrong."

A third guard, his voice trembling, breathed, "I've never seen anything like it. It's... it's unnatural."

William's brow furrowed as he processed this information. His mind raced, trying to connect these clues to Lilly and Elizabeth's disappearance. He ran a hand through his hair, frustration evident in his movements.

"Olivia," he murmured, catching her eye. In that brief moment, a silent communication passed between them. Her emerald gaze reflected his own concern and determination.

"You heard that too?" Olivia whispered, her voice tight with worry.

William nodded. "Something's happening inside the Troll Market. It could be related to Lilly and Elizabeth."

Thaddeus, ever observant, leaned in. "What's going on?" he asked, his weathered face a mask of curiosity and apprehension.

"Not sure yet," William replied, his voice low. "But whatever it is, it's got the trolls spooked."

The atmosphere around them grew heavy with unspoken concerns and mounting tension. William felt it pressing down on his shoulders, his muscles coiling with anticipation. The wolf within him stirred restlessly, sensing the danger that lurked just beyond their reach.

Olivia shifted closer, her emerald eyes scanning the crowd. "We need to find a way in," she breathed.

"Agreed," William nodded, his gaze fixed on the Market's sealed entrance. "But how?"

Thaddeus stroked his bushy beard thoughtfully. "Perhaps we could... persuade one of the guards?"

William shook his head. "Too risky. They're already on edge."

As they stood there, surrounded by the agitated crowd and nervous guards, William couldn't shake the feeling that they were on the precipice of something far bigger and more dangerous than they had initially imagined. The mystery of the Troll Market's closure and the disappearance of their friends seemed to be intertwining, creating a web of intrigue that threatened to ensnare them all.

"Whatever's happening in there," William muttered, his eyes narrowing, "I have a feeling it's just the beginning."

Olivia nodded grimly, her emerald eyes flashing with determination. "Then we'd better be ready for what comes next."

WILLIAM'S HEART RACED as he watched Olivia approach the agitated trolls. Her chestnut hair caught the morning light, swaying gently in the breeze. He couldn't help but admire her courage, even as worry gnawed at his insides.

"She's got this," Thaddeus murmured beside him, his weathered face a mask of concentration.

William nodded, not trusting his voice. The mist swirled around Olivia's feet, giving her an almost ethereal appearance. He noticed the subtle changes in her posture - shoulders back, chin up. Confidence radiated from her, but his keen eyes caught the slight tremor in her hands as she smoothed her jacket.

As Olivia neared the trolls, their gravelly voices reached William's ears, though he couldn't make out the words. He strained to listen, fingers twitching near his concealed weapon.

"Easy now," Thaddeus whispered, sensing William's tension. "Any sudden moves could muck this up right proper."

William forced himself to relax, watching as the trolls' expressions shifted from suspicion to recognition. Olivia's voice, though too quiet to hear clearly, carried a note of authority that seemed to give the massive creatures pause.

"What do you think she's saying?" William asked, unable to bear the silence any longer.

Thaddeus shrugged. "Can't rightly say, but whatever it is, it's got their attention."

Minutes crawled by like hours. Olivia gestured emphatically, her body language conveying urgency without aggression. The trolls shifted uneasily, their massive forms casting long shadows in the morning light.

Finally, Olivia turned back towards them. William held his breath, searching her face for any clue. Her expression remained neutral, but there was a glimmer in her emerald eyes that sparked hope in his chest.

As she approached, William couldn't contain himself. "Well?" he asked, his voice a mix of anticipation and dread.

Olivia's lips curved into a small smile. "They're willing to listen," she said, her voice low. "But we're not out of the woods yet."

William let out a breath he didn't realize he'd been holding. "You were brilliant out there," he said, fighting the urge to pull her into an embrace.

"Save the compliments for when we're safe," Olivia replied, but the warmth in her eyes betrayed her appreciation. "Now, let's see if we can turn this willingness to listen into something more substantial."

WILLIAM WATCHED INTENTLY as Olivia approached the trolls again, his heart pounding in his chest. The massive creatures towered over her, their stony faces etched with suspicion. He held his breath, muscles tense, ready to spring into action at the slightest sign of danger.

The trolls' animated chatter died abruptly as Olivia drew near. Their enormous heads swiveled towards her, eyes narrowing. William caught a flicker of recognition in their gazes, followed by a mix of wariness and grudging respect.

The largest troll, his skin a patchwork of moss and stone, stepped forward. William's hand instinctively moved towards his weapon, but he forced himself to remain still. The troll inclined his head slightly, acknowledging Olivia's presence.

The other trolls huddled closer, their gravelly whispers barely reaching William's ears. He strained to catch their words, but the low rumble of their voices made it impossible to discern anything meaningful.

Olivia stood her ground, her posture radiating a calm authority that William couldn't help but admire. Her chin was lifted, shoulders back, exuding confidence despite being dwarfed by the trolls' massive forms.

The trolls exchanged meaningful glances, their expressions inscrutable to William. He could almost feel the weight of their deliberation, the air thick with tension. His palms grew sweaty as he waited, every second stretching into an eternity.

Finally, the moss-covered troll nodded, a slow, deliberate movement that sent a ripple of relief through William's body. The troll gestured for Olivia to approach, his massive hand moving with surprising grace.

The other trolls formed a protective circle around Olivia and their leader, effectively cutting off William's view. He took an involuntary step forward, fighting the urge to rush in after her. Thaddeus's hand on his arm held him back, a silent reminder to trust in Olivia's abilities.

WILLIAM'S HEART POUNDED as Olivia approached, her face a canvas of worry. He could almost hear the blood rushing in his ears, anticipation building with each step she took.

"What's the news?" he asked, his voice barely above a whisper.

Olivia's green eyes darted between William and Thaddeus. "There's an emergency council meeting," she murmured, her words carrying the weight of impending doom.

William's fingers tightened around his cane sword, the cool metal a stark contrast to his clammy palms. "What's happened?"

"Something's threatening the market," Olivia continued, her auburn hair catching the dim light as she leaned in closer. "Something they've never seen before."

Thaddeus adjusted his spectacles, his bushy eyebrows shooting up. "Good heavens," he muttered. "What could possibly rattle the trolls?"

William's mind raced, conjuring images of monstrous creatures and dark magic. He swallowed hard, trying to keep his voice steady. "How bad is it?"

Olivia's gaze met his, her expression grim. "They're closing the market to outsiders until further notice."

The words hit William like a physical blow. He stumbled back a step, his cane sword clattering against the cobblestones. "Blast it all," he hissed. "We need that market."

Thaddeus nodded, his weathered face etched with concern. "Indeed, my boy. Our entire plan hinges on the resources we could acquire there."

William ran a hand through his dark hair, frustration bubbling up inside him. "There has to be a way in," he insisted. "We can't let this derail everything we've worked for."

Olivia placed a gentle hand on his arm. "William, think about it. If something's got the trolls spooked, it's not to be trifled with."

He met her gaze, seeing the fear she was trying to hide. A knot formed in his stomach as the reality of their situation sank in. "You're right," he admitted. "But what does this mean for Elizabeth and Lilly?"

The trio fell silent, the weight of their missing companions hanging heavy in the air. William's mind whirled, trying to connect this new threat to the disappearances that had brought them here.

Thaddeus cleared his throat. "We must adapt, my friends. Perhaps this new development is somehow connected to our quest."

William nodded slowly, his resolve strengthening. "You're right, Professor. We'll find a way through this, just like we always do."

As they huddled together in the shadows, plotting their next move, William couldn't shake the feeling that they were stepping into something far bigger and more dangerous than they had ever imagined.

WILLIAM'S JAW CLENCHED, the muscles in his neck coiling like taut springs. His heart pounded against his ribs, each beat a thunderous reminder of the gravity of the situation. This couldn't be a mere coincidence. He locked eyes with Olivia, his piercing blue gaze burning with an intensity that made her breath catch in her throat.

"Olivia," he said, his voice low and strained, "this has to be connected to Lilly and Elizabeth's disappearance." The words tumbled out, each syllable heavy with frustration and a flicker of hope. "We can't be left in the dark now. Not when we're so close."

He took a step closer, invading Olivia's personal space. She could see the flecks of silver in his blue eyes, like stars in a turbulent sky. His hands trembled slightly as he fought to maintain his composure.

"You have to convince them," William urged, his tone softening but losing none of its urgency. "We need to be at that meeting. We might have the missing piece they need."

Jaxon nodded vigorously, his wire-rimmed spectacles sliding down his nose. He pushed them back up with a gnarled finger, his eyes alight with the thrill of intellectual pursuit. "Indeed," he chimed in, his gravelly voice carrying the weight of decades of experience. "Our combined expertise could prove invaluable in this crisis. We can't afford to be sidelined."

Olivia hesitated, her brow furrowing as she weighed their request. William watched the conflict play out across her face - the desire to help warring with the need for caution. He held his breath, acutely aware of how much hinged on her decision.

"And if they refuse?" Olivia asked, her voice barely above a whisper. "What then?"

William's lips pressed into a thin line. "Then we find another way. But we have to try this first."

The seconds stretched like hours as Olivia considered. William could almost hear the gears turning in her mind, calculating risks and possibilities. Finally, her expression shifted. The doubt in her eyes gave way to determination, and she nodded, a new resolve settling over her features.

William felt a wave of relief wash over him, his tense muscles relaxing ever so slightly. He released a breath he hadn't realized he'd been holding.

"Alright," Olivia said, her voice steady and sure. "I'll do it. I'll convince them to let us attend."

"Thank you," William breathed, a small smile tugging at the corners of his mouth.

Olivia held up a warning finger. "But we need to be careful. One wrong move and we could lose our only chance to find Elizabeth and Lilly. Are you prepared for that responsibility?"

William nodded solemnly. "More than you know."

Jaxon clapped his hands together, the sound sharp in the tense atmosphere. "Well then," he said, a hint of excitement creeping into his voice, "shall we prepare our arguments? We have a meeting to crash, after all."

OLIVIA FELT THE WEIGHT of responsibility settle upon her shoulders, as tangible as a heavy cloak. Her heart thundered in her chest, but she forced her breathing to remain steady. She locked eyes with William, his blue gaze a swirling tempest of hope and anxiety, trust and fear.

"You can do this, Olivia," William whispered, his voice barely audible. "We're all counting on you."

The intensity of his stare sent butterflies fluttering in her stomach, but Olivia pushed the feeling aside. Now wasn't the time for distractions.

"I know," she replied, her voice low but firm. "I won't let you down."

Thaddeus caught her eye, his weathered face etched with determination. He gave her a slight nod, lips pressed into a thin line.

"Remember," Thaddeus growled, "trolls respect strength. Show no weakness."

Olivia inhaled deeply, the scent of magic and ancient stone filling her lungs. Her mind raced, crafting arguments to appeal to the trolls' sense of duty and their connection to the magical world.

"What if they don't listen?" William asked, worry creasing his brow.

"Then we'll cross that troll bridge when we come to it," Olivia answered, trying to sound more confident than she felt.

She turned back towards the gate, her fingers instinctively brushing against the Celtic rune bracelet on her wrist. The cool metal grounded her, a reminder of her own strength and the magic flowing through her veins.

The troll guards loomed before them, massive forms casting long shadows in the flickering torchlight. Olivia lifted her chin, meeting their wary gazes with unwavering confidence.

"Here goes nothing," she muttered, taking a step forward.

"Wait," William called softly. Olivia turned, seeing a mix of concern and admiration in his blue eyes. "Be careful."

She nodded, allowing herself a small smile before facing the guards again. Her mind raced with strategies as she approached. Appeal to duty first, then curiosity. If that failed, play on their fear of the unknown threat. And if all else failed... well, she had a few magical tricks up her sleeve.

"Greetings, noble guardians," Olivia called out, her voice clear and strong. "We seek an audience with your leaders on a matter of great importance."

The larger of the two trolls grunted, eyeing her suspiciously. "And why should we grant you passage, human?"

Olivia straightened her spine, channeling every ounce of authority she could muster. "Because the fate of both our worlds may depend on it."

THE MOSS-COVERED TROLL regarded her with a mixture of curiosity and wariness. Olivia's emerald eyes met his, unflinching.

"Honored guardians," she began, her voice low but clear, "I understand your hesitation. But the threat we face isn't confined to your market alone. It's spreading, affecting both our worlds."

The other trolls leaned in, listening intently. Olivia felt a surge of hope in their interest.

"My companions and I," she gestured towards William, Jaxon, Gabriel, Connor, and Thaddeus, "possess unique skills that could prove invaluable in this crisis. William's supernatural senses can detect traces of dark magic that might elude others. And Professor Ironheart here is one of the foremost experts on arcane artifacts and vampire lore in all of London."

The guards exchanged glances, their stony faces unreadable. Olivia pressed on, her words gaining urgency.

"We believe the disturbances in your market are connected to recent disappearances in the human world. If we pool our knowledge and resources, we stand a better chance of unraveling this mystery before it's too late."

She paused, letting her words sink in. The larger troll shifted his weight, causing the ground to tremble slightly.

"And what do you bring to this fight, human?" he rumbled, his voice like grinding stones.

Olivia straightened her spine, meeting his gaze with unwavering confidence. "I am a practitioner of protective magic, specializing in wards and shielding spells. My skills could help fortify your defenses against whatever dark force threatens the market."

The trolls murmured among themselves, their gravelly voices too low for Olivia to make out. She held her breath, acutely aware of William and Thaddeus's anxious presence behind her.

Finally, the moss-covered troll turned back to Olivia. "Your words carry weight, human. But words alone are not enough to grant you passage."

Tension built as Olivia waited for the guard's final decision, the fate of their mission hanging in the balance.

WILLIAM'S KNUCKLES whitened as he gripped his cane sword, the cool metal a stark contrast to his clammy palms. His eyes never left Olivia's animated form, drinking in every gesture, every inflection in her voice.

"Come on, Liv," he muttered under his breath. "You've got this."

The air felt thick, almost suffocating. William could almost taste the tension, metallic and bitter on his tongue.

Beside him, Thaddeus's fingers danced through the air, tracing arcane symbols. The vampire hunter's lips moved in a silent incantation.

"Steady on, old chap," Thaddeus whispered, eyes fixed on the trolls. "Our dear Olivia has this well in hand."

The scent of ozone tickled William's nostrils. He glanced at Jaxon, who was shifting from foot to foot like a nervous schoolboy.

"Bloody hell," Jaxon hissed. "Why'd we let her do the talking again?"

Gabriel's face hardened. "Because she's the only one who can keep a civil tongue around these brutes."

Connor nodded, his werewolf instincts clearly on high alert. William found comfort in the pack's presence, a reminder they weren't alone in this fight.

As time crawled by, William's anxiety warred with hope. Olivia's gestures became more emphatic, her emerald eyes flashing with determination. The trolls' stony faces began to crack, skepticism giving way to consideration.

"Gentlemen," Olivia's voice carried over, clear and strong. "We represent not just humans, but the Fae and Werewolf communities as well in this matter."

The largest troll leaned down, his moss-covered face inches from Olivia's. William's muscles coiled, ready to spring. But Olivia stood her ground, chin lifted in defiance.

"And why," the troll rumbled, voice like grinding stones, "should that matter to us?"

"Because this threat concerns us all," Olivia countered. "The disappearances, the magical disturbances – they don't discriminate. We need access to the Troll Market to follow our only lead."

William held his breath. Their entire investigation hung in the balance.

The troll straightened, eyes narrowing. The silence stretched, taut as a bowstring.

Finally, he spoke. "Very well, human. You may enter. But know this – one false move, and you'll wish you'd never set foot in our domain."

Olivia nodded, relief evident in the slight sag of her shoulders. As she turned back, William caught her eye and gave her a small, proud smile.

"Well done, Liv," he murmured as she rejoined them.

"I thought he was going to eat you for a moment there," Jaxon quipped, his earlier nervousness dissolving into humor.

Olivia rolled her eyes. "Please, Jaxon. I'm hardly a troll's idea of a snack."

"No, but you're certainly a treat for the eyes," Connor teased, earning a playful swat from Olivia.

"Focus, everyone," Gabriel growled, but there was a hint of amusement in his eyes. "We're in, but the real challenge begins now."

William nodded, his grip on the cane sword relaxing slightly. "Indeed. Let's not waste this opportunity. The Troll Market awaits, and with it, hopefully, some answers. The next step will be to find out more intel, some of us should meet with Silas, and Barty Quill is a good info broker we should harras a bit I think... Also there is the activist Celeste Moonfellow, Gabriel and Connor should probably be the ones to talk with her."

As they moved forward, William couldn't shake the feeling that they were stepping into the unknown. But with Olivia's quick wit, Thaddeus's magic, and the strength of their unlikely band, he dared to hope they might just unravel this mystery after all.

Earning Respect

William's nostrils flared as he stepped through the hidden entrance, his wolf senses instantly on high alert. The air shifted, thick with magic that prickled his skin like static electricity. A familiar scent tickled his nose—sweet, ethereal faerie dust mingling with the earthy musk of trolls.

"Do you smell that?" he whispered to Olivia and Thaddeus, his companions close behind.

Olivia nodded, her green eyes wide with wonder. "It's intoxicating," she breathed.

As they moved deeper into the market, William's ears pricked up, catching the low hum of incantations. The words, though indistinct, pulsed with an otherworldly rhythm that seemed to resonate in his very bones.

Narrow corridors wound before them, carved from living stone. Troll architecture surrounded them, all rough edges and primal strength. William's hand brushed against a wall, feeling the cool, damp surface beneath his fingers.

"Watch your step," he murmured to the others, noting the uneven floor. "These trolls aren't known for their smooth craftsmanship."

Thaddeus chuckled, his deep voice echoing slightly in the confined space. "Aye, I'd rather not break my neck before we even reach the market proper."

As they navigated the twisting passages, memories flooded back to William. He recalled his first visit years ago, wide-eyed and overwhelmed by the sheer magic of it all. Now, older and wiser, he felt a different kind of awe—tinged with caution and purpose.

Olivia's voice broke through his reverie. "It's even more incredible than I remembered," she whispered, her auburn hair catching the soft glow of the fungi that lined the walls.

Thaddeus grunted in agreement. "Aye, but don't let the wonder distract you. We're here on business, remember?"

William nodded, his blue eyes scanning their surroundings. "Right, you are, old friend. Keep your wits about you."

As they rounded a corner, the passage widened, revealing glimpses of the market proper. Stalls crammed with magical curiosities lined the cavern walls, their wares glinting in the soft, otherworldly light.

William paused, allowing his senses to adjust to the cacophony of sights, sounds, and smells. The Troll Market was a feast for the supernatural senses, a place where the impossible became mundane and the extraordinary was commonplace.

"Well," he said, a hint of excitement creeping into his voice, "shall we dive in?"

Olivia grinned, her eyes sparkling with anticipation. "Lead the way, William. I can't wait to see what wonders—and dangers—await us."

Thaddeus hefted his walking stick, a glint in his eye. "Just remember, you two. In a place like this, everything comes with a price. Best be prepared to bargain with more than just coin."

With a shared nod of understanding, the trio stepped forward into the bustling heart of the Troll Market, ready to face whatever magical challenges lay ahead.

GABRIEL'S HEART RACED as he stepped into the cavernous market, his senses overwhelmed by the kaleidoscope of sights, sounds, and smells. Vendors' voices echoed off stone walls, hawking wares that defied imagination. A troll with skin like cracked leather haggled with a delicate pixie over a glowing crystal, while a gnome bartered with a creature that seemed to shift forms with each blink.

"Well, I'll be damned," Connor muttered, his gruff voice barely audible over the market's din. He ran a hand through his salt-and-pepper hair, amber eyes wide with wonder. "It's like stepping into another world."

William inhaled deeply, his nostrils flaring as he caught the intertwining scents of exotic spices and raw magic. "It never ceases to amaze me," he said, a smile playing on his lips. "No matter how many times I visit."

Olivia's emerald eyes sparkled as she gazed at a nearby stall. Shimmering potions in glass vials caught the light, casting rainbow reflections across her face. "I could spend days exploring this place and still not see everything," she breathed, reaching out to touch a bottle before thinking better of it.

Thaddeus grumbled, his gnarled hand tightening on his walking stick. "Trust me, you wouldn't want to," he warned, rheumy eyes darting suspiciously from stall to stall. "Some things here are best left undiscovered."

Jaxon chuckled, clapping Thaddeus on the shoulder. The old professor stumbled slightly, shooting Jaxon a withering glare. "Always the optimist, eh, Professor?" Jaxon grinned, unfazed. "Come on, let's head to my shop. It's just around the corner."

As they weaved through the crowd, Gabriel couldn't help but stare. A group of goblins huddled near a stall, their beady eyes following passersby with unsettling intensity.

Connor noticed Gabriel's unease. "Watch your pockets," he warned in a low voice. "Some of these folk have sticky fingers."

William snorted, his blue eyes twinkling with mischief. "Speak for yourself," he quipped. "I seem to recall a certain werewolf with a penchant for 'borrowing' things in his youth."

Connor growled playfully, baring teeth that seemed just a bit too sharp. "That was a long time ago, old friend. Besides, I always returned what I borrowed... eventually."

Their banter was cut short as Jaxon's voice rose above the market's clamor. "Here we are," he announced, gesturing to a shop front. A weathered wooden sign swung gently in the breeze, 'Organized Chaos' etched in swirling script.

The group filed into the shop, the door's bell tinkling softly as it closed behind them. Gabriel blinked, his eyes adjusting to the dimmer light. Towering stacks of books threatened to topple at any moment, while shelves groaned under the weight of arcane trinkets. Jaxon moved through the clutter with practiced ease, straightening a crooked tome here, and adjusting a mysterious artifact there.

"Welcome to my humble abode," Jaxon said, pride evident in his voice. He turned to face them, his hazel eyes gleaming. "Feel free to look around, but please, don't touch anything unless you're prepared for the consequences. That goes double for you, Connor," he added with a wink.

Connor raised his hands in mock surrender. "I'm reformed, I swear," he chuckled, but his eyes lingered on a jeweled dagger displayed near the counter.

Gabriel took a tentative step forward, his fingers itching to explore. A leather-bound book caught his eye, its spine adorned with symbols he didn't recognize. As he reached for it, Olivia's hand gently caught his wrist.

"Remember what Jaxon said," she murmured, her voice tinged with both caution and curiosity. "In a place like this, even the most innocuous object could be more than it seems."

Gabriel nodded, withdrawing his hand. As he turned to explore another corner of the shop, he couldn't shake the feeling that some of the objects were watching him. In Jaxon's Organized Chaos, it seemed, nothing was quite as it appeared.

THE BELL ABOVE THE door chimed, a delicate tinkling that belied the chaos Olivia was about to step into. She slipped out of Jaxon's shop, her heart pounding so hard she could feel it in her throat. The moment she crossed the threshold, the Troll Market hit her like a tidal wave.

Shouts from vendors hawking their wares pierced the air. "Fresh dragon scales! Get your scales here!"

"Enchanted trinkets! Ward off evil spirits!"

The clinking of coins and the hum of a thousand conversations blended into a dizzying symphony. Olivia blinked rapidly, trying to process the sensory overload. She took a deep breath, filling her lungs with the scent of incense and exotic spices.

Her emerald eyes darted from face to face, searching for any clue about Elizabeth and Lilly. The crowd surged around her, a living sea of magical beings. A troll lumbered past, its stone-like skin catching the lamplight. Olivia had to sidestep to avoid being crushed.

Overhead, faeries flitted by, trailing stardust in their wake. One winked at her, its tiny face mischievous. Olivia couldn't help but smile, despite the tension coiling in her stomach.

A group of pixies zoomed past, their gossip carried on glittering wings. Olivia's ears perked up. She leaned in, careful not to draw attention.

"Did you hear?" one pixie chirped, its voice high and reedy. "Another disappearance last night!"

"That's the third this week," another replied, worry etched on its tiny face. "What in the name of the Fae queen is going on?"

Olivia's pulse quickened. She sidled up to a nearby stall, pretending to examine a collection of enchanted trinkets. Her fingers traced the outline of a silver locket, but her attention was fixed on the pixies' conversation.

The vendor, a wizened gnome with a beard that pooled at his feet, fixed her with a suspicious glare. "Interested in protection charms, miss?" he growled. His voice was like gravel in a blender. "Dark times we're living in, mark my words."

Olivia saw her chance. She met the gnome's gaze, feigning innocence. "Oh? What sort of dark times?"

The gnome's bushy eyebrows shot up so high they nearly disappeared into his hairline. He leaned in, his voice dropping to a conspiratorial whisper. "People vanishing without a trace, that's what. Some say it's the work of an ancient artifact - the Loom of Fate."

Olivia's breath caught in her throat. "The Loom of Fate?" she repeated, fighting to keep her voice steady. Her mind raced, connecting dots she hadn't even known existed.

The gnome nodded gravely, his eyes darting left and right as if afraid the very walls had ears. "A terrible power, it is. Weaves the very fabric of reality. In the wrong hands..." He trailed off, shaking his head.

"That sounds... terrifying," Olivia managed, her mind racing. "Thank you for the warning."

As she moved deeper into the market, snippets of similar conversations reached her ears. Whispered fears of an unseen threat, rumors of a power that could reshape the world. The air felt thick with tension, as if the entire market was holding its breath.

A cloaked figure bumped into Olivia, nearly knocking her off balance. She caught a glimpse of piercing glowing eyes before the stranger melted into the crowd. A chill ran down her spine, and she couldn't shake the feeling of being watched.

With a growing sense of unease, Olivia made her way back to Jaxon's shop. The bell above the door chimed as she entered, and her companions turned to her expectantly. William's blue eyes locked onto hers, filled with a mix of curiosity and concern.

"Well?" he asked, his voice tight with anticipation. "What did you find out?"

Olivia took a deep breath, her gaze sweeping over the familiar faces. Jaxon leaned against his cluttered counter, while Thaddeus fidgeted with a pocket watch. The tension in the room was so thick you could cut it with a knife.

"It's worse than we thought," she began, her voice barely above a whisper. "There have been more disappearances, not just Elizabeth and Lilly. And they're all connected to something called the Loom of Fate."

William's brow furrowed, creating a deep crease between his eyebrows. "The Loom of Fate? What in blazes is that?"

Olivia shook her head, her emerald eyes clouded with worry. "I don't know exactly, but from what I gathered, it's some kind of ancient artifact. Powerful enough to 'weave and alter the fabric of reality,' according to one particularly paranoid gnome."

Jaxon let out a low whistle. "Blimey, that sounds like trouble with a capital T, and like something we've heard before."

"You're telling me," Olivia agreed, running a hand through her hair. "And that's not all. The whole market is on edge. People are disappearing left and right, and nobody knows why or how."

Jaxon's usually jovial face turned grim. "This Loom of Fate... if it's as powerful as they say, it could explain a lot. But who could be wielding such a thing?"

William's eyes widened, a spark of realization igniting in their blue depths. "Wait a minute," he said, his voice low and urgent. "Doesn't this sound familiar? Remember what we heard about Lord Everett Wentworth?"

Thaddeus stopped fidgeting with his pocket watch, his face paling. "By Jove, you're right! Didn't those rumors mention something about him searching for an artifact that could alter reality?"

Olivia felt her stomach drop. "And now people are disappearing... It can't be a coincidence."

Jaxon nodded slowly, his expression grave. "If Lord Everett Wentworth has gotten his hands on this Loom of Fate..."

"Then we're in even more trouble than we thought," William finished, his jaw set in determination.

A heavy silence fell over the group as the implications sank in. Olivia's mind raced, piecing together the fragments of information she'd gathered. One thing was clear: they were in over their heads, and time was running out.

WILLIAM'S FOOTSTEPS echoed in the cramped confines of Jaxon's shop as he paced back and forth, his brow furrowed in concentration. The floorboards creaked beneath his feet, a counterpoint to the ticking of the ornate clock on the wall. He ran a hand through his hair, his blue eyes unfocused as he searched his memory.

Suddenly, he stopped, his body going rigid. "I've seen something like this before," he muttered, his voice barely above a whisper.

Olivia's head snapped up, her emerald eyes wide with interest. "You have?" she asked, leaning forward. "Where?"

William's shoulders slumped as he shook his head. "I can't... it's like trying to grasp smoke," he said, frustration etching lines across his face. "It's there, just out of reach."

Jaxon and Thaddeus exchanged glances, their expressions a mix of curiosity and concern. The silence in the shop grew thick, broken only by the steady tick-tock of the clock.

Olivia chewed her lower lip, her mind racing. Suddenly, her face lit up. "What about Silas?" she blurted out, excitement coloring her voice.

William blinked, his blue eyes focusing on her. "Silas?" he repeated, confusion evident in his tone.

"Yes, the old elf!" Olivia explained, her words tumbling out in a rush. "You know, the one with all those connections to information gathering and market history? If anyone knows about this Loom of Fate and its connection to the disappearances, it would be him."

William's expression cleared, a spark of hope igniting in his eyes. "Olivia, you brilliant woman," he said, a small smile tugging at the corners of his mouth. "Silas has been around for centuries. If there's any lore about this Loom, he'd know it."

Thaddeus nodded, stroking his chin thoughtfully. "And if there's a connection to the recent disappearances in London, he'd be the one to ask," he added. "The old codger's got ears everywhere. Probably knows what the Queen had for breakfast this morning."

Jaxon snorted, a rare sound of amusement. "Knowing Silas, he probably supplied the tea leaves himself."

William's posture straightened, determination radiating from him. "It's settled then," he declared, his voice firm. "We need to find Silas and pick his brain about this Loom of Fate and its possible connection to the rest of this mystery."

Olivia stood, smoothing out her skirts. "Well then, gentlemen," she said, a mischievous glint in her emerald eyes, "shall we go elf-hunting?"

GABRIEL'S SILVER-STREAKED fur shimmered in the dim light of Jaxon's cluttered shop. He locked eyes with William, his voice a low rumble that seemed to vibrate through the floorboards. "Connor and I will track down Celeste. She may not trust us, but we share a common enemy."

Connor, a mountain of muscle and fur, grunted his agreement. His massive paws flexed, leaving faint claw marks on the worn wooden floor.

Jaxon's eyes glinted with excitement behind his wire-rimmed spectacles. He rubbed his hands together, a mischievous smile playing on his lips. "Leave Barty to me. That goblin's been dodging my calls, but he owes me more than a few favors."

"Just don't scare him off," William warned, a hint of amusement in his voice. "We need information, not another enemy."

As the trio departed, their footsteps fading into the bustling sounds of the Troll Market outside, William turned to face Thaddeus and Olivia. His sapphire eyes blazed with intensity, reflecting the flickering lamplight.

"We need that map," he said, his voice low and urgent. "It's the key to unraveling this whole mess."

Olivia's brow furrowed, her fingers absently tracing the intricate patterns on her sleeve. "But William, it's back at your house. That's quite a journey from here, isn't it?"

Thaddeus stroked his salt-and-pepper beard, his eyes distant as he considered their options. After a moment, he snapped his fingers. "What about a little detour? Silas and Slygrin were already on the agenda, right? They might have some valuable insights for us, and taking a visit to them both on the way get us two flies in one strike so to speak."

William's gaze brightened, a flicker of optimism kindling in his expression. "Thaddeus, you clever old fox!" he declared, already striding toward the exit. "They're en route, and their expertise might be precisely the asset we require."

As they stepped out into the Troll Market, a cacophony of sounds and smells assaulted their senses. The air was thick with the aroma of exotic spices and less savory odors. Creatures of all shapes and sizes bustled about, haggling over glowing potions and mystical artifacts.

William led the way, his heightened senses on high alert. He navigated the crowded streets with practiced ease, occasionally placing a protective hand on Olivia's arm to guide her through particularly dense throngs.

Olivia leaned in close, her voice barely audible above the market's din. "Do you really think Silas will be willing to help? He's not exactly known for his generosity."

William's jaw tightened, a muscle twitching beneath his skin. "He'd better be," he muttered through clenched teeth. "We don't have time for his usual cryptic nonsense and riddles."

The cacophony of the market faded to a distant hum, replaced by the hollow echo of their footsteps. Ahead, a dilapidated building loomed, its windows like dead eyes staring back at them.

"Charming place," William muttered, his blue eyes scanning the crumbling facade.

Thaddeus grunted in agreement, his hand drifting to the hilt of his weapon. "Silas always did have a flair for the dramatic."

As they drew closer, William noticed moss creeping up the stonework like grasping fingers. A faint, eerie glow seeped from beneath the door, casting an otherworldly sheen on the grimy street.

"This is it," Thaddeus whispered, his weathered face taut with tension. "Silas's den of secrets. Let's hope he's in a charitable mood."

William squared his shoulders, feeling the weight of their mission settle upon him like a lead cloak. He pushed aside his doubts, focusing on the task at hand. "Well," he said, reaching for the tarnished door handle, "let's find out if the old snake is feeling chatty today."

The door creaked open, revealing a dimly lit interior that smelled of musty books and something acrid William couldn't quite place. As their eyes adjusted to the gloom, a gravelly voice called out from the shadows.

"Well, well. What brings the likes of you to my humble abode?"

Silas emerged from behind a towering bookshelf, his silver hair glinting in the strange light. His mismatched eyes – one blue, one brown – fixed on William with unsettling intensity.

"We're here about the Loom of Fate," William said, trying to keep his voice steady.

Silas's thin lips curled into a smirk. "Ah, that old thing. Funny you should ask. Another gentleman was here not long ago, asking about the very same artifact."

William's heart quickened. "Lord Everett Wentworth?"

"I don't kiss and tell, boy," Silas chuckled, moving to a cluttered desk. "But I will say this – the Loom is more than just a pretty bauble. It's a key to unraveling the very fabric of reality."

Thaddeus stepped forward, his patience wearing thin. "Cut the riddles, Silas. What do you know?"

Silas's eyes narrowed. "I know that Wentworth is a fool playing with forces beyond his comprehension. And I know that you three are in way over your heads."

William felt a chill run down his spine. Silas's words only confirmed his suspicions – the Loom of Fate was indeed the artifact Lord Wentworth sought, and its power was more terrible than they had imagined.

THE CACOPHONY OF THE Troll Market assaulted William's senses. Exotic spices tickled his nose, while the clamor of haggling voices echoed in his ears. His eyes, sharp as a hawk's, darted from stall to stall, searching for any sign of Elizabeth and Lilly.

"Watch your pockets," Thaddeus grumbled, his hand resting on the hilt of his weapon.

Olivia rolled her eyes. "We're here to find our friends, not fret over pickpockets."

William was about to interject when a gnarled hand grasped his sleeve. He spun, muscles tensing, ready for a fight. But the sight before him made him pause.

An old woman stood there, her eyes gleaming with an uncommon light. Wisdom and urgency radiated from her gaze, stopping William in his tracks.

"You seek the missing ones," she croaked, her voice barely a whisper above the market's din.

William's heart thundered in his chest. "Elizabeth and Lilly? Have you seen them?"

The old woman's head bobbed slowly, her eyes darting nervously. "Aye, I have. But speaking of such things here..." Fear etched deep lines in her weathered face.

Thaddeus stepped forward, his posture protective. "We can ensure your safety, madam. Any information could be crucial."

The woman shook her head vigorously, silver hair catching the light. "No, no. My safety is not assured, even with your protection." She leaned in, her breath warm against William's ear. "But know this – they were taken against their will. Dark forces are at play."

Olivia knelt beside the woman, her green eyes filled with concern. "Please, if there's anything more you can tell us, we'd be grateful. These women are our friends."

The old woman's gaze softened. She glanced around once more before speaking. "I am Ms. Jenny. I've seen more than most in this market, but what I witnessed that night..." A visible shudder ran through her frail frame. "I dare not speak of it here. The very walls have ears."

William's fists clenched at his sides, hope and frustration warring within him. "Ms. Jenny, is there anywhere we could speak more freely?"

Ms. Jenny's eyes flickered with that strange light again. "Perhaps. But not now, not here. Too many eyes, too many dangers." She pressed a small, intricately carved, and polished stone into William's hand. It felt unnaturally warm against his palm.

"If you truly wish to know more, use this when the moon is highest," she whispered. "But be warned – knowledge comes at a price."

Before William could respond, Ms. Jenny melted into the crowd, leaving only questions in her wake.

"Well, that was certainly cryptic," Thaddeus muttered, eyeing the stone in William's hand.

Olivia frowned. "What do you think she meant by 'use it when the moon is highest'?"

William turned the stone over in his fingers, feeling its unnatural warmth. "I don't know, but I intend to find out. Whatever the price, it's worth paying if it leads us to Elizabeth and Lilly."

As they continued through the market, the weight of the stone in William's pocket served as a constant reminder of the mystery that lay ahead. The crowd surged around them, but William's mind was elsewhere, already racing with possibilities of what the night might bring.

WILLIAM'S FINGERS TRACED the contours of the warm stone nestled in his pocket, his mind a whirlwind of possibilities. Ms. Jenny's cryptic words echoed in his ears, a dissonant melody of hope and foreboding. He cast a sidelong glance at Olivia and Thaddeus, their faces mirroring his own concern.

"We can't just abandon her," William said, his jaw clenched with determination. "Whatever she knows, it's put a target on her back. We have to protect her."

Thaddeus quirked an eyebrow, his skepticism was evident. "And how exactly do you propose we do that? We don't even know where the old bird roosts."

William's eyes darted across the bustling market, searching for any sign of the enigmatic woman. The cacophony of haggling voices and clattering carts seemed to mock their predicament.

"We'll find a way," William insisted, his voice low but resolute. "We always do."

As they wove through the maze of stalls, the scent of spices and unwashed bodies assaulting their senses, William's frustration began to simmer. "Bloody hell," he muttered, kicking at a loose cobblestone.

"Why is it always riddles and world-ending catastrophes? Can't we ever have a simple case of pickpocketing?"

Olivia's emerald eyes softened with sympathy, but William was too caught up in his tirade to notice.

"Remember the chaos with Frost and that blasted 'Heart of Empathy'?" he continued, his voice rising. "The city's barely stopped smoldering, and here we are again, knee-deep in another potential disaster."

He ran a hand through his dark hair, his exasperation palpable. "It's always some artifact or ancient prophecy. Just once, I'd like to investigate a normal theft or a straightforward murder."

Thaddeus snorted. "Careful what you wish for, mate. Knowing our luck, even a 'simple' murder would probably involve a resurrected corpse or a vengeful ghost."

William shot him a withering look. "You're not helping, Thaddeus."

As William's complaints continued, Olivia's patience began to wear thin. She placed a gentle but firm hand on his arm, halting him mid-rant.

"William, love," she said, her voice soft but unyielding. "That's quite enough. We can't change what's happening, but we can choose how we respond to it."

William's shoulders slumped, the fight draining from him like water from a cracked basin. He met Olivia's gaze, his blue eyes softening as they locked with her emerald ones.

"You're right," he admitted, his voice barely above a whisper. "I'm sorry. It's just..." He ran a hand through his tousled brown hair, searching for the right words. "The future, Liv. It terrifies me. What if all this," he gestured vaguely around them, "changes everything between us?"

Olivia's brow furrowed, concern etching lines across her forehead. "Will, look at me," she said, her voice gentle but firm. She cupped his face in her hands, her touch warm against his stubbled cheeks. "Whatever comes, we face it together. Always."

William leaned in, pressing a quick, tender kiss to her cheek. The gesture spoke volumes – an apology, a promise, a reaffirmation of their bond.

Thaddeus cleared his throat, breaking the moment. "Well," he drawled, a hint of amusement in his steel-gray eyes, "now that we've sorted out William's existential crisis, shall we get back to the matter at hand? We've got an old woman to find and a city to save... again." He emphasized the last word with a dramatic eye roll.

William couldn't help but chuckle. "Right you are, friend," he said, clapping Thaddeus on the shoulder. "Let's see what trouble we can stir up this time. Maybe we'll even set a new record for property damage."

"Don't jinx us," Olivia groaned, but a smile tugged at her lips.

With renewed purpose, the trio plunged deeper through the market. The cacophony of haggling voices and clanging pots surrounded them as they wove among the crowded stalls. William's hand instinctively drifted to his pocket, fingers brushing against the warm stone within. Its presence was a constant reminder of the mystery that lay ahead, a comforting weight anchoring him to their mission.

As they approached the Troll Gate leading out towards the general direction of William's house, the stone seemed to pulse with otherworldly energy. William exchanged a knowing glance with his companions.

THE COBBLESTONES ECHOED with their hurried footsteps as Olivia, William, and Thaddeus raced through the familiar streets of London. The city's eerie quiet pressed in around them, a stark contrast to the usual bustle.

Olivia's emerald eyes darted from shadow to shadow, her mind piecing together the fragments of information they'd gathered. She tucked a strand of her auburn hair behind her ear, a nervous habit she'd never quite shaken.

"Alright, let's take stock," she said, her voice low but urgent. "What do we know for certain?"

William's brow furrowed, his blue eyes intense with concentration. "Silas said Elizabeth and Lilly were last seen near the docks, right? Something about a magical disturbance."

"Right," Olivia nodded. "And Slygrin was practically shaking in his boots about increased vampire activity in that area. I've never seen him so nervous."

Thaddeus, his wiry frame taut with tension, chimed in. "Don't forget those whispers in the market. 'Gathering of shadows' and 'blood offerings.' Gave me the bloody creeps, it did."

A shudder ran through Olivia, the implications chilling her to the bone. "It all points to some sort of ritual, doesn't it? But for what?"

"The Loom," William breathed, his voice barely audible over their footsteps. "It has to be connected to the Loom of Fate somehow."

They turned down a narrow alley, a shortcut to William's townhouse. The shadows seemed to deepen, and Olivia found herself instinctively moving closer to her companions.

"There's more," she said, her mind racing. "Silas mentioned Lord Wentworth's been unusually active. His minions are all over the city, searching for... something."

"Or someone," Thaddeus interjected grimly, his dark eyes scanning their surroundings.

Olivia nodded, a spark of determination flashing in her eyes. "We need to face facts. Elizabeth and Lilly might have stumbled onto something big. Something Wentworth wants to keep quiet."

William's jaw tightened, the muscles in his face visibly tensing. His usually smooth forehead creased with worry lines, marring his handsome features. He ran a hand through his dark hair, his blue eyes darting nervously.

"Kidnapping two well-known investigators?" he muttered, his voice low and strained. "That's a bold move, even for Wentworth."

Olivia leaned in close, her auburn hair brushing against William's shoulder. Her green eyes widened as a thought struck her. "Unless," she whispered, her breath warm against his ear, "they're not just victims. What if they're part of whatever Wentworth is planning?"

The trio hurried through the darkening streets, their footsteps echoing off the cobblestones. As they turned into William's neighborhood, a sense of relief washed over them. They slowed their pace, catching sight of a small, lush garden tucked behind a wrought-iron fence.

"Let's catch our breath," William suggested, gesturing to a wooden bench nestled among fragrant roses.

They sank onto the seat, the wood creaking slightly under their weight. Thaddeus let out a nervous chuckle, his face lightly flushed from their brisk walk.

"Well," he said, wiping his brow with a handkerchief, "at least we're not short on excitement, eh? Who needs a quiet evening at the pub when you've got vampires, rituals, and missing friends to worry about?"

William's lips quirked into a wry smile. He reached into his pocket, his fingers closing around the warm stone he'd been carrying. As he toyed with it, he felt its comforting heat seep into his skin.

"Your optimism is truly inspiring, Thaddeus," he quipped, his tone a mix of amusement and exasperation.

Olivia couldn't help but smile, despite the knot of worry in her stomach. She watched as William fiddled with the stone, noting the way the lamplight caught the flecks of werewolf gold in his blue eyes.

"We'll figure this out," she said softly, placing a reassuring hand on his arm. "Whatever Wentworth's planning, whatever's happened to Elizabeth and Lilly, we're in this together."

As they sat in the quiet garden, the sweet scent of roses mingling with the crisp night air, Olivia couldn't shake the feeling that they were on the edge of something monumental. The weight of their task pressed down on her, but as she looked at her companions – William's determined expression, Thaddeus's grim but unwavering presence – she felt a surge of hope. Whatever challenges lay ahead, they would face them as one.

WILLIAM PULLED THE small box from his coat pocket, turning it over in his hands. The intricate carvings caught the dim lamplight, casting eerie shadows across its surface.

"We can't forget about this," he said, his voice low. "Found it at the first crime scene, remember? Right before Elizabeth and Lilly vanished."

Olivia leaned in, her brow furrowed as she studied the box. "Those symbols... they're similar to the sigils we saw carved around the city, aren't they?"

Thaddeus nodded grimly. "Aye, and not just in one place. I've spotted 'em in at least five different locations. Always in spots with a clear view of the sky."

William's mind raced, connecting the dots. "It's not just Elizabeth and Lilly, is it? There have been other disappearances."

"More than we realized," Olivia confirmed, her voice tight with concern. "I've been digging through reports at the Yard. At least a dozen people have gone missing in the last month alone. And the ones they've found..." She trailed off, shuddering.

"No apparent cause of death," Thaddeus finished for her. "Just... gone. Like the life was sucked right out of 'em."

William ran a hand through his hair, frustration evident in every line of his body. "And now we're hearing whispers about this 'Loom of

Fate.' An ancient magical artifact that can... what? Rewrite reality, just like we would change the text in a missive?"

Olivia nodded slowly. "That's what the rumors say. And more than one person has mentioned it in connection with the disappearances. Remember that old woman in the market? She was terrified, and kept muttering about 'the Loom weaving a dark future.'"

Thaddeus leaned back, his face grim. "It's all connected, isn't it? The box, the sigils, the disappearances... and this bloody Loom. Whatever's happening, it's big. And it's only getting started. Olivia, it just occurred to me that Frost was also known as the Weaver of Shadows, at least he is a part of the past,"

The trio fell silent, the weight of their realization settling over them like a heavy cloak. The gentle rustling of leaves in the night breeze seemed to whisper of darker things to come.

GABRIEL LEANED FORWARD, his elbows resting on the rough wooden table. The flickering candlelight cast dancing shadows across his face, accentuating the worry lines etched around his eyes. He glanced at Connor and Jaxon, their faces equally tense in the dim corner of the Troll Market.

Celeste Moonfellow's wild, untamed hair seemed to crackle with energy as she leaned in close. Her fierce eyes, a startling shade of amber, darted around the bustling market before settling on the trio.

"Listen carefully," she whispered, her breath warm against their ears. "The disappearances aren't random. They're targeting those with latent magical abilities."

Connor's brow furrowed, his golden-flecked eyes clouding with confusion. "But why? What could they possibly gain from-"

"Power," a gravelly voice interrupted. Barty Quill materialized from the shadows, his goblin features twisting into a sly grin. "Raw, untapped magical potential. Perfect fuel for ancient rituals."

Jaxon's eyes widened, the usual mischievous glint replaced by genuine fear. "The Loom of Fate," he breathed. "It's not just a myth, is it?"

Celeste shook her head grimly, her wild striped mane swaying with the movement. "I've seen the evidence myself. Symbols are carved into the very bones of the city. They're preparing for something big."

Gabriel felt a chill run down his spine. "How long do we have?"

Celeste's amber eyes met his, filled with determination. "Not long enough."

Across the city in a small secluded private garden, William ran a hand through his dark hair, his blue eyes intense as he addressed Thaddeus and Olivia. "We need that map," he insisted. "All these pieces... they're connected somehow. But we can't see the full picture without it."

Olivia nodded, her auburn curls bouncing slightly. "Agreed. And with what Silas and Slygrin told us about the lunar cycles..."

"It's time we head back," Thaddeus concluded, his weathered face set in grim determination. "We've learned all we can here for now."

As they navigated the winding streets of London, the weight of their discoveries pressed down on them. The gas lamps cast long shadows, and every alley seemed to hide potential dangers.

Approaching William's townhouse, Olivia's sharp eyes caught something out of place. "William, look," she pointed, her voice hushed. "There's a package on the steps."

William approached cautiously, his footsteps barely audible on the cobblestones. He picked up the small parcel addressed to him, turning it over in his hands. "No sender," he muttered, a crease forming between his brows.

Inside, Ms. Potts' cheerful voice greeted them. "Oh, Mr. Blackwood! I'll fetch some tea right away," she called, disappearing into the kitchen with a swish of skirts.

As they climbed the stairs to William's study, a soft meow broke the tension. Midnight, William's winged cat, stretched lazily on a nearby bookshelf, her obsidian fur gleaming in the lamplight.

"Hello, old girl," William smiled, reaching out to scratch behind the cat's ears. Midnight purred contentedly, her wings fluttering slightly.

Olivia settled into a plush armchair, her eyes fixed on the mysterious package. "Should we open it?" she asked, her voice tinged with both curiosity and apprehension.

Thaddeus frowned, studying the parcel intently. "Carefully," he warned. "We don't know what tricks our enemies might be playing."

William nodded, his fingers tracing the edges of the package. The room fell silent, broken only by the gentle clink of china as Ms. Potts entered with a tray of steaming tea.

"Well," William said, a hint of forced lightness in his tone, "shall we see what new mystery awaits us?"

Strands of Fate

William's heart thundered against his ribs as he stared at the package on his desk. The brown paper seemed to taunt him, concealing secrets that both beckoned and terrified. He reached out, his hands quivering like autumn leaves in a gale.

"Steady on, old chap," he muttered, inhaling deeply. The familiar scent of his study—leather-bound books and aged wood—failed to soothe his frayed nerves. His usually nimble fingers fumbled with the twine, betraying his anxiety.

The door creaked open, and Gabriel's concerned face appeared. His piercing eyes scanned the room before settling on William. "Everything alright? You look like you've seen a ghost."

William forced a smile that didn't reach his eyes. "Just a... challenging package. Come in, please."

Gabriel stepped inside, followed by Connor, Olivia, and Jaxon. The latter was locked in a heated debate with Ms. Potts about the evening's menu.

"I'm telling you, Ms. Potts, a good Irish stew would hit the spot," Jaxon insisted, his voice carrying from the hallway.

"And I'm telling you, young man, that we're having roast beef, and that's final," Ms. Potts retorted, her tone brooking no argument.

The group gathered around William's desk, curiosity etched on their faces. William's fingers trembled as he peeled back the paper, revealing a simple wooden box underneath.

A familiar scent wafted up, and William's heart skipped a beat. "Elizabeth," he whispered, his voice barely audible.

Olivia leaned in, her emerald eyes widening. "That's her perfume, isn't it? The one she makes herself?"

William nodded, his stomach clenching with a potent mixture of longing and dread. The innocent-looking box belied the weight of its contents. He hesitated, his hand hovering over the lid.

"Come on, mate," Connor urged, his Irish lilt tinged with concern. "Whatever it is, we're here with you."

Gabriel placed a reassuring hand on William's shoulder. "Connor's right. You don't have to face this alone."

William took a deep breath, steeling himself. "Right then. Here goes nothing." He slowly lifted the lid, revealing a small vial of amber liquid and a folded piece of parchment.

Jaxon peered over William's shoulder, his dark eyes gleaming with curiosity. "What's that? Some kind of potion?"

"Jaxon," Olivia hissed, elbowing him in the ribs. "Give William some space."

William carefully unfolded the parchment, his eyes scanning the elegant script. The color drained from his face, and he sank into his chair, the letter clutched tightly in his trembling hands.

"William?" Gabriel's voice was laced with concern. "What does it say?"

William looked up at his friends, his eyes haunted. "She's in trouble. Elizabeth... she needs our help."

With a swift motion, William lifted the lid further. Two locks of hair nestled inside, tied together with a black ribbon. One, a rich fiery red; the other, a deep raven black.

"Oh, God," Jaxon breathed, his dark skin paling. "That's Elizabeth's hair, isn't it? And Lilly's?"

William's breath caught. He reached out, fingers ghosting over the strands. "Oh, my dears," he murmured, voice thick with emotion.

A folded piece of paper beneath the hair caught his eye. Dread pooled in his stomach as he plucked it from the box.

"What does it say?" Gabriel asked, his gold-flaked piercing eyes narrowing.

William's face hardened as he read. The words dripped with casual cruelty, detailing their friends' captivity.

"Bastards," William growled, crumpling the paper. Rage and fear battled within him.

The wolf inside howled for release. William's eyes flashed with an inner glow, his canines elongating into wicked fangs.

"William, control yourself!" Olivia hissed, grabbing his arm. Her emerald eyes blazed with intensity. "We need you thinking clearly, not running wild!"

With great effort, William took slow, deep breaths. His features slowly returned to normal.

"Sorry," he muttered, smoothing out the paper. "I just... I can't bear the thought of them in danger."

Connor squeezed his shoulder. "We'll find them, mate. Together."

William nodded, forcing himself to read the note again. This time, he approached it as a detective, his supernatural senses picking up traces of the writer's scent.

"I will find you," he promised, voice low and dangerous. "And when I do, may God have mercy on your souls, for I certainly won't."

Jaxon shivered. "Remind me never to get on your bad side, William."

Despite the gravity of the situation, a wry smile tugged at William's lips. "Noted, my friend. Now, let's get to work. Elizabeth and Lilly are counting on us."

"Right," Gabriel said, his pale blue eyes gleaming with determination. "Where do we start?"

William stood, his resolve hardening. "We start by following the scent. Connor, I'll need your tracking skills. Olivia, your knowledge of magical artifacts might come in handy. Jaxon, your street smarts could be crucial."

"And what about me?" Gabriel asked, a hint of amusement in his voice.

William clapped him on the shoulder. "You, my friend, are our voice of reason. Someone needs to keep us from charging headlong into danger."

"Fat chance of that," Jaxon muttered, but there was a grin on his face.

As they prepared to leave, William cast one last glance at the locks of hair. "Hold on, my dears," he whispered. "We're coming for you."

WILLIAM'S HANDS SHOOK as he clutched the intertwined locks of hair. The fiery red strands of Elizabeth's hair tangled with Lilly's raven-black tresses, a stark reminder of their absence. He lifted the locks to his nose, inhaling deeply.

"No," he whispered, his voice cracking. "This can't be happening."

The familiar scents of his friends mingled with unfamiliar, threatening odors. Traces of their captors clung to the strands, igniting a primal rage within him. It coursed through his veins like liquid fire, setting every nerve alight.

A low growl rumbled in William's chest, starting as a quiet vibration and building to a thunderous roar. His piercing blue eyes flickered, alternating between their usual hue and the amber glow of the golden-flecked iris of his wolf form. The room seemed to shrink around him, the walls closing in as his heightened senses picked up every minute detail.

"Control," he muttered through gritted teeth. "I must maintain control."

But the beast within, usually kept tightly leashed, surged forward with unprecedented force. William's muscles tensed, his body quivering with the effort of restraint. His fingernails lengthened slightly, threatening to become claws. The taste of copper filled his mouth as his canines sharpened, pricking his lower lip.

For a heart-stopping moment, William teetered on the edge of losing himself completely. The wolf howled in his mind, rabid, demanding release, yearning to hunt down those who had taken his friend and sister.

"It would be so easy," he thought, his inner voice a mixture of desperation and temptation. "To let go, to let the animal take over and tear through the city until I find them."

The intensity of his reaction shocked William to his core. He'd always prided himself on his control, on keeping his dual nature in check. But now, faced with the tangible evidence of his friends' captivity, he was forced to confront the full power of what lurked beneath his human facade.

William squeezed his eyes shut, taking deep, ragged breaths as he fought to regain control. The wolf's rage pulsed through him, demanding action, but a small part of his rational mind clung to reason.

"No," he growled, his voice a mixture of human and beast. "Losing control now will only put them at greater risk of harm. I need to think, to plan."

He opened his eyes, now a swirling mix of blue and golden flakes, and stared at the locks of hair in his trembling hand.

"Hold on, Elizabeth, Lilly," he whispered, his voice thick with emotion. "I'm coming for you. And heaven help those who took you from me."

William straightened, his jaw set with determination. He would use both sides of his nature – the man's cunning and the wolf's strength – to save his friends. The hunt was on, and he wouldn't rest until they were safe.

WILLIAM'S CHEST HEAVED as he struggled to contain the storm raging within him. His hands trembled, clutching the locks of hair that had triggered this internal tempest. Suddenly, the chaos stilled, like the eye of a hurricane.

He blinked, his piercing blue eyes widening with sudden clarity. The room, which had seemed to close in on him moments ago, now expanded, revealing details he'd overlooked in his turmoil.

"What's happening to me?" he whispered, his voice barely audible.

The answer came not in words, but in a feeling. The constant battle between his human and wolf sides ceased, replaced by an unexpected harmony. It wasn't a conquest of one over the other, but a perfect fusion.

William's racing heart steadied, and his breathing evened out. He looked down at the hair in his hand, no longer seeing it as a trigger for blind rage, but as a clue - a beacon guiding his path.

"I need both sides of myself," he realized aloud, his voice stronger now. "The detective and the wolf. Together."

He closed his eyes, focusing on this newfound equilibrium. When he opened them again, flecks of amber danced in the blue, a visual testament to the balance he'd achieved.

William stood, his muscles relaxed yet coiled with potential energy. He moved to the window, gazing out at the fog-shrouded London streets.

"I'm coming for you, Elizabeth. You too, Lilly," he vowed, his voice low and determined. "And God help anyone who stands in my way."

He turned back to the room, his keen detective's eye now working in tandem with his heightened wolfish senses. Details he'd missed before jumped out at him - the faint scent lingering on the package, the barely visible fingerprints on the envelope.

A small smile played at the corners of his mouth. For the first time since receiving the package, William felt truly in control. Not by suppressing part of himself, but by embracing his whole being.

"Time to hunt," he murmured, his voice a blend of human determination and wolfish anticipation. William Blackwood, detective, and werewolf, was ready to use every facet of his nature to bring Elizabeth and Lilly home.

WILLIAM'S NOSTRILS flared as he turned his attention back to the package. His heightened senses, a gift of his lycanthropic nature, picked up traces that would elude ordinary humans. The musty scent of stagnant water and mold clung to the paper, painting a vivid picture in his mind.

"Interesting," he muttered, bringing the package closer to his nose. A metallic tang tickled his senses. "Old machinery, a steam engine perhaps?"

Gabriel leaned in, his curiosity piqued. "What do you smell, William?"

William's deep blue eyes, seeming to glow with an inner fire and golden flecks, met Gabriel's gaze. "Rust, coal, and... something else. It's faint, but unmistakable."

Connor crossed his arms, skepticism etched on his face. "And what might that be?"

"Fear," William replied grimly.

Olivia's hand flew to her mouth. "Oh, those poor souls!"

Jaxon, ever the pragmatist, cut in. "Can you trace it, William? Find where they're being held?"

William's fingers danced across the paper's surface, feeling for any irregularities. Tiny indentations, invisible to the naked eye, told a story of their own. His brow furrowed as he pieced together the clues.

"Written on a rough surface," he mused aloud. "But where?"

The ink caught his attention next. It wasn't the standard writing ink he was accustomed to seeing. This was something different, more... industrial.

Realization struck William like a bolt of lightning. "A factory near the river. It has to be."

His mind raced, recalling his earlier conversation with Thaddeus. The grizzled vampire hunter's words echoed in his memory.

"There's a whole world beneath our feet, William," Thaddeus had said, his voice gruff but tinged with respect. "Tunnels that creatures use to move unseen. The knowledge that could save your hide one day."

William's lips curled into a grim smile. "And today might just be that day, friend."

A plan began to form in his mind, wild and dangerous, yet playing to both his human intellect and wolfish instincts.

"It's mad," William chuckled darkly. "But it just might work."

He turned to his companions, determination blazing in his eyes. "We're going to mount a two-pronged attack. Thaddeus and I will create a diversion aboveground. Meanwhile, you four will slip into the tunnels."

"The tunnels?" Olivia's voice quavered. "But we don't know the way!"

William reached into his coat pocket, producing a small vial. "This contains my scent. Follow it, and it will lead you straight to me – and to Elizabeth and Lilly."

Connor's eyebrows shot up. "That's... actually brilliant."

"It's also incredibly dangerous," Jaxon pointed out. "If we're caught down there..."

"We won't be," Gabriel said firmly, his hand resting on the hilt of his sword. "We can't let fear stop us now."

William nodded, gratitude warming his chest. "The risks are enormous, I won't lie. But it's our best shot at rescue."

His hand clenched into a fist as he whispered fiercely, "Hold on, Elizabeth. Hold on, Lilly. We're coming for you."

With a deep breath, William steeled himself for the dangerous path ahead. The weight of responsibility settled on his shoulders, but as he looked at the determined faces of his friends, he knew they were ready to face whatever challenges lay ahead. Together, they would brave the unknown depths and bring their loved ones home.

WILLIAM'S FOOTSTEPS echoed through his office, each step purposeful and measured. His deep brown eyes, holding centuries of wisdom, darted from corner to corner.

"Will, you got everything?" Gabriel's voice called from the doorway, his silver hair catching the lamplight.

William nodded, reaching for his weathered coat. "Almost. Can't forget you, old friend," he murmured to the garment.

As he slipped it on, the familiar weight settled on his shoulders. His fingers danced across hidden pockets, each touch a reminder of life-saving tools.

Connor leaned against the desk, his green eyes twinkling. "Checking your secret stash, eh?"

William chuckled, opening a drawer to reveal small vials. "You know me too well."

The glass clinked as he selected a few, tucking them into his coat's inner lining.

"Wolfsbane, silver nitrate, holy water," he whispered.

Jaxon, lounging in a chair, raised an eyebrow. "Essential as your morning coffee, I bet."

"You have no idea," William replied, his gaze falling on the silver-tipped arcane cane sword leaning against the wall.

As his fingers wrapped around the handle of the Cane Sword of Cardan, energy surged through his veins. William closed his eyes, savoring the sensation.

"You and me, Cardan," he said softly. "We've got work to do."

Thaddeus, his dark eyes serious, pointed to a locked cabinet. "Don't forget the special gear, Will."

William nodded, fishing out a key from around his neck. The lock clicked open, revealing supernatural tools.

Olivia, her auburn hair gleaming, peered over his shoulder. "Ooh, the mirror with the runes. Always comes in handy."

William carefully selected items: the small mirror, a pouch with splinters of mountain ash, and a set of humming lock picks.

As he tucked each away, a sense of completeness washed over him.

Catching sight of himself in a wall mirror, William paused. The man staring back wasn't the same one who had entered earlier. His jaw was set, eyes glinting with purpose.

"Well, look at you," he chuckled to his reflection. "Finally figured it out, eh?"

Gabriel clapped him on the shoulder. "About time, cub."

For the first time in months, William felt truly whole. He was embracing every part of himself – detective, werewolf, protector.

With a deep breath, he straightened his coat and gripped his cane sword.

"Time to face the music," he muttered.

Jaxon grinned, falling into step beside him. "Let's see what the night has in store for us."

WILLIAM STOOD BEFORE his desk, his gaze fixed on the cherished illustrations of Elizabeth and Lilly. Their frozen smiles seemed to reach out to him, urging him forward. He traced the edge of Elizabeth's picture with a trembling fingertip, his jaw clenched with determination.

"I'll find you," he whispered, his voice barely audible. "Both of you. I swear it."

Gabriel's tall frame filled the doorway in his hybrid form. His emerald eyes swept the room before settling on William.

"You're not planning on going alone, are you?" Gabriel asked, his tone a mixture of concern and amusement.

William turned, a half-smile tugging at his lips. "I wouldn't dream of it. Where's the rest of our motley crew?"

As if on cue, Connor's shock of gray hair appeared behind Gabriel, followed by Thaddeus's broad shoulders. Jaxon squeezed past them, adjusting his spectacles, while Olivia gracefully slipped into the room last.

"We're all here, mate," Connor said, his Scottish lilt filling the room. "Couldn't let you have all the fun, now could we?"

Jaxon nodded, his hazel eyes serious. "We're in this together, William. Whatever it takes."

Thaddeus cleared his throat. "I've been analyzing the clues we've gathered. I believe I've narrowed down their possible locations."

Olivia stepped forward, her golden hair catching the lamplight. "And I've reached out to my contacts in the supernatural community. We're not without allies."

William felt a surge of gratitude wash over him. He turned back to the window, the sprawling city of London stretching before him, a maze of streets and shadows hiding countless secrets. But it was his reflection that caught his attention, drawing him in.

The man staring back at him was familiar, yet changed. Gone was the uncertainty that had clouded his hazel eyes for so long. In its place, a quiet confidence radiated from him. His posture was straighter, his shoulders set with purpose.

"William?" Olivia's soft voice broke through his reverie. "Are you alright?"

He turned to face his friends, really seeing them for the first time. Each of them stood ready, determination etched on their faces.

"I am," he said, surprised to find it true. "I think... I think I've finally accepted who I am. What I am."

Gabriel's eyebrow arched. "And what's that?"

William took a deep breath. "A detective. A werewolf. A protector. All of it."

Connor clapped him on the shoulder. "About bloody time, cub."

Thaddeus nodded approvingly. "It suits you."

Jaxon pushed his glasses up his nose. "Fascinating. The merging of your dual natures could potentially enhance your abilities."

Olivia smiled warmly. "We've always seen you that way, William. It's good you finally see it too."

William felt the weight of this realization settles over him. The responsibilities were immense, but he was no longer alone.

"Whatever happens," he said, looking at each of his friends in turn, "there's no going back. Our lives have changed irrevocably."

"Well then," Jaxon said with a grin, "let's make sure we change them for the better. Shall we go rescue some ladies and save London while we're at it?"

William nodded, a newfound determination coursing through him. "Let's go."

As they filed out of the room, William cast one last glance at the photographs on his desk. "Hold on," he whispered. "We're coming."

WILLIAM'S FINGERS TREMBLED as he adjusted his cravat, the silk smooth against his skin. He took a deep breath, steadying himself before reaching for the doorknob. The cool brass grounded him, a final anchor to the familiar world he was about to leave behind.

"Ready?" Gabriel's voice called from the hallway, a mix of excitement and concern.

William swallowed hard. "As I'll ever be."

He pulled open the heavy oak door, revealing the bustling London streets beyond his home. The city assaulted his senses, a cacophony of sights, sounds, and smells he'd never experienced before.

Beside him, Connor whistled low. "Quite the change, eh?"

William blinked rapidly, trying to process the kaleidoscope of colors and shapes dancing at the edges of his vision. The cobblestones beneath his feet seemed to pulse with energy, sending tingles up his legs.

"Steady on," Thaddeus murmured, placing a steadying hand on William's arm. "The first few minutes are surely the most disorienting."

Olivia's hair caught the late afternoon sun as she stepped out behind them. "Oh, do give him some space," she purred. "Let the man breathe."

Jaxon brought up the rear, his hazel eyes scanning the street warily. "We should move," he said, voice low. "We're attracting attention."

William nodded, forcing himself to take a step forward. The world tilted alarmingly for a moment before righting itself. He gripped his cane sword tightly, the feel of it reassuring in his hand.

As they walked, William's heightened senses picked up on subtle magical signatures woven into the very fabric of the city. A group of fae, disguised as street performers, caught his eye. They nodded almost imperceptibly as he passed, acknowledging his newfound awareness.

"Don't stare," Gabriel murmured, his silver hair glinting as he leaned in close. "They don't like to be noticed."

William's grip on his cane tightened. "There's so much I never saw before," he whispered, awe and trepidation warring in his voice.

The scents of the city assaulted him – acrid smoke from factories, the earthy smell of the Thames, and beneath it all, the unmistakable tang of magic. A shadow flitted across an alleyway, too quick for human eyes to catch. William's muscles tensed instinctively.

"Relax," Connor said, his eyes twinkling with amusement. "You're broadcasting your nerves to every supernatural within a mile radius."

William forced himself to take a deep breath. "Right. Confidence, not fear."

"That's the spirit," Olivia smirked, sauntering ahead of them. "Though a little fear can be... invigorating."

Thaddeus peered at William through his spectacles, brow furrowed. "How are you feeling, my boy?"

William shook his head. "Nothing beyond the expected sensory overload. It's... overwhelming, but exhilarating."

"Well, well," a silky voice purred from nearby. They turned to see a woman with striking violet eyes watching them intently. "If it isn't our newly awakened 'Protector.'"

Jaxon stepped forward, positioning himself between the group and the newcomer. "Move along," he growled. "This doesn't concern you."

The woman laughed, a sound like tinkling glass, before melting back into the crowd.

William caught sight of his reflection in a shop window. The man looking back at him stood taller, and moved with more assurance. He was no longer trying to blend in, to hide his true nature. Instead, he embraced it, letting it guide his steps.

"Well then," William said, straightening his shoulders. "Shall we give them something to talk about? I believe we have work to do."

Gabriel grinned, a predatory gleam in his eyes. "Now you're talking. Welcome to the hunt, William. London's supernatural underbelly won't know what hit it."

As the group moved off into the gathering twilight, William felt the weight of his decision – to fully commit to this dangerous path. But with that weight came a sense of liberation, of finally being true to himself. He knew the challenges ahead were formidable, but for the first time, he felt truly equipped to face them. William's gaze swept across the sprawling cityscape, his eyes alight with determination. The industrial landscape stretched before them, a maze of brick and iron, smoke and shadow. He turned to Olivia, her auburn hair catching the fading sunlight.

"We should start our search among the factories and warehouses," he suggested, his voice low but filled with newfound purpose. "That's where the themes of industry are strongest."

Olivia quirked an eyebrow, a smirk playing at the corners of her lips. "Oh? And here I thought we'd begin with a nice cup of tea and a chat about the weather."

William chuckled, shaking his head. "Your wit never fails to surprise me, Olivia."

She fell into step beside him, her skirts swishing softly against the cobblestones. "So," she drawled, her green eyes sparkling with mischief, "where shall we begin? The textile mills or the ironworks?"

William paused, considering. The weight of their task pressed upon him, but for once, it didn't feel suffocating. Instead, it ignited a fire within him, a burning desire to uncover the truth.

"Why not both?" he replied, a smile spreading across his face. The confidence in his voice surprised even him.

Olivia's eyebrows shot up. "My, my, William. Who are you and what have you done with our timid PI?"

He laughed, the sound echoing off the nearby buildings. "Perhaps he's finally found his courage."

As they set off towards the industrial district, William felt a surge of excitement course through him. The city unfurled before them, a labyrinth of secrets and shadows waiting to be explored. Steam hissed from nearby vents, and the distant clang of machinery provided a steady rhythm to their steps.

For the first time in his life, William felt ready to face whatever lurked in the darkness. With Olivia by his side and his newfound resolve, he knew they could unravel the mysteries that lay ahead. The adventure was just beginning, and he couldn't wait to see where it would lead them.

The Tide Turns

The little-known park with its ancient oaks looming overhead, their gnarled branches stretching out like protective arms felt like a tranquil balm on their nerves. William led the group through the dappled shadows, his footsteps barely audible on the soft grass. He could feel the weight of their mission pressing down on him, as heavy as the humid air that clung to his skin.

"This should do," William murmured, coming to a stop in a secluded corner of the park. He turned to face his companions, noting the tension etched on their faces.

Thaddeus stood rigid, his weathered features set in a grim mask. The vampire hunter's eyes, hard as flint, scanned their surroundings with practiced vigilance.

William cleared his throat. "Right then. Let's go over what we know again."

He reached into his coat pocket, withdrawing a small package wrapped in brown paper. With careful fingers, he peeled back the layers, revealing locks of hair and a folded note.

Gabriel leaned in, his nostrils flaring. "The scent," he said, his voice barely above a whisper. "It's faint, but unmistakable."

Thaddeus nodded, reaching out to trace the edges of the paper. "Typical vampire theatrics," he growled. "They can't resist their little games."

Olivia frowned, her green eyes narrowing as she studied the contents. "Can you make sense of it, Thaddeus?"

The older man's lips thinned. "Perhaps. There are... patterns they tend to follow."

THE LOOM OF MS. JENNY

As Thaddeus began to dissect the hidden meanings in the note, William found himself impressed by the hunter's insights. Years of experience were etched into every line of the man's face, a living testament to battles fought in the shadows.

"Here," Thaddeus said suddenly, jabbing a finger at a particular phrase. "This is a reference to an old vampire hunting ground. They're trying to lead us astray, but it narrows down our search area."

Connor stepped closer, his massive frame blocking out what little light filtered through the leaves. "So we have a general location," he rumbled. "What's our next move?"

William felt a surge of determination course through him. "We split up," he said, his voice firm. "Cover more ground, but stay in pairs. No one goes alone."

Jaxon nodded, a hint of approval in his hazel eyes. "Smart thinking. We'll need to coordinate our efforts, though. Can't have us stumbling over each other in the dark."

As they delved deeper into planning, William marveled at how seamlessly they had fallen into working together. The earlier mistrust had evaporated, replaced by a shared sense of purpose. Each member of the group contributed their unique skills and knowledge, building a strategy that grew more refined with every passing minute.

"What about you, William?" Olivia asked, her voice cutting through his thoughts. "You've been quiet. Any brilliant ideas brewing in that head of yours?"

William couldn't help but smile. "Just trying to keep up with all of you," he replied. "But I do have a thought or two. Let's start by..."

As the sun dipped lower in the sky, casting long shadows across their makeshift war council, William felt a glimmer of hope. They were no longer a group of comrades together by circumstance. They were indeed a team, forged in the crucible of their shared mission. And together, he thought, they just might have a chance of succeeding.

WILLIAM'S NOSE TWITCHED as he caught a whiff of something otherworldly. The scent hung in the air, a mix of decay and ancient magic that made his wolf instincts bristle. He glanced at Thaddeus, the vampire hunter's steely gray eyes scanning the shadows.

"You smell that?" William whispered, his golden-flecked blue eyes gleaming in the dim light, his werewolf form letting itself show.

Thaddeus nodded, his hand resting on the hilt of his silver dagger. "Aye. We're getting close."

The cobblestone streets of London had given way to twisting alleys and hidden passages. Here, in the supernatural underbelly of the city, the very air felt charged with unseen power. William's enhanced senses were on high alert, picking up traces of magical energy that normal humans would never detect.

"Remind me why we split up again?" William muttered, stepping over a puddle that seemed to glow with an eerie blue light.

Thaddeus smirked, his scarred face softening for a moment. "Because Gabriel and Connor make a better team, apparently... And Jaxon wouldn't let Olivia out of his sight when you and I work together."

William chuckled softly, but his amusement was short-lived. As they delved deeper into this hidden realm, the contrast between the London they knew and this supernatural underbelly became stark. Eerie glows pulsed from strange fungi clinging to damp walls, and the ground beneath their feet seemed to shift and breathe.

Whispered conversations in languages William didn't recognize reached his sensitive ears. Shapes darted in the corners of his vision, always just out of focus. The werewolf detective felt a chill run down his spine.

"I don't like this," he growled softly. "It feels like we're being watched."

Thaddeus paused at an intersection, his brow furrowed in concentration. He pointed down a particularly dark and forbidding alley. "This way," he murmured, his voice barely audible. "The vampiric energy is growing stronger. Hmm... I have an idea about how we should start the hunt, follow my lead in this."

William nodded, steeling himself for what lay ahead. As they pressed on, he couldn't help but marvel at the duality of the city he'd sworn to protect. This hidden world, teeming with supernatural life and danger, existed right alongside the London that most people knew.

"You ever get used to this?" William asked, his eyes darting from shadow to shadow.

Thaddeus's lips quirked in a humorless smile. "To the monsters? Never. To the hunt? Always."

As they ventured deeper into the supernatural labyrinth, William felt the wolf inside him stir. Whatever awaited them in the depths of this hidden London, he knew they'd face it together – a werewolf and a vampire hunter, united against the darkness that threatened their city.

WILLIAM'S NOSE TWITCHED, a familiar tingle that always preceded danger. The dilapidated tavern loomed before them, its weathered sign creaking in the night breeze. Faded letters, barely visible, spelled out "The Crimson Fang."

"Looks abandoned," William muttered, his keen eyes scanning the seemingly deserted exterior.

Thaddeus chuckled, a low rumble in his chest. "Appearances can be deceiving, my friend. Listen."

William's ears perked up, catching the low murmur of voices and the clink of glasses filtering through the decrepit walls. His muscles tensed instinctively.

Thaddeus stepped forward, his movements fluid and practiced. He rapped on the door, his knuckles creating an intricate rhythm that echoed in the quiet street.

"Secret knock?" William raised an eyebrow.

"Insurance," Thaddeus winked.

For a heartbeat, silence reigned. Then, with a bone-chilling creak, the door swung open. A wave of smoky air assaulted William's sensitive nose, carrying with it a cocktail of supernatural scents.

"Brace yourself," Thaddeus whispered as they crossed the threshold.

The dim interior came into focus, revealing a scene far from empty. In shadowy corners, vampires reclined with predatory grace, their eyes gleaming like polished gems in the low light. They tracked William and Thaddeus's every move, their gazes almost tangible.

Near the bar, a cluster of Fae huddled close, their whispers a melodic undercurrent. Their otherworldly beauty seemed at odds with the seedy surroundings, yet they lounged with casual ease.

"Don't stare," Thaddeus warned under his breath. "Fae don't take kindly to unwanted attention."

William's gaze shifted to the bar itself, where shapeshifters perched on stools. One moment, a man with wolfish features gripped a tankard; the next, a lithe feline figure lapped delicately at a saucer.

The weight of dozens of eyes pressed down on them as they ventured further inside. The tavern's atmosphere crackled with tension, a collective intake of breath as the patrons assessed the newcomers.

"Well, well," a silky voice purred from the shadows. "What have we here? A pair of lost lambs?"

Thaddeus's hand brushed against his weapon, a subtle movement that didn't go unnoticed. The tension in the room ratcheted up a notch.

William's muscles coiled, ready for action. "We're here on business," he growled, meeting the glowing eyes in the darkness.

"Business?" the voice chuckled. "How delightful. And what sort of... business might that be?"

Thaddeus stepped forward, his voice steady. "The kind that doesn't concern you, unless you've got information about recent disappearances in the Nightshade District."

A hush fell over the tavern. William could almost taste the sudden spike of fear in the air.

"Brave words," the voice replied, a hint of respect coloring its tone. "Or foolish ones. Time will tell which."

William couldn't shake the feeling that they'd just stepped into the lion's den as they moved deeper into the smoky interior. And they were most certainly not the lions.

THE ACRID SMELL OF pipe smoke and stale ale assaulted William's nostrils. His keen eyes, a deep brown that almost appeared black in the low light, scanned the room. Every muscle in his body tensed, ready to react at a moment's notice.

"Quite the menagerie we've got here," William muttered under his breath, his gaze lingering on a group of patrons huddled in a shadowy corner.

Thaddeus grunted in response, his massive frame casting an imposing shadow as they moved further into the room. "Keep your wits about you, lad. This ain't no place for the faint of heart."

William nodded, his attention drawn to a pale figure seated alone at a table near the back. A vampire, her porcelain skin a stark contrast to the grimy surroundings. She lifted a goblet to her ruby lips, the dark liquid within catching the light. Their eyes met, and she inclined her head ever so slightly.

"Seems we've been noticed," William whispered, returning the gesture with equal subtlety.

Thaddeus's weathered hand came to rest on William's shoulder, a silent reminder of their purpose. The older man's presence seemed to ripple through the room, causing a palpable shift in the atmosphere.

"Ironheart," a gruff voice nearby muttered, the name spreading through the crowd like wildfire.

William felt a familiar tingle across his skin, the telltale sign of supernatural energy permeating the air. He resisted the urge to scratch as his body's reaction caused him to grow fur along his back, very uncomfortable under his clothing. Though, knowing any sign of discomfort could be perceived as a weakness he kept still.

"Well, well," Thaddeus rumbled, his steel-gray eyes fixed on a group near the bar. "Looks like we've got some high-born company."

William followed his gaze, his breath catching at the sight of the Fae. Their otherworldly beauty seemed out of place in the seedy tavern, yet they commanded attention, patrons drifting in and out of their orbit like moths to a flame.

"Think they might have what we're looking for?" William asked, his voice low.

Thaddeus nodded, a grim smile playing at the corners of his mouth. "Only one way to find out. Ready to dance with the fair folk, lad?"

William squared his shoulders, meeting Thaddeus's gaze. "As ready as I'll ever be."

They made their way across the room, each step measured and deliberate. The crowd parted before them, a mix of fear and curiosity etched on their faces.

As they approached the Fae, William could feel the weight of centuries-old grudges and complex alliances pressing down on them. He took a deep breath, steeling himself for the delicate dance of words and gestures that lay ahead.

"Evening, gentlefolk," Thaddeus said, his gravelly voice carrying a hint of forced politeness. "Mind if we join your little soirée?"

The lead Fae, a tall, willowy creature with hair like spun silver, turned to regard them with eyes of liquid gold. "Ironheart," she purred, her voice like honey laced with poison. "To what do we owe the... pleasure?"

William felt the tension in the air thicken, raw magic pulsed like a heartbeat emanating from the individuals in front of him, knowing that their next words could mean the difference between success and a tavern-wide brawl. He silently prayed that Thaddeus's silver tongue wouldn't fail them now.

WILLIAM'S NOSTRILS flared as he stepped forward, his keen eyes scanning the group of Fae. The scent of magic hit him like a wave—sweet and intoxicating, mingling with an ancient earthiness that tickled his senses. His gaze settled on a willowy figure that seemed to glow in the dim light. Her hair cascaded down her back like spun moonlight, and her eyes sparkled with the intensity of distant stars.

He caught Thaddeus's eye and gave a subtle nod. The hunter's hand twitched near his concealed weapons, ready for action. William approached the ethereal being, his heart quickening despite his calm exterior.

"Evening," William said, his voice a low rumble that seemed to vibrate in his chest. "Might we have a moment of your time?"

The silver-haired Fae turned, curiosity dancing across her delicate features. Her eyes, like twin pools of starlight, fixed on William with an intensity that made him want to look away. But he held her gaze, refusing to show weakness.

"What brings a wolf and a hunter to our circle?" she asked, her voice melodious like wind chimes in a gentle breeze. The words seemed to hang in the air, shimmering with an otherworldly quality.

William leaned in, the scent of magic growing stronger. It made his head swim, but he pushed through the disorientation. "We're seeking information about recent vampire activities," he murmured, his voice barely above a whisper. "Any unusual movements or gatherings?"

The Fae's starlight eyes narrowed, but William caught a flicker of interest. He pressed on, carefully choosing each word. He wove a tapestry of half-truths, dancing around outright lies. His werewolf instincts prickled, alerting him to the subtle shifts in the Fae's demeanor—a slight tilt of her head, a twitch of her fingers.

"Vampires, you say?" the Fae mused, a hint of amusement in her tone. Her lips curved into a smile that didn't quite reach her eyes. "And what makes you think the Sidhe would know anything about those primitive blood-suckers?"

William's lips curled into a wry smile. He could feel Thaddeus's presence at his back, a silent sentinel. The hunter's vigilance allowed William to focus on this delicate dance of information gathering.

"Let's just say a little birdie told us the Fae have their fingers on the pulse of the city," William replied, his tone light but his eyes sharp.

The silver-haired Fae hesitated, then leaned in close. Her unearthly beauty and sensual movements stirred thoughts in William's mind that he quickly pushed aside. Focus, he told himself sternly.

Her breath tickled William's ear as she whispered, "There have been whispers... of increased activity in the old tunnels beneath the city."

William nodded, committing the information to memory. He could smell no deceit on the Fae, but his instincts told him she was holding something back. He pressed further, his questions precise and probing.

"These tunnels," William said, his voice low and urgent. "Any idea what they're up to down there?"

The Fae's starlight eyes darted around, as if checking for eavesdroppers. She drew back, standing straighter. "Nothing good, I'd wager. But that's all I know, truly..."

As the conversation unfolded, William marveled at how naturally he and Thaddeus worked together. The hunter's intimidating presence complemented William's investigative skills perfectly, creating a formidable team.

With each carefully extracted piece of information, William began to piece together a picture of the vampires' recent movements. The puzzle was far from complete, but it was a start.

"Thank you for your time," William said, straightening up. "You've been most helpful."

As they turned to leave, the Fae woman called out, her voice carrying a hint of warning, "Be careful, wolf. The night has many eyes, and not all of them are friendly."

William nodded, a chill running down his spine despite the warmth of the evening. He exchanged a meaningful glance with Thaddeus. The hunt was on, and the stakes were higher than ever.

As they walked away, Thaddeus muttered, "Well, that was about as clear as mud. You think she's telling the truth?"

William shrugged, his mind racing. "No, the Fae can not lie to a mortal while in our world. But there's more to this than she's letting on and they are masters at misdirection. We need to check out those tunnels."

Thaddeus grunted in agreement. "Into the belly of the beast, eh? Just another day's work for us."

William couldn't help but chuckle. "Just remember, if we run into any vampires—"

"Yeah, yeah," Thaddeus interrupted with a grin. "Aim for the heart, not the head. I've been doing this a while, you know."

As they disappeared into the night, William's thoughts turned to the challenges ahead. The city's supernatural underbelly was a dangerous place.

WILLIAM'S HEART POUNDED as he pieced together the fragments of information they'd gathered. The tapestry of truth unfolding before him was far more intricate than he'd ever imagined. He glanced at Thaddeus, noting the deep creases etched across the hunter's forehead.

As they stepped out of the tavern into the cool night air, a familiar silver-haired figure materialized from the shadows. The Fae woman approached them, her ethereal presence sending a shiver down William's spine.

"Gentlemen," she whispered, her voice as soft as a breeze, "there's more you should know."

William's muscles tensed. "What is it?"

The Fae's eyes, luminous in the dim light, darted around before settling on William's face. "Whispers speak of turmoil among the vampire elders. A power struggle brews."

Thaddeus leaned in, his voice gruff. "What kind of struggle?"

"One tied to an ancient prophecy, they say," she replied, her slender fingers twisting nervously.

William's breath caught in his throat. "A prophecy? What does it foretell?"

The Fae shook her head, silver locks swaying. "Details are scarce, but it's said to predict a monumental shift in power. Some believe it could upend the very foundations of the supernatural world."

William's stomach lurched as the implications crashed over him like a tidal wave. He turned to Thaddeus, their eyes locking in a moment of shared dread. The hunter's weathered face mirrored the dawning horror in William's mind.

"Elizabeth and Lilly," William murmured, his voice barely audible. "Their abduction..."

Thaddeus nodded grimly. "It's a piece of a much larger, more dangerous puzzle."

The weight of this revelation settled on William's shoulders like a lead cloak. What he'd hoped would be a straightforward rescue had morphed into a labyrinth of supernatural politics and ancient prophecies.

"We need to move," Thaddeus growled, his hand instinctively moving to the hilt of his weapon. "And fast."

William nodded, his mind racing. If Elizabeth and Lilly's kidnapping was entangled in this web of power and prophecy, the danger they faced was far greater than he'd feared.

"Thank you," William said to the Fae, his voice thick with emotion. "You may have saved more than just two lives tonight."

As they hurried away from the tavern, the cool night air did little to calm William's nerves. Each step felt heavier than the last, the gravity of their situation sinking in with every passing moment.

"You know," Thaddeus muttered, breaking the tense silence, "I was hoping for a quiet night of hunting. Maybe a rogue vampire or two. But no, we had to stumble into a bloody vampire prophecy."

Despite the dire circumstances, William couldn't help but crack a wry smile. "When has anything in our lives ever been simple, friend?"

Thaddeus snorted. "Fair point. Still, I can't help but wonder where this will lead us."

As they disappeared into the labyrinthine streets of London in the direction of vampire-filled tunnels, William felt the familiar cocktail of determination and dread churning in his gut. The stakes were very high indeed, and he knew that every choice they made from this moment on could ripple through the supernatural world. The weight of responsibility pressed down on him, but with it came a steely resolve. Whatever challenges lay ahead, he would face them head-on. For Elizabeth, for Lilly, and for the delicate balance of the world he'd sworn to protect.

THE STENCH OF DECAY assaulted William's nostrils as he stood at the tunnel entrance. His gold-flecked blue werewolf eyes narrowed, scanning the shadows. Every muscle in his body tensed, ready for action.

"You smell that?" Thaddeus whispered, his silver-edged blade catching what little light filtered through the gloom.

William nodded, his lips curling back to reveal slightly elongated canines. "Vampires. And something worse."

As if summoned by his words, pale figures materialized from the darkness. Their eyes, cold and hungry, fixed on Thaddeus.

"Well, well," one of them sneered, fangs glinting. "If it isn't the famous hunter and his pet wolf."

Thaddeus's knuckles whitened around his weapon's hilt. "Charming as ever, I see. Did you practice that line in the mirror? Oh wait, you can't see your reflection, can you?"

The lead vampire's face contorted with rage. "Get them!"

"Down!" William roared. He shoved Thaddeus aside, feeling the whoosh of a hurled rock slice through the air where his friend's head had been moments before.

Chaos erupted. William's muscles coiled, werewolf strength surging through him. He caught the first vampire's wrist, twisting until bone splintered beneath his grip. The creature's shriek of pain was cut short as William hurled it into its companions.

"Watch your back!" Thaddeus called out.

William ducked instinctively, feeling the rush of air as Thaddeus's blade whistled over his head. A wet thud and a gurgle told him the strike had found its mark.

"Thanks," William grunted, driving his fist into another vampire's jaw. The satisfying crunch of shattering bone reverberated through his arm.

They moved in perfect sync, a deadly dance honed by fighting side by side. William's heightened senses tracked each threat, his body responding with inhuman speed and power.

A vampire blurred towards Thaddeus, fangs bared for the kill. William's hand shot out, fingers closing around the creature's throat. "Not today," he growled, slamming it into the ground. The impact left a small crater in the stone floor.

Thaddeus spun, his blade slicing through a vampire aiming for William's exposed back. "Getting sloppy in your old age?" he quipped, a hint of a smile playing at his lips despite the dire situation.

William snorted, ducking under a wild swing. "You're one to talk, old man. How many centuries have you been swinging that letter opener around?"

The air crackled with supernatural energy. Vampires attacked from all directions, their inhuman speed making them little more than blurs in the dim light. Magical attacks sizzled past, leaving smoking scorch marks on the tunnel walls.

"We need to move," Thaddeus said, his voice barely audible over the din of combat. "The deeper tunnels are to our left, but we should probably aim for the streets instead at this point."

William nodded, grabbing a loose boulder. His muscles strained as he hurled it into the densest cluster of attackers. The sickening crunch of breaking bones and parting flesh bought them precious seconds.

They edged closer to their escape route, each covering the other's blind spots. William's world narrowed to the ebb and flow of combat, his senses hyper-focused on the immediate threats surrounding them.

"Lovely evening, eh?" Thaddeus called out, his blade leaving smoking furrows in vampire flesh.

William grinned, a feral light of swirling gold in his blue eyes. "Never a dull moment with you around, that's for sure."

Thaddeus laughed, a sound at odds with the violence surrounding them.

As they fought their way free of the tunnels, William couldn't help but marvel at their unlikely partnership. A werewolf and a vampire hunter, bound by friendship and a common cause.

"You know," William panted, driving his elbow into a vampire's face, "when this is over, we're overdue for a good beer."

Thaddeus grinned, decapitating another attacker with a fluid motion. "Agreed. Somewhere sunny. Very, very sunny and... A beer."

WILLIAM'S LUNGS BURNED as he sprinted through the winding alleys, Thaddeus hot on his heels. The sounds of pursuit echoed behind them, growing fainter with each turn. His werewolf speed gave him an edge, but he made sure not to outpace his companion.

"Left!" Thaddeus hissed, grabbing William's arm and yanking him into a narrow passage barely visible in the gloom.

They pressed themselves against the damp stone, hearts pounding. William's enhanced hearing picked up the frustrated snarls of their pursuers as they lost the trail.

"Nice trick," William whispered, a grin spreading across his face despite the danger.

Thaddeus nodded, his eyes gleaming with a mixture of excitement and caution. "Plenty more where that came from. Follow me."

They darted from shadow to shadow, Thaddeus leading them through a maze of hidden paths and forgotten alleyways. William marveled at the vampire hunter's intimate knowledge of London's underbelly.

As they emerged onto a deserted street, the distant sounds of pursuit finally faded entirely. William leaned against a wall, catching his breath. The adrenaline coursing through his veins made him feel more alive than he had in years.

"We make a pretty good team," he said, glancing at Thaddeus.

The older man chuckled, wiping sweat from his brow. "That we do. Your speed and strength, my knowledge of the city's secrets... I dare say we're becoming quite the formidable pair."

William nodded, feeling a newfound respect for his unlikely partner. The heat of battle had forged a bond between them that no amount of planning or discussion could have achieved.

"So," William said, straightening up, "where to next?"

Thaddeus grinned, a mischievous glint in his eye. "I know just the place. It's time we compared notes and planned our next move."

As they set off into the night, William couldn't help but feel a surge of optimism. With Thaddeus by his side, he was beginning to believe they might actually have a chance of unraveling the mystery and saving their friends.

WILLIAM AND THADDEUS slowed their pace as they reached a deserted square, their eyes scanning the area for any signs of pursuit. Satisfied they'd lost their vampires, they ducked into a shadowy alcove beneath an old clock tower.

William leaned against the cool stone, his breath coming in controlled pants. He closed his eyes, focusing on his heightened senses to ensure they were truly alone. Beside him, Thaddeus pulled out a small notebook, his brow furrowed in concentration.

"Let's go over what we know," Thaddeus said, his voice low.

William nodded, his mind racing. "The Fae mentioned increased vampire activity in the old tunnels. And that bit about unrest among the elders..."

Thaddeus scribbled furiously. "Yes, and don't forget the prophecy. It's all connected somehow."

As they spoke, the pieces began to fall into place. The kidnapping of Elizabeth and Lilly, the strange symbols at the crime scenes, the whispers of an ancient artifact - it all pointed to something far larger than they'd initially suspected.

"We're not just dealing with a rogue vampire lord or two," William muttered, a chill running down his spine. "This is a conspiracy."

Thaddeus nodded grimly. "And not just any conspiracy. I'd wager we're up against some of the oldest and most powerful vampires in London."

The enormity of the challenge ahead hit William like a physical blow. These weren't just any opponents - they were creatures who had survived centuries, accumulating power and influence beyond imagination.

Yet, as he met Thaddeus's steely gaze, William felt a surge of determination. They'd come too far to back down now. Elizabeth and Lilly's lives hung in the balance, and the fate of London itself might well rest on their shoulders.

"It won't be easy," Thaddeus said, voicing William's thoughts.

William straightened, his jaw set. "No, it won't. But we don't have a choice. We have to see this through."

Thaddeus nodded, a hint of a smile playing at the corners of his mouth. "Indeed we do, wolf. Indeed we do."

THE FIRST RAYS OF SUNLIGHT crept over London's skyline, painting the city in hues of gold and pink. William and Thaddeus stood side by side on a rooftop, their eyes scanning the awakening metropolis below. The night's events had left them battered and bruised, but a newfound energy coursed through their veins.

William inhaled deeply, the crisp morning air filling his lungs. He glanced at Thaddeus, noticing the vampire hunter's stance had relaxed slightly. The tension that had initially defined their partnership had mellowed into something more akin to mutual respect.

"We make a good team," William said, breaking the silence.

Thaddeus nodded, a hint of a smile playing at the corners of his mouth. "Indeed. Your instincts are... surprisingly useful."

William chuckled, recognizing the compliment hidden beneath Thaddeus's gruff exterior. "And your experience saved our hides more than once tonight."

As they watched the sun climb higher, William felt a sense of purpose solidify within him. The challenges ahead were daunting, but for the first time since Elizabeth and Lilly's disappearance, he felt a glimmer of hope.

"So," Thaddeus said, turning to face William fully. "What's our next move?"

William's mind raced, piecing together the information they'd gathered. "We need to dive into the tunnels. That's where the vampire activity is concentrated, as we found out tonight..."

Thaddeus nodded, his expression grim but determined. "It won't be easy. We'll be in their territory."

"True," William agreed. "But we have something they don't expect - each other and our other friends."

William watched as the vampire hunter's eyebrows twitched upward, a flicker of surprise crossing his weathered face. Instead of arguing, the man reached into his coat pocket, producing a small, well-worn map of London's underground.

"We should start here," he said, his calloused finger tracing a path along the paper before tapping decisively near the Thames. The faint smell of alchemy and leather wafted from him as William leaned closer.

William peered at the map, his keen eyes taking in every detail. "Interesting choice. Any particular reason?"

The hunter's lips quirked into a half-smile. "Call it a hunch. These old bones have a way of sensing trouble."

As they bent over the map, plotting their next move, William felt a surge of renewed resolve course through him. The night's events had proven they could work together effectively, their strengths complementing each other in ways he hadn't anticipated.

"We make quite the team, don't we?" William mused, a hint of amusement in his voice.

The hunter grunted in agreement. "Never thought I'd say this, but you're not half bad for a wolf."

With the first rays of dawn painting the sky in hues of pink and gold, they decided to regroup with the others at William's house. The familiar streets of London began to stir as they made their way back, the city slowly awakening from its slumber.

Upon arriving, they found Gabriel, Connor, Jaxon, and Olivia already waiting. Gabriel's piercing eyes scanned them for injuries, while Connor paced restlessly, his fingers drumming against his leg.

"About time you two showed up," Jaxon quipped, his hazel eyes glinting with a mix of relief and mischief. "We were starting to think you'd eloped."

Olivia elbowed him playfully, her hair catching the early morning light. "Ignore him. Are you both alright?"

William nodded, sinking into a nearby armchair. "We're fine. Just need a moment to catch our breath and plan our next move."

As they settled in, sharing their findings and theories, the group fell into a comfortable rhythm. The hunter, initially tense, gradually relaxed as he recounted their night's adventures.

"I hate to admit it," Connor said, running a hand through his dark hair, "but it sounds like you two work well together."

William smiled wryly. "Surprising, isn't it? The night's full of wonders."

They rested for a while with scones and tea, the conversation flowing easily between them as they ate. As the sun climbed higher in the sky, a sense of anticipation began to build. London's supernatural underworld awaited, and they were ready to face whatever challenges lay ahead.

"Well," Gabriel said, standing up and stretching, "shall we get this show on the road?"

With renewed energy and determination, the group set out once more into the bustling streets of London, ready to unravel the mysteries that lurked in the city's shadows.

The Loom's True Power

T he last rays of sunlight painted London's skyline in hues of gold and crimson as William and his companions stepped out of his townhouse. The familiar streets they'd traversed countless times by day now seemed to shimmer with otherworldly energy, unveiling a hidden realm that thrived in the gathering darkness.

William's heightened senses prickled, every nerve ending alive with awareness. His emerald eyes widened as he caught glimpses of the supernatural world emerging around them. Fae lights danced in shadowy alcoves, their ethereal glow casting long, twisting shadows across worn cobblestones.

"Do you see them?" William whispered, his voice barely audible above the city's nocturnal hum.

Olivia squeezed his hand, her touch grounding him amidst the sensory onslaught. "I do," she murmured, her own green eyes scanning their surroundings. "Focus on my voice, Will. Don't let it overwhelm you."

Thaddeus moved with the fluid grace of a predator, his centuries of experience evident in every calculated step. His weathered hand never strayed far from the weapon concealed beneath his coat, Steel gray eyes darting from shadow to shadow.

"Stay alert," he growled softly. "The night has teeth."

Gabriel and Connor flanked the group, their postures tense and ready. Jaxon brought up the rear, his boyish face a mask of wonder and trepidation.

"Blimey," he breathed, nearly stumbling as he gaped at a cluster of will-o'-wisps floating lazily above a nearby rooftop.

Connor chuckled, the sound low and rumbling. "Welcome to London after dark, lad. Best keep your wits about you, really need to get your senses in order."

As they turned a corner, William's nostrils flared. The air was thick with scents both familiar and alien – the musk of wet fur, the acrid tang of alchemy, and something else, something ancient and primal that made the hairs on the back of his neck stand on end.

"Crimson Paw," Gabriel said proudly, his golden eyes fixed on the rooftops above.

William followed his gaze, catching sight of sleek, lupine forms prowling the skyline. The patrol by Gabriel's pack moved with fluid grace, their keen eyes scanning the streets below. One of the wolves, its black fur with speckles of white on his muzzle gleaming in the moonlight, locked eyes with Gabriel. A silent exchange passed between them, an acknowledgment of respect.

"Friend of yours?" Olivia asked, her tone light despite the tension in her shoulders.

Gabriel's lips quirked in a half-smile. "That is Damien, let's just say he knows his place in my pack."

They pressed deeper into the heart of supernatural London, each step taking them further from the familiar and into a realm where shadow and wonder intertwined. The night air thrummed with possibility and danger in equal measure.

"Remember," Thaddeus cautioned, his voice barely above a whisper, "in this world, beauty and peril often wear the same face. Trust nothing but each other."

William nodded, his grip on Olivia's hand tightening. The city he thought he knew had transformed into a labyrinth of magic and mystery. As they ventured further into the unknown, he couldn't shake the feeling that they were being watched – not just by the Crimson Paw patrol, but by countless unseen eyes, some curious, others hungry.

The night was young, and their journey had only just begun.

WILLIAM'S EARS TWITCHED, catching a faint, haunting sound that drifted through the misty air. He glanced at his companions - Gabriel, Connor, Jaxon, and Olivia - their faces etched with a mix of curiosity and apprehension.

"Did you hear that?" William whispered, his voice barely audible.

Gabriel nodded, his eyes scanning the darkness. "It's coming from over there," he murmured, pointing towards an abandoned churchyard looming ahead.

As they drew closer, the mournful wail grew louder, sending icy fingers of dread down William's spine. Every hair on his body stood on end, his werewolf instincts screaming danger.

Connor's hand instinctively moved to the hilt of his sword. "I don't like this," he growled, his muscular frame tense.

Jaxon, ever the scholar, pushed his glasses up his nose. "Fascinating," he breathed, eyes wide with wonder. "Could it be a-"

"Banshee," Thaddeus interrupted, his weathered face a mask of calm. The old vampire hunter's eyes, steel-gray, betrayed no emotion. "Follow my lead."

They crept through the rusted gates, overgrown grass crunching beneath their feet. Olivia stumbled, her hair catching on a thorny bush. "Blasted plants," she hissed, untangling herself.

In the center of the graveyard, an ethereal figure hovered. Her long white hair billowed in an unseen wind, her translucent form flickering like a candle flame. Her mouth opened in another piercing cry, and William fought the urge to cover his ears.

"Sweet mercy," Jaxon muttered, eyes wide with awe and fear.

Thaddeus stepped forward, hands raised in a placating gesture. "We mean you no harm, lady of sorrow," he called out, his voice steady and respectful.

The banshee's hollow eyes fixed on them, her expression twisting with hostility. She drifted closer, her spectral form pulsing with an eerie light.

"Why do you disturb my vigil, mortals?" Her voice echoed with centuries of grief, each word a dagger of sorrow.

"We seek information to prevent deaths, not cause them," Thaddeus replied, holding her gaze.

The banshee paused, her hostile demeanor softening slightly. "Prevent death? A noble but futile goal, death halts for no one."

William watched in amazement as Thaddeus engaged the spirit in conversation, his words carefully chosen and his tone measured. Gradually, the banshee's hostility faded, replaced by a reluctant cooperation.

"A gathering darkness festers in the city's catacombs," she intoned, her voice carrying the weight of prophecy. "Ancient powers stir, hungry for the lives of the innocent."

As they left the churchyard, the banshee's wails fading behind them, William turned to Thaddeus with newfound respect. "That was incredible," he admitted. "I've never seen anyone handle a situation like that so smoothly."

Thaddeus offered a small smile, the corners of his eyes crinkling. "Centuries of practice, my friend. Sometimes, the most powerful weapon we have is our words."

Jaxon scribbled furiously in his notebook. "The implications of this encounter are staggering! A real banshee, and one willing to share information, no less!"

Olivia rolled her eyes, but couldn't hide her smile. "Only you would be excited about meeting a wailing harbinger of death, Jax."

Connor grunted, his hand still resting on his sword hilt. "I'd rather face a dozen angry vampires than another of those screaming specters."

Gabriel chuckled, clapping Connor on the back. "Come on, cub. Let's get back to the city. I think we all need a stiff drink after that."

As they walked away, William cast one last glance at the churchyard. The banshee's words echoed in his mind, a chilling reminder of the dangers that lay ahead. But with his friends by his side and Thaddeus's wisdom to guide them, he felt ready to face whatever darkness awaited in the catacombs below.

WILLIAM'S BOOTS CRUNCHED on the gravel path as he and Thaddeus entered the moonlit park. The silver light painted everything in stark contrasts, turning familiar landscapes into a chiaroscuro dreamscape. Shadows danced and shifted with each step, playing tricks on their heightened senses.

"I don't like this," William muttered, his hand resting on the hilt of his cane sword. The young man's eyes darted from shadow to shadow, searching for threats.

Connor nodded in agreement, his face set in grim lines. "It's too quiet. Even for midnight."

Jaxon, ever the voice of reason, spoke up. "Let's not jump at shadows. We're here for information, nothing more."

Olivia placed a calming hand on Gabriel's arm. "Stay alert, but don't let fear cloud your judgment."

As if summoned by their whispered conversation, a figure materialized from the inky darkness beneath an ancient oak. She moved with an otherworldly grace and sensuality that set William's teeth on edge, every instinct screaming danger.

As she drew closer, William caught sight of her eyes – quicksilver pools that seemed to shift and change with each blink. Impossible to read, yet undeniably captivating.

"Well, well," the newcomer drawled, her voice like honey laced with poison. A sardonic smile played at the corners of her mouth. "What brings London's most unlikely protectors – and their motley crew – to my humble corner of the night?"

Gabriel tensed beside him, a low bass growl rumbling in his chest. William laid a steadying hand on his partner's shoulder before taking a step forward.

"Vesper Gloaming, I presume?" Thaddeus kept his tone polite, but wary.

The Fae shapeshifter's smile widened, revealing teeth that seemed just a touch too sharp. "The vampire hunter remembers his manners. How quaint."

William felt the weight of her gaze, sensing the ancient power that lurked beneath her deceptively casual demeanor. He chose his words carefully, aware that verbal sparring with the Fae was a dangerous game.

"We're seeking information about Lord Everett Wentworth's recent activities," William said, meeting her mercurial gaze steadily. "I believe you might be able to help us."

Vesper's form seemed to shimmer slightly in the moonlight, her expression turning evasive. "And why would I involve myself in the affairs of vampires and werewolves?"

"Because you're curious," William countered, his voice low and intense. "Because whatever Wentworth is planning, it's big enough to send ripples through all the supernatural communities of London. Including the Fae."

For a heartbeat, Vesper's mask of indifference slipped. William caught a glimpse of genuine fear in her ever-changing eyes. She glanced around, as if checking for unseen watchers, before speaking in a hushed voice.

"Wentworth's been gathering power, more than he should be able to," Vesper admitted, her words barely above a whisper. "He's calling in old debts, making alliances that shouldn't be possible. The balance is... shifting."

As Vesper spoke, the weight of her words settled over the group like a shroud. William became acutely aware of the complex web of politics and alliances that bound the supernatural world together. He realized that by seeking Vesper's help, he might be entangling himself and his companions in Fae matters that could prove just as dangerous as Wentworth's schemes.

Jaxon stepped forward, his hazel eyes narrowed in thought. "What kind of alliances are we talking about?"

Vesper's gaze flicked to the young man, a hint of amusement coloring her features. "The kind that makes even creatures like me lose sleep, little shadow."

Connor, ever the forward enforcer, spoke up. "Is there anything we can do to help stabilize things?"

Vesper's laugh was like shattered glass. "Oh, you mortals. Always thinking you can fix everything." Her expression softened, almost imperceptibly. "But your heart's in the right place. Perhaps that's why She chose you."

Before anyone could question her cryptic statement, Vesper's form began to blur at the edges. "Be careful, detectives. The game you're playing has rules you don't yet understand."

With that, she melted back into the shadows, leaving the group with more questions than answers.

William exhaled slowly, feeling the weight of responsibility settle on his shoulders. He turned to face his companions, their faces a mix of determination and uncertain confusion in the silvery moonlight.

"Well," he said, a wry smile tugging at his lips, "I'd say that went about as well as could be expected when dealing with the Fae."

Thaddeus grunted in agreement. "Which means we're in deeper trouble than we thought... and after this, even more than we were before."

As they made their way out of the trees, William couldn't shake the feeling that they had just taken their first steps down a very dangerous path. But with his trusted allies by his side, he was ready to face whatever challenges lay ahead.

WILLIAM'S SKIN CRAWLED as they stepped out of the park, an invisible hand tracing icy fingers up his spine. He locked eyes with Thaddeus, a silent conversation passing between them. In a heartbeat, the shadows around them solidified, morphing into a pack of vampires with eyes gleaming like hungry wolves in the dim streetlight.

"Scouts," Thaddeus spat, his weathered hand instinctively reaching for the weapon at his hip. The gray of his hair glinted in the moonlight like silver, a stark contrast to the darkness closing in around them.

Before William could respond, a vampire lunged at him, fangs bared. He ducked, feeling the whoosh of claws grazing his cheek. The scent of his own blood filled his nostrils, igniting a primal rage within him. Years of training took over as he pivoted, his foot connecting with the vampire's gut in a powerful kick. The creature flew backward, crashing into a nearby lamppost with a sickening crunch.

"Behind you!" Gabriel's voice cut through the chaos, his usually calm demeanor replaced by urgency.

Thaddeus moved like liquid silver, a stake materializing in his hand as if by magic. He plunged it into an approaching vampire's chest with practiced precision. The creature's scream faded as it crumbled in a heap, the clothes scattering in the night breeze.

"Nice move, old man," Connor quipped, dodging a swipe from another attacker. His eyes sparkled with a mix of adrenaline and aggression, in the face of danger.

William's world narrowed to a whirlwind of fists and fangs. He caught glimpses of Thaddeus weaving through the fray, each strike of his weapon finding its mark with deadly accuracy. The vampire hunter's steel-gray eyes were focused, betraying years of experience in this deadly dance.

William relied on the raw power of his werewolf blood, his knuckles crunching against vampire flesh and bone. The satisfying crunch of breaking ribs echoed in his ears as he drove his fist into a vampire's chest.

Suddenly, searing pain exploded in William's shoulder as fangs sank deep into his flesh. He roared, a sound of both agony and rage that reverberated through the street. "Get off me, you bloodsucking bastard!" he growled through gritted teeth.

Before he could react, Olivia appeared, her blade singing through the air. The vampire's head hit the cobblestones with a dull thud, its body following a moment later.

"Watch your back," Thaddeus grunted, dancing past them, already turning to face the next threat. A thin line of blood trickled down his forehead, but his eyes remained sharp and alert.

William nodded, gratitude for his companions surging through him. "Right back at you," he managed, pressing a hand to his bleeding shoulder. "Didn't know you cared so much, old man."

They moved in sync, covering each other's blind spots, their fighting styles meshing like gears in a well-oiled machine. William's brute strength complemented Thaddeus's finesse, creating a deadly combination that the vampires struggled to overcome.

"Jaxon, on your left!" Olivia's warning rang out, followed by the sharp twang of her crossbow. A bolt whizzed past William's ear, embedding itself in the chest of a vampire that had been sneaking up on Jaxon.

As the last vampire fell, an eerie silence descended. William stood, chest heaving, his body humming with leftover adrenaline. He met Thaddeus's gaze, seeing his own shock reflected in the vampire hunter's steel-gray eyes.

"They knew we were here," William said, his voice low and grim. He ran a hand through his dark hair, matted with sweat and vampire dust.

Thaddeus nodded, his face etched with hard lines. "We're not as under the radar as we thought." He wiped his blade clean on his coat, leaving a dark smear on the worn fabric.

"Well, that's just bloody fantastic," Connor muttered, brushing vampire dust from his sleeve with exaggerated disgust. "And here I thought we were going for a pleasant evening stroll."

As the reality of their situation sank in, a chill that had nothing to do with the night air settled over William. They'd won this round, but the encounter was a stark reminder of the dangers lurking in the shadows of their world. The taste of copper lingered in his mouth, a metallic reminder of how close they'd come to disaster.

"We need to move," Thaddeus said, his eyes scanning the darkness. "They might have sent word to others." His hand rested on the hilt of his weapon, ready for any further surprises the night might hold.

William nodded, his mind already racing with possibilities. "Back to my townhouse?"

"For now," Thaddeus agreed. "We need to regroup and figure out our next move." He paused, a rare hint of uncertainty crossing his features. "This changes everything."

As they melted into the night, William couldn't shake the feeling that this was just the beginning of something much bigger. The shadows seemed to stretch longer, hiding untold dangers in their depths. William's eyes now held a steely determination. Whatever came next, they would face it together.

THE GAS LAMPS FLICKERED, casting long shadows as William and Thaddeus navigated the narrow cobblestone streets of London.

William's breath misted in the chilly night air, his heart pounding with a mixture of anticipation and dread. The pair had deliberately chosen to venture out alone, hoping to avoid drawing unwanted attention.

As they approached their destination, William's eyes fixed on a weathered sign swinging gently in the breeze. "Ned's Final Rest," it proclaimed in faded gold lettering that had seen better days. The mortuary's facade was unremarkable, blending seamlessly with the surrounding buildings.

William's hand hovered over the door, his knuckles mere inches from the worn wood. He turned to Thaddeus, his blue eyes clouded with uncertainty. "Are you absolutely certain about this, Thaddeus? A necromancer, of all things?"

Thaddeus's face was a mask of grim determination, his steel-gray eyes glinting in the dim light. "Sometimes, William," he said, his voice low and gravelly, "to fight the darkness, we must dabble in it ourselves."

Before William could respond, the door creaked open, revealing a young man who looked as if he hadn't slept in days. His hair was a disheveled spiked mess, and dark circles rimmed his bloodshot eyes. He peered at them nervously, his gaze darting between the two men.

"We're closed," he mumbled, attempting to shut the door.

William stepped forward, his voice soft and reassuring. "Ned? We need to talk."

Recognition flashed across Ned's face, followed quickly by panic. He tried to slam the door shut, but Thaddeus was faster, wedging his foot in the gap.

"Please," William said, his tone empathetic. "We're not here to cause trouble. We need your help."

Ned's eyes widened, fear evident in his trembling hands. "I don't know anything," he stammered. "I'm just a mortician. Nothing more. A bad one to boot."

Thaddeus leaned in, his imposing figure casting a shadow over the younger man. "We know what you are, Ned," he said, his voice stern but not unkind. "And we know you have information about the vampire prophecy."

The color drained from Ned's face, and he stumbled backward into his shop. William and Thaddeus followed, closing the door behind them with a soft click.

The interior of the mortuary was dimly lit with oil lamps, the air heavy with the scent of formaldehyde and something else—something older and more sinister. William's eyes adjusted to the gloom, taking in the rows of gleaming instruments and the sheet-covered forms on nearby tables.

"I can't help you," Ned whispered, his voice cracking. He wrung his hands nervously, his eyes darting to the shadows as if expecting something to emerge from them. "They'll kill me if they find out I talked."

William approached him slowly, hands raised in a placating gesture. "We can protect you, Ned," he said, his blue eyes locked on the necromancer's face. "But we need to know what's happening. People's lives are at stake."

Ned's resolve wavered visibly. His gaze flicked from Thaddeus's imposing figure to William's earnest face and back again. "You don't understand," he said, his voice barely above a whisper. "The things I've seen... The rituals they're performing..."

Thaddeus stepped forward, his patience wearing thin. The movement caused Ned to flinch, pressing himself against a nearby workbench. "Speak plainly, necromancer," Thaddeus demanded. "What rituals?"

Ned winced at the word 'necromancer' as if it physically pained him. He took a deep, shuddering breath, his shoulders slumping in defeat. "They're sacrificing people," he finally admitted. "Not just for blood, but for some kind of dark magic. It's tied to the prophecy, something about reshaping reality."

As Ned spoke, William felt a chill run down his spine, his skin prickling with gooseflesh. The pieces of the puzzle were starting to fit together, forming a picture more terrifying than he'd dared imagine.

"Reshaping reality?" William echoed, his voice hollow.

Thaddeus's expression darkened, his jaw clenching. "Something far worse than we anticipated, sacrifices."

Ned nodded miserably, his eyes haunted. "You have no idea," he whispered. "No idea at all."

EQUIPPED WITH NED'S fresh intel, the pair navigated the crowded Troll Market, hunting for mystical safeguards and hex-breaking relics. The sensory overload assaulted their faculties as they maneuvered through the throng. They approached a shadowy nook housing a ramshackle stall, its time-worn placard barely discernible: "Uncommon Relics and Oddities."

William's nose twitched as they neared the shop, catching a whiff of musty parchment and exotic spices. His keen eyes locked onto the shopkeeper—a creature that looked ancient beyond measure, its skin resembling sun-baked leather, crisscrossed with deep furrows. In the dim light, the being's eyes glowed with an eerie, amber luminescence.

As they approached, the shopkeeper's gaze snapped to them, a mix of suspicion and intrigue etched across its weathered features.

"What brings you to my humble establishment?" the creature rasped, its voice like stones grinding together.

William stepped forward, dipping his head in a respectful bow. He met the shopkeeper's gaze steadily, careful not to appear confrontational. "We come seeking items of power, good sir. Our cause is just and urgent."

The shopkeeper's eyes narrowed to glowing slits. "Just and urgent, you say? I've heard such claims before. They often lead to chaos and destruction. How can I trust that you won't misuse what you seek?"

Beside William, Thaddeus tensed, his hand inching towards the concealed weapon at his hip. William placed a calming hand on his friend's arm, feeling the coiled energy beneath.

"Easy, old friend," he murmured. To the shopkeeper, he said, "Your caution is wise and appreciated. Perhaps this might ease your concerns." William reached into his coat, withdrawing a small, intricately carved stone.

The shopkeeper's eyes widened, recognition flashing across its face. "A truth charm," it breathed, gnarled fingers reaching out. "Rare indeed."

William placed the smooth, flat coin in the creature's palm. "We offer this as a token of our sincerity. It binds us to our word."

The shopkeeper turned the stone over in its hands, studying it intently. After a long moment, it nodded. "Very well. What is it you require?"

As William began listing their needs, Thaddeus kept his senses alert, scanning their surroundings. He noticed several shadowy figures lurking nearby, their interest in the proceedings all too apparent.

"William," he muttered, "we've got company."

William nodded almost imperceptibly, continuing his negotiations without missing a beat. His silver tongue danced through the complex web of supernatural etiquette, offering favors and rare ingredients in exchange for the items they sought.

Suddenly, a hulking troll lumbered towards them, its intentions hostile. Thaddeus stepped forward, his hand resting casually on the hilt of his sword. The troll's eyes widened in recognition, and it quickly retreated into the shadows.

The shopkeeper's eyebrows rose. "Your companion's reputation precedes him," it remarked, a hint of newfound respect in its gravelly voice.

William seized the opportunity. "Indeed. And I'm sure a purveyor of such fine wares as yourself can appreciate the value of a solid reputation. Surely we can come to an arrangement that benefits us both?"

The shopkeeper's lips curled into what might have been a smile. "You drive a hard bargain, wolf. But I find your terms... acceptable."

As they concluded their transaction, William felt a mixture of relief and unease settle in his gut. They had acquired what they needed, but he couldn't shake the feeling that they'd drawn unwanted attention.

"Let's not linger," he murmured to Thaddeus as they turned to leave. "I fear we may have stirred up more than we bargained for."

Thaddeus nodded grimly, his hand never straying far from his weapon. "Story of our lives, old friend. Story of our lives."

AS THE FIRST RAYS OF dawn painted the London sky in hues of pink and gold, William and Thaddeus walked side by side through the winding backstreets. The city was just beginning to stir, the quiet broken only by the distant clatter of horse hooves and the occasional cry of a seagull.

William's mind raced, replaying the night's events. The encounter in the Troll Market, the cryptic information from Ned, and the tense negotiation with the ancient shopkeeper—all pieces of a puzzle that was growing more complex by the hour.

"Thaddeus," he said, breaking the silence, "I can't shake the feeling that we've stumbled into something far bigger than we anticipated."

Thaddeus nodded, his weathered face etched with concern. "Aye, my friend. The vampires' increased activity, this prophecy... it's all connected to the Loom somehow. And I fear we've only scratched the surface."

William's hand unconsciously went to the pouch at his belt, feeling the weight of the mystical items they'd acquired. "These artifacts might give us an edge, but at what cost? We've made ourselves known to forces that would rather see us dead."

They turned a corner, the familiar sight of William's townhouse coming into view. Thaddeus placed a hand on William's shoulder, stopping him.

"William, we knew the risks when we started this. Elizabeth and Lilly are counting on us. London itself might be at stake. We can't back down now."

William met his friend's gaze, seeing the same determination he felt mirrored there. He nodded, squaring his shoulders. "You're right, of course. We need to gather the others, and share what we've learned. Plan our next move carefully."

As they approached the townhouse, William felt the weight of responsibility settle more firmly on his shoulders. The coming days would test them all, but he was grateful to have Thaddeus and the others by his side.

Don't miss out!

Visit the website below and you can sign up to receive emails whenever Johan Sparr publishes a new book. There's no charge and no obligation.

https://books2read.com/r/B-A-IJJEB-XKRDF

BOOKS 2 READ

Connecting independent readers to independent writers.

Also by Johan Sparr

The StainedSteam Saga
Phantom of StainedSteam
The Near Voice of Empathy
The Loom of Ms. Jenny

Watch for more at www.johansparrbooks.com.

About the Author

Johan Sparr has always had a passion for fantasy and science fiction, ever since he first read Terry Pratchett's Discworld series as a teenager. He was immediately drawn into the witty world of magic, adventure, and imagination.

After his time studying Computer Science and Biology at Uppsala University, Johan began writing his own mystical fantasy stories set in magical worlds. He was inspired by authors like Terry Pratchett, Neil Gaiman, and Jim Butcher.

When he's not writing, Johan enjoys reading urban fantasy literature, watching science fiction movies, studying history, and adding to his collection of exotic plants. He also loves exploring the wilderness which has a rich sense of folklore and magic, just like in his stories.

Johan currently lives in the small town of Bollnäs in Sweden with his wife, two children, a cat called Purr, and more books than can fit on his shelves. He is busy working on the next installments in The StainedSteam series, taking readers deeper into the secrets of a magical Victorian London.

Read more at www.johansparrbooks.com.

Milton Keynes UK
Ingram Content Group UK Ltd.
UKHW031214111124
451035UK00007B/695